Denise Robertson

Blue remembered hills

———————

Constable · London

First published in Great Britain 1987
by Constable and Company Limited
10 Orange Street London WC2H 7EG
Copyright ©1987 by Denise Robertson
Photoset in Linotron Ehrhardt 11pt
and printed in Great Britain by
Redwood Burn Limited, Trowbridge, Wiltshire

British Library CIP Data
Robertson, Denise
Blue remembered hills.
I. Title
823′.914[F]   PR6068.O18

ISBN 0 09 467690 9

The lines from John Betjeman's *Collected
Poems* on pages 108 and 110 are reproduced
by permission of John Murray (Publishers)
Ltd. The lines from *The Collected Poems by
W. B. Yeats* on page 130 are reproduced by
permission of A. P. Watt Ltd on behalf of
Michael B. Yeats and Macmillan London Ltd.

1

The pub at lunch-time was usually cold and always seedy. Dust showed in the folds of the leatherette seats, and the floor was scarred by a hundred stubbed-out cigarettes. Today, though, end-of-term euphoria lent it a cosy air. 'Move along,' Gwen said, squeezing behind a table. 'Thank God that's over.'

Fran nodded. 'The last two weeks have dragged. I'm not going to think about work for a month. Then I'll get down to some real graft.'

It was June 1985. Their second year of teacher training was over, the third and critical year still twelve weeks away. Time to unwind.

'One lager, one lager and lime. The snowball's for Jenny ... God knows how she can drink that muck ... and that's Gordon's Exhibition.' Tony Lund emptied his tray and returned to the bar.

'He fancies you,' Gwen said, licking froth from her upper lip.

'Hush!' Fran tried to sound nonchalant. 'The others'll be here in a moment. We don't want them hearing nonsense!'

Gwen was not to be deterred. 'He fancies you – hence the drinks all round. I'm not averse to a free half, but watch your step. He's a bit too fly, that one.'

Tony was waiting for his change, dark hair unruly above an open-necked shirt, as befitted a sociology tutor. His navy jacket was shiny in places but his shoes were custom-made and must have been expensive. Fran suspected he was a bit of a fraud –

anti-establishment on the outside and an elitist where it didn't show. He was affable with all the students but lately she had found his attention to her disconcerting. He seemed always to be secretly amused by her, putting her completely off lectures and making her respectable end-of-term mark in his subject a blatant fraud.

Now he sat opposite trying to catch her eye, grinning when he succeeded. She snatched away her gaze. 'Damn men,' she thought. Still, it was nice to be fancied, why deny it? And why worry about it, when there were other and more frightening things with which to contend? Tomorrow she had promised to take Martin to Seaham Harbour to try out his new fishing tackle. Not only the sea to fear, but a complex mass of rod and line!

'Cheer up!' Gwen said suddenly. 'This is out of school drinkies we're having, not a wake!'

Fran smiled and raised her glass. 'Here's to crime,' she said recklessly, the first words that came into her mind.

'I'll drink to that.' Tony grinned and clinked glasses and Fran felt a blush begin. Of all the ridiculous things to say! Trust him to twist it ... there was no mistaking what he meant.

The conversation turned to holidays and she sat back to contemplate her fellow students. No chance of a holiday for her this year, so she had nothing to contribute. Not that she had a hankering for foreign parts; just to be at home for three whole months would be bliss.

Gwen was going to Greece with Lewis, her husband. The oldest 'mature' on the course, her face was alight at the thought of sunshine and food. 'I'm going to lose half a stone before I go, then I can just enjoy without any mad guilt feelings.'

Fran smiled. Gwen's attempts to diet were notorious for their failure to produce results. She would go to Greece at thirteen stone and come back five pounds heavier, but she was the most reassuring person Fran knew and could be forgiven any amount of wishful thinking.

Jenny and Gordon were young and earnest and in love. They were going to do France the hard way, on foot with half a ton of

[2]

equipment on their backs. Fran closed her eyes as they talked, remembering long French roads lined with poplars. She and David had spent two weeks of honeymoon in France, weeks filled with laughter and love-making that no longer needed to be illicit.

She opened her eyes to find Tony watching her. 'I'm tired,' she said defensively. He seemed always to be teasing. Even when he said nothing, the challenge was there. David had been dead for two years but still she felt on edge with men.

There had been one other man – Steve, who had loved her and then gone back to his wife – she had never really felt comfortable with him unless they were close together, limbs entwined, cheek to cheek, so that it was impossible for eyes to meet and transmit disconcerting messages. Now it was happening again.

'Can I give you a lift?' The others were rising to go and Tony was between her and the door.

'Thanks, but I've got the car.' Not for the first time she blessed the Mini, a haven on wheels. Once inside it, she was safe.

They all came out into the sunlight, suddenly anxious to get away. It was always like that at the end of term. You thought you would miss your fellow students, even promised to keep in touch, and then suddenly you were free and wanted to forget them.

'Take care.' Gwen's cheek was soft and powdery, reminding Fran of her mother's cheek which had always smelled of 4711 cologne.

'And you! Enjoy Greece and don't forget to come back.' The inane exchanges continued until Gwen turned the corner and Jenny and Gordon were striding purposefully in the other direction.

'Well, if I can't give you a lift let me see you to your car.' There was no escape and, worst of all, he was grinning at her discomforture.

Fran felt a sudden anger. 'Haven't you a home to go to?'

Her heart sank at the sound of her own voice. She didn't sound distant and superior, as she had intended. She sounded as though she were checking up on him, and that would imply interest. He was shepherding her over the zebra crossing towards the car-park and his reply was detached. 'Two actually . . . the flat here and a house in York.' They were on the pavement but he still held her arm loosely, above the elbow. 'But there's no little woman waiting, just cold empty rooms.' So he *had* thought she was probing! 'You're supposed to say "Aaah" when I say that,' he said mildly and she found herself grinning.

'I'm not in the least sorry for you.' The door of the Mini was open, safety just inches away. She could afford to be generous. 'But I hope you have a good holiday.'

He was winding down the window and closing the door. 'I'm here for at least a week, tying up ends. We might have a meal one night?'

Nothing to do but nod and smile. She eased into reverse and the car was under way. 'Bye!' She was out on the road, steering with one hand and winding up the window with the other before she realized that she was quite glad about the invitation. It would probably never come to anything but it might be nice if it did.

She was wandering through C & A, looking at racks of bright holiday clothes, when she saw Min. She was six months pregnant now but still glamorous, black hair a shining cap, limbs tanned from two weeks in Tenerife. She was riffling through maternity dresses, rattling hangers disdainfully along the rail as each one failed to please.

'Min, what are you doing here?'

Min turned from the dresses and clutched Fran's arm. 'Slumming, darling. Dennis is on one of his economy drives and says no more maternity wear. "Let something out," he said at lunchtime. Men? Give me alligators! Anyway, I'm glad you're here. I was dying for tea and cream cakes but it's so naff to sit by oneself. There's nowhere to put your eyes.'

Useless to say she didn't feel like cream cakes at two in the afternoon. Min was normally determined; pregnant, she was unstoppable. Fran watched her across the table as she ordered.

'And some of those choux buns with cream. Lemon with the tea and we'd like a toasted tea-cake to start.' Her throat and face were the colour of caramel above the beautifully cut white silk shift.

'How much did that cost?' Fran said.

'A lot!' For a moment Min looked guilty. 'But it's not every day you have a baby, is it? And it's such a drag. I need something to cheer me up.'

Min's baby had been conceived to cement her reconciliation with Dennis, her husband, after a brief affair she'd had with another man. 'I'm quite pleased about it really,' she said as she poured the tea. 'You know I am, so don't look so disapproving. But you get fed up with feeling like a tank and being trapped in the house all the time.'

Fran could not conceal her smile. 'You're just back from Tenerife!'

Min was unrepentant. 'I know, but that was a wash-out … apart from the sunshine, which was bliss. But it's no fun on your own, not when you've got a bump. I said to Dennis, "You don't need to worry about me being good. I couldn't give it away looking like this."'

The tea-cake had arrived and Min fell on it with gusto. 'Thank God I don't put on weight. You sure you don't want some? Good! Now stop looking like Mary Whitehouse and tell me your news. I hope you've done something wicked. If I can't do it myself, hearing about it's the next best thing.'

For a moment Fran was tempted to remind Min that less than a year ago she had been grovelling to Dennis for forgiveness, and forswearing even unchaste thoughts; but it would be a waste of time. They had been friends since school and there was no hope of Min's changing now. Not that Fran would want her to change.

'I'm sorry to disappoint you, darling, but there's more shena-nigans in the Vatican than in my life at the moment. Although I *have* just been propositioned by my sociology tutor … at least I think I have. But I doubt it'll come to anything.'

Min's eyes were suddenly wise. 'You mean you hope it won't

come to anything. You can't mourn David forever, you know. He wouldn't want you to. You're thirty-four years old, Fran. Someday you'll find someone. Not the same as David, but just as good. Anyway, that's what we all hope.'

Fran felt her eyes prick. 'Thanks but no thanks, Min. I've got enough on my plate bringing up Martin and attempting the course. If I can just qualify and get a decent school to teach at, I'll ask for nothing more.' She could have pointed out that she had already tried replacing David: her affair with Steve had been traumatic and Min knew it. Instead she changed the subject. 'How's Dennis?'

Min was on to the choux buns. 'Vile. All he talks about is business and that ghastly strike.' Fran groaned inwardly. Min had never forgiven her for living in a mining village, holding her personally responsible for the year-long miners' strike! 'He says it's worse since they went back to work. Nobody's buying furniture. All their branches are flat; even the Sunderland shop's struggling. They've got rid of ever so many staff and that makes Dennis feel guilty. No one likes putting people on the dole, not even me. Especially when there's no other work available. But that's business. If you can't stand the heat, and everything. And Harold doesn't help, going on about all the liquidations he's handling. Accountants are vultures, nothing more. They get fat on other people's downfall. If we hadn't been friends with Eve and Harold since school, I'd cut them dead. Eve's so smug. She'd like to see Dennis go broke.'

Loyalty to Eve made Fran demur. 'I'm sure you're wrong, Min. Eve can be a bit of a pain sometimes but she's very loyal.' They had all grown up together, pairing naturally at sixteen into Harold and Eve, Dennis and Min, David and Fran. Pairing, they had believed it would last for ever – until David's death had shown them all the transience of happiness.

'She may be loyal, Fran, but she's sanctimonious. She says I should humour Dennis. She doesn't have to live with him. It's a good job I'm preggers because I doubt if he's got the energy for sex. Still, the baby'll take his mind off his troubles when it

[6]

arrives, and things'll pick up for Christmas. They always do.'

She rattled on through another choux bun while Fran marvelled at her certainty. The baby would be born safely and the business would pick up: no thought of still birth or liquidation. And yet businesses were folding left and right – every night the *Echo* told the dismal story. The strike had been over for three months but still the ripples were widening.

'What about Martin? You must bring him over in the holidays. The kids were asking about him last night.' Min let out a tiny burp. 'That's better.'

Fran smiled. 'Martin's fine. He's developed this sudden passion for sea-angling. We went to Seaham a couple of weeks ago and he saw some anglers on the pier. I thought it was just a phase, but he went on and on and then Bethel found this ancient rod which had belonged to her husband and he just went mad. So tomorrow I'm taking him to try it out, and I'm terrified.'

'Trust that old witch to cause trouble.' Min's token feud with Fran's char was of long standing, but Bethel meant much more to Fran than a cleaning-woman and she sprang to her defence. 'She's very fond of Martin, you know that, Min. The rod means a lot to her ... it's jolly kind of her to give it to him.'

Min pulled a face. 'Sorry, I forgot I mustn't criticize Mother Teresa. I'll try not to do it again.'

She was paying the bill now, changing a five-pound note. 'No, Fran. It's my treat. Besides, if Dennis cuts my allowance much more it'll be you treating me next time.'

They parted at the entrance to the beauty salon. 'I've got a manicure at three. Don't forget about bringing Martin over. Anyway, I'll ring you. And don't think I've forgotten about the sociology tutor. I'll await developments.' She patted her belly. 'That's all I can do at the moment.'

As Fran drove back towards Belgate she thought about Dennis and Min. His family's furniture business, Fellowes', had boomed in the 'fifties and 'sixties. When they married they had moved into a custom-built, split-level luxury home and Min had a new car every year. Their two children went to private schools and

Min's perfume cost £42 a bottle.

But Fellowes' shops were situated in colliery areas, their customers mostly miners who bought on credit. They must have felt the draught. Impossible to believe they could go bust, but it was bound to be difficult for a while. There were still strained faces in Belgate, and if Bethel was to be believed things would not get better in the near future. A Russian paper had reported Scargill as claiming that the miners had scored 'a brilliant victory'. If it were true, they had paid a terrible price for it in broken and scarred relationships. Fran felt a sense of despair now whenever she thought about the strike. Bitterness seemed to have increased. Myths abounded, and increasingly people forgot that a ballot had been denied the men, even those who had fought vociferously to obtain one. It was all talk, now, of the Government against the miners and not a hint that miner had been against miner, father against son.

The fading graffiti on the railway bridge caught her eye: '*Scabs are shits!*' And a new slogan, white and bright and startling: '*UDM is Scum*'. No one in Belgate had joined the breakaway union but in Sunderland there were quite a few members.

Fran changed gear for the roundabout and saw the chimneys of her own home ahead. The strike was over, no point in thinking about it now. What was real and imminent and frightening was the prospect of that bloody fishing-rod. They would never get it put together, and if they did they would never catch anything. Since David's death she couldn't bear to see Martin disappointed. Still, as long as he didn't fall into the sea nothing else mattered. She glanced at her watch. Only half-past three, and no need to settle to her books tonight. Suddenly she felt like a kid out of school and it was a pleasant feeling.

2

Now that she was on holiday a Saturday morning lie-in was no longer a luxury, so she was up by eight o'clock, drawing back her bedroom curtains on an unkempt garden. Officially this was the front of the house. In fact, the comings and goings of Belgate were via the back yards and Fran's house was no exception.

It was painful to see the flowers David had planted run to seed. Aquilegia and marigolds were lost in waist-high grass. Today, however, she was full of good intentions. Some time during the holiday she would transform the garden from a wilderness to a perfumed pleasure place.

She had always liked alliteration in English classes. Now she repeated the felicitous phrase aloud twice before she acknowledged its idiocy. She was as capable of creating a garden as she was of writing Italian opera. Still, at least she could tidy it up.

Not today, though. Today, unless the gods were kind and sent rain, she was taking Martin fishing. The sky was leaden, so she might have a lucky escape. She brushed her hair off her face and skewered it with hairpins. Later on there might be time for a bath but first she must riddle the boiler.

As she squatted gingerly among the ash, trying to break up clinker, she wondered once more if it might have been wiser to move back to Sunderland after David's death. Her friends had urged her and there was no denying this house was too big. Its heating system burned money and gave back very little in return. She gave one last vicious twist of the poker and shut the door. There had been a small patch of red glowing faintly through the grey: with luck there would be hot water.

Martin had not made a sound yet. Perhaps he'd forgotten about the fishing trip? If he had, she would take him somewhere else. Somewhere they could do things together, things she could manage.

This was when she missed David most, in the upbringing of his son. No one to talk to about Martin's character, his good and bad points. If you discussed your offspring with outsiders you felt a traitor and they felt compelled to say the child was a saint, so constructive discussion was out. Only with the other parent could you talk freely.

She sat down at the kitchen table and riffled through the morning paper. Wimbledon was front-page news, McEnroe and Navratilova expected to retain the titles they'd won in 1984. Their winning would be predictable and therefore boring unless McEnroe threw a tantrum. But his tennis was bliss, so the next two weeks would at least be pleasurable.

She was reading her fortune ('not a good day for excursions. Stay close to home') when Nee-wan sat up, ears pricked. The next moment there was a bang on the back gate. As she padded down the yard, dog at her heels, a fine drizzle touched her face.

Michael Malone stood in the back street, red hair beaded with rain. 'Is your Martin in?'

Fran ushered him into the yard, retrieved the dog who was keen to explore, and re-bolted the door. 'He's still in bed, Mike, but you can go up if you like.' She made a quick calculation and decided to be brave. 'We're going through to Seaham shortly, to try out his fishing-rod. Want to come?'

For a moment interest gleamed in the blue Malone eyes but it was transient. 'No thanks.'

As he vanished upstairs Fran reflected on how much he had changed in the last eighteen months. Before the strike he had been a fairly normal nine-year-old, outwardly streetwise, inwardly naïve. But the strike had split his family, setting militant brother against rule-book father. Today they passed one another in the street as though they were strangers but it was the little boy who had suffered most. He had to cope with divided loyalties.

He was coming down from the bedroom now, clutching a borrowed football under his arm. 'See you this saffa,' he called back upstairs.

Martin hung over the banister to reply. 'Yeah. Gerra game fixed termorrer and I'll play.'

Fran's smile was pained. Talking to his friends, her son was an elocutionist's nightmare.

When he came down his enunciation had returned to normal. 'It's a nice day,' he said firmly as he ate his muesli, daring her to contradict. 'Just right for fishing.' Outside the sky glowered, the yard gleamed wetly.

'It'll be awful on that pier,' Fran said doubtfully, wanting to put him off, no longer able to say a straight 'no', now that his twelfth birthday was in sight.

He grinned at her. 'I'm still going, mam. You get more fish when the sea's a bit rough. They bash their heads on the rocks and it knocks them silly. Then you just dangle the hook ...' he made a cast with an imaginary line ... 'and you've got fish and chips.'

She was consumed with love for him and proud of his persuasiveness until a new and terrible thought struck her. 'You're not expecting me to clean them, are you? Because I couldn't.'

In the end they agreed that any catch would be admired, measured and thrown back, and he went off to get ready. 'Wrap up!' she called after him and received the predictable short reply.

She was stacking the breakfast things when the yard door rattled. 'It's me, Bethel.' Five days a week Bethel cooked and cleaned for Fran for a peppercorn wage. On Saturdays she paid social calls. 'That tea's stewed,' she said, feeling the pot. 'Get the kettle on.'

As they drank their tea Bethel recounted the local gossip. Her tongue was acid but her heart was kind. The deeds and misdeeds of the neighbourhood were catalogued and graded, and local funerals listed. Bethel would be attending the Methodist church at 2 p.m. to see off her second cousin. 'Never was strong ... a chest like an old tin can.' After the funeral she was expecting company.

'Anyone special?' Fran enquired but Bethel's lined face

remained impassive.

'Walter ... I doubt you'd call him owt special.' Walter was Bethel's seventy-year-old boy-friend. Lamed in the pit, he booled around Belgate in an invalid car.

'Do you think he'll pop the question today?' Fran asked innocently.

Bethel sniffed. 'He can pop as much as he likes, the answer'll be the same.'

'Go on,' Fran urged. 'Admit you love him.'

Bethel stood up and reached for her hat. 'I can see I'll have to go. You're in one of them moods. Impudent! I'm old enough to be your mother, so show some respect.'

Fran wound her arms around Bethel's neck, against only token resistance. 'You know I love you, Bethel. I only want what's best for you. Let Walter make an honest woman of you. I'll be bridesmaid.'

'Let me out.' Bethel broke free and rammed her hat on to hair that was thinning with age. 'I can see how it's going to be. Twelve weeks of torture. That college of yours wants to get down to some work instead of letting the likes of you loose to torment decent old women.'

In spite of her outrage she stayed long enough to fettle the boiler and wipe down the draining-board. 'I'll be in on Monday, and make sure you've simmered down by then. You're worse than the bairn.'

There was no sign of the sun as they drove out of Belgate but the drizzle had eased. Perhaps they would get on and off the pier without mishap. 'You mustn't go near the edge,' she warned for the umpteenth time.

'I know, mam. You've already told me.' His tone was weary and she made a mental note not to be so over-protective. Kids survived, even kids who were unsupervised, sometimes unloved. That thought created a fresh terror: perhaps she loved Martin too much, so that he was almost singled out for disaster? She glanced at the landscape for diversion.

Belgate was a small colliery village perched above the North Sea, the houses radiating from the pit. It had one main street, two pubs, two churches, a miners' Welfare and a cenotaph. Everyone knew everyone else's business and, on the whole, they got on together very well. Or they had done until the strike.

The last house flashed past and there was a brief interlude of fields before the outskirts of Seaham began. Seaham was a town, boasting three working pits and a shopping centre. Last week she had taken Martin to see the harbour. Now she wished she hadn't, for he had gone on and on about the anglers ever since. Bethel had overheard and appeared next day with an ancient rod. Martin had gone into ecstasies, Bethel glowed with benevolence, and Fran had found herself promising to mount an expedition for which she was totally unfitted.

A wooded dale led towards the sea. The road was lined with neat houses and green spaces where people were exercising their dogs. Nee-wan lay on the ledge behind the back seat, looking out at the other dogs and occasionally uttering a token growl.

'We can't take the dog on the pier,' Fran said. 'It isn't safe.' To her relief Martin didn't argue. He was too taken up with the rod. Its massive handle was bound tight with string that had turned yellow with the sweat of its owner's palm. Bethel's husband had died in the pit forty years before, aged twenty-nine. He must have come up from the darkness of the shaft and revelled in open air and sea.

'You're lucky to have that rod,' she told Martin. 'Take care of it.'

His eyes, when they met hers, were exasperated. 'I know, I know. It belonged to her husband. I'm not daft, you know, mam.'

Fran's anxiety increased when they got to the pier. She tried to ignore the swirling water below the sheer drop, by concentrating on the assembly of the rod. 'It's easy,' Martin grimaced, trying to force one length into another.

'It screws,' Fran said. The brass ends were grooved but the pieces refused to join.

[13]

A sea-bird waddled forward to get a closer look. Fran was about to offer help when she saw the set of Martin's lips. It had become a matter of honour now, a challenge. 'Look,' she said, trying to sound reasonable, 'let's lay the pieces out in order and then try again.'

His fingers were stained with rust and suddenly looked immature, the hands of a child. He looked up and saw her sympathetic face. 'It's a bugger, isn't it?' he said.

'Don't swear,' Fran said automatically but they both knew more was at stake here than words. They needed David. They needed a man to flick the pieces of rod into place and make everything simple.

She looked towards the end of the pier. Two men were hunched over their rods. Even if she dared walk out that far, they would hardly appreciate interruption. She was still staring seawards when the voice came from behind. 'Need a hand?' She let out her breath in a sigh of relief and turned.

Martin was already holding out the segments of the rod. The newcomer was dressed in a grey sweater and slacks, too well pressed for the pier, but the hands manipulating the rod were deft. He wasn't from around here, though. The accent was southern, even a little Cockney. His eyes flicked up and caught Fran's. 'I used to have one like this ... well, something like this. They're mostly fibreglass nowadays.' They grinned in mutual appreciation of the rod's venerable age.

'There now.' The last segment clicked into place and he handed the completed rod to Martin. 'Watch what you're doing.' He had laid a pipe and tobacco pouch down to handle the rod; now he picked them up.

'Watch him,' he said to Fran, in a lowered tone. 'The rod's a bit big ... if he swings it too enthusiastically it could topple him.' A wedding ring gleamed on his left hand. 'I'd stay, but I have to get back.'

Fran nodded. 'I'll be careful. You've been very kind.' He wanted to be away now and she turned her back to set him free.

'It's not as easy as I thought,' Martin admitted after a half-dozen abortive casts.

To the north, over Sunderland, the sky was turquoise and streaky. Down below, the beach stretched into infinity: golden sand, free from rocks, but almost empty because of the weather. It was always cold here. If this beach were in the south or on the west coast, it would be renowned. But if it were anywhere else it would have lost its trademark – the faint patina of coal dust that lodged at the tide-line like the black edge of a mourning card.

She turned to the south. Below, in the small dock, brightly coloured fishing-boats bobbed at anchor. Once this harbour had throbbed with life. They still sold fish here, fresh-caught and silver, but it was a hard trade and one made no easier by bureaucracy. Over in the main harbour a ship was moving through the gates. Sailors home from the sea. Behind the pit bulked, mountains of coal and foothills of scrap iron: industry and dereliction. She felt love well up in her for this place, this bleak coastline that was her heritage.

'You're not scared, are you?' Martin was looking at her, wide-eyed.

'No.' She shook her head and blinked her eyes. Impossible to explain patriotism. She didn't even understand it herself. 'I was thinking about the lifeboat.'

He let the rod sag, interest aroused. 'Where is it?'

Fran shook her head. 'They don't have one any more, they share Sunderland's. They had one once, when I was your age. It went out on a rescue and then it went down and they were all drowned. We had a collection at school, and everyone was sad.'

Martin's face was sombre as he went back to his fishing. Perhaps mention of the lifeboat had put the sea into perspective. It could lap your feet at the tide's edge, or swallow you up like a flake of foam.

The drizzle had returned and the greening stones of the pier were slippery. Once or twice Fran took a grip of the middle of his jacket, only to have her hand shaken angrily away. 'It's raining,' she said, looking gratefully at the sky. 'We could come back next week.'

Martin lowered the rod, honour satisfied. 'OK. I'll be better at it by then.'

They couldn't dismantle the rod completely but managed to separate it into two halves. 'There's a pub on the sea-front,' Fran said. 'We could get lunch there if you'd like?'

Martin was in a good mood, grateful that she had not ordered him off the pier. 'Can we afford it?' he said.

She felt a surge of goodwill towards him. 'Definitely. Providing you don't want champagne and caviar, you can have anything you like.'

He settled for fish and chips. 'Fish is better in batter.' He chewed for a moment. 'I was a bit worried about catching anything. I mean, they flap around. I've seen it on the telly.'

Fran nodded. 'I know. You're supposed to hit them on the head or something.'

He crunched his batter. 'We'll find out before next week.' They both knew there would be no second expedition but the myth had to be sustained for the time being.

They were on to dessert when the man from the pier came in. The barmaid greeted him like an old friend. 'Eating in today?' So he was a resident! Fran turned away, anxious lest he saw them and was caused embarrassment.

'What do you want to do?' she asked. 'Go to the casino?'

Martin's eyes gleamed. 'OK, but I can only afford 50p, and we can't leave the dog much longer.'

The money vanished into the fruit machine like snow from a griddle. 'It's a mug's game,' Fran said, 'it never pays out.' And was turned into a liar as the bandit gushed out silver for the person who had taken Martin's place.

They drove into a wooded dene beside an ancient church and set free the dog. Fran watched it run, wild with delight, turning at intervals to make sure they were following. A dog was a responsibility but worth every ounce of effort. 'I'm enjoying myself,' Fran thought and hugged the idea to her until the damp grass penetrated her flimsy summer shoes and brought her back to reality.

[16]

They called at Treesa's on the way home. It was six weeks since Treesa and her baby had left them for her new council house. Every time Fran passed the spare bedroom door she felt like pushing it open to see the small head rear up from the pillow and smile a welcome.

'Come in. I was hoping you'd come round.' Genuine pleasure showed on Treesa's face – pleasure and pride. The tiny living-room was packed with new furniture and the shag-pile carpet ran from wall to wall.

'It's lovely,' Fran said but each woman knew what was in the other's mind. The money that had furnished the room had been blood money, bought with a death in the pit. 'I'll pop up and get the bairn,' Treesa said. 'He's ready to wake up and he'll be pleased to see you.'

A new stereo gleamed in the corner, and a video under the TV. You needed such things when you were alone, Fran thought, remembering how she had clung to music after David died, to records that would make her cry and let her emotions run free.

'There now, look who's here.' The baby was still sleepy but his eyes lit up at the sight of Martin.

'I've got him.' Martin was proud of his skills with the baby, and the two women relaxed.

'You must stay to tea,' Treesa said. 'I'll be glad of a bit company. You don't feel like eating when it's just yourself.'

Fran nodded. 'I lived on cottage cheese after David died. Just cottage cheese off a spoon. I never set a table. Still, you've got to look after yourself. Don't your family come round ... or the Malones?'

Treesa twitched out a non-existent ruck in the new hearthrug. 'Me mam comes sometimes, and the bairns call round. Me dad's been once, to see how I'd got the place. He liked it.' She was picking at an imaginary hang-nail until she looked up defiantly. 'And Terry comes round ... just to see there's nothing needs doing. Well, he is the bairn's uncle.'

[17]

Fran wanted to reach across and soothe the jerky young hands, but it wouldn't do. 'He's a very kind young man. Just like Brian. You remember how kind Brian was to me when I was on my own? Well, you used to come with him sometimes, didn't you? After Brian died, Terry just took over. I don't know what I'd have done without him. Still don't know.'

She was getting better at fending for herself but there were times when a man's strength was indispensable. The day before yesterday Terry Malone had forced back the bent mud-guard on Martin's bike and stopped it from scraping the tyre.

Treesa stood up. 'I'll pop the kettle on and then we can talk. I've got heaps to tell you.' There was an air of excitement about her under the unease, and Fran understood the emotional turmoil that engulfed Treesa. She had been seventeen when she became pregnant, eighteen when Brian had died on the eve of their wedding, crushed between tubs in the pit.

Since then she had given birth, had moved in with Fran to escape her unsympathetic mother, fought as an unmarried mother to establish her right to compensation for Brian's death, and set up a home. All in the space of eighteen or twenty months. And now Terry was in love with her and that love was returned: Fran had seen signs of it before Treesa moved out, and had sensed how afraid of her feelings the girl had become. It was hard to acknowledge that life and love went on after bereavement. Fran knew that from experience.

When Treesa came back into the room she made a determined effort to change the conversation. 'I'm taking the bairn to a playgroup twice a week. He likes the company.' In the corner the baby rocked back and forward, trying to force a plastic bucket into its mouth, eyes bright with laughter at Martin's antics with a jack-in-the-box. 'He's good with babies, your Martin. It's a pity ...' Treesa's words died away as she realized their implication but Fran didn't mind. Lately she had come to terms with the fact that Martin was her only child and likely to remain so.

'We'd been trying for another baby for years,' she said, smiling to show she was not upset. 'In and out of clinics. They couldn't find any reason, it was just one of those things. If David had lived we'd have persevered. We might even have adopted eventually.'

Treesa was still embarrassed. 'Well, you still might ... I mean...'

She was floundering and Fran came to her rescue. 'Tell me about your new neighbours. Are they nice?'

Treesa launched at once into an account of neighbours right, left, and opposite. Right and left were elderly people who kept themselves to themselves. It was opposite that interested Treesa. 'He was sacked after the strike. He was taken to court and fined, but he lost his job just the same. You can't say that's fair.'

Fran shook her head. 'No. If that's true it's not fair.' The plight of the sacked miners was a sore point in mining areas. Fran did not believe that men who had done bodily harm to others should get off scot-free, but she had heard too many stories like Treesa's to be happy about the situation. 'Can't he appeal?'

Treesa's laugh was scornful. 'Appeal? Who to? It's been left to the area directors and we all know whose pocket they're in.'

As Treesa went to scald the tea, Fran fought hard to restrain a smile. The sacked miners were no laughing matter; what was funny was the way Treesa's voice and attitudes were beginning to mirror Terry's. He had always been militant, a Scargill follower. Now, unless Fran was much mistaken, he was spending a lot of time with Treesa and his opinions were rubbing off.

Over the tea it emerged he was coming round that night. 'He wants to fix the tiles in the toilet,' Treesa said. 'There's nothing in it, I mean, I wouldn't. Even if he was interested ... which he's not ... well, you know I wouldn't get up to anything.'

She was still vowing chastity when she waved Fran and Martin off. 'Be happy,' Fran said as she left. 'Don't worry about anything else.'

The trouble with being cryptic was that it didn't work. Treesa would take no notice and go on worrying just the same.

'Are you stopping in tonight?' Martin asked as she got out to

[19]

open the garage doors.

'Don't I usually?' she answered dryly.

He shrugged. 'How do I know? Anyway, if you are, you can't watch mush on the telly. Sports Special's on.'

Fran gave a theatrical groan. 'I'll go to bed then. Poor old mum. Thirty-four years old and no rights.'

He was smiling, relieved that she had not given him an argument. Secretly, she was pleased. She didn't need telly. A nice long bath, with nothing to prepare for the morning. Bliss!

She was turning on the immersion heater when the telephone rang. 'Frances?'

Her heart leaped and then steadied to beat twice as fast as usual. 'Hallo. I didn't expect to hear from you.' It was true, she had not expected Tony Lund to ring, in spite of his words.

'I suggested a meal, didn't I? When are you free?'

They arranged to meet on Tuesday night and she put the phone down slowly, waiting to hear the click at the other end before she let go. 'Who was that?' Martin called as she crossed the hall.

'No one. Well, no one special.'

When she was safely in the bath, suds up to her chin, she thought about Lund. He wasn't special. Quite a typical lecturer except for the disturbing eyes. He had nice hands, good fingernails, his hair touched his collar, and his breath quite often smelled of exotic food. Par for the sociology course. So why the agitation?

She had arranged to meet him in Sunderland. She still couldn't bear the thought of another man picking her up here, in David's house, but she was looking forward to the meeting. Some sixth sense told her that, like Byron, Tony would be mad, bad and dangerous to know, and she was in the mood for some excitement. She reached for the loofah and began to scrub.

3

She had looked forward to the ritual of dressing-up but when it came it was an ordeal. Foundation caked as she applied it, mascara clogged and beaded, and had to be wiped away, leaving her chipmunk-eyed. She sat on the edge of the bath and drew breath. She was going out for a meal with a man, that was all. No big deal. David had been dead for two years. No one could expect her to live in purdah, no one except herself.

She put on her navy suit with the red and white blouse and lapels, then decided it was too formal and changed into a pink linen shift-dress. Now her red lipstick clashed and had to be replaced. She cursed gently as she tried to wipe it away. Somewhere in Sunderland Tony Lund was washing his face, perhaps changing his shirt – no more. Men had all the luck. Thoughts about the chore of daily shaving intruded but she put them resolutely aside. It was her turn to feel deprived and no one was going to stop her.

Bethel arrived as Fran was making Martin's supper. 'Leave that to me. You don't want your best dress mucked up.'

Fran sat down gratefully and watched Bethel bustle about. Three years ago they had been strangers. Well, almost strangers. Bethel had come twice a week to clean the house and it was David who had joked with her and drawn her out of her shell. Then David had died and Bethel had taken over.

'She's like a mother to me,' Fran thought, emotion pricking pepper-like at her nostrils.

The older woman was stooping to peer under the grill. 'It's not the same,' she said gloomily. 'Not that anything is nowadays, but toast has no taste. The bread's pap and you can't beat a fork to the fire.'

Suddenly Fran understood. Bethel was angling to keep open

the living-room fireplace. During the strike Terry Malone had opened it up, after years of disuse, and they had kept a fire going with whatever came to hand. Now the strike was over Fran was preparing to have it blocked off again, but if it stayed open Bethel could give her part of her concessionary coal – and she was determined the fireplace should remain.

'You never wanted me to open up that fireplace,' Fran said accusingly, but Bethel was not abashed.

'That was because you set a madman loose on it. If you'd gone about it sensibly I'd have been all in favour. Anyroad, stop raking old coals. It's open now and it's daft to shut it. You could keep a fire going for next to nothing, and burn all your rubbish besides. And you wouldn't get cardboard when you wanted toast.' She banged two pieces of toast on the bench to illustrate her point. 'It's a good job that lad of yours has a good set of teeth.'

Fran promised to reconsider the fireplace and made her good-byes. 'I won't be late and I won't do anything you wouldn't do and I'll try to be a lady.' Bethel's snort of disbelief followed her through the hall.

Tony was already at the town-centre hotel, lager in front of him and the *Guardian* open at the leader page. While he collected her drink she glanced at the headlines. 'I thought you'd read this,' she said, indicating the paper as he slid into his seat.

'Compulsory,' he said, returning her grin. 'No good sociologist is complete without it.'

So far, so good, Fran thought. Away from the college environment he seemed more vulnerable, less of a threat. 'Tell me about yourself,' he said suddenly and set the alarm bells ringing once more.

'You know all about me.' She sounded defensive and the teasing gleam returned to his eye.

'Not the important bits. What makes you tick, Frances Drummond?' He was going to probe! Worse than that, he was going to analyse. He had probably invited her out as part of some terrible sociological research project and he was waiting for an answer.

'What makes me tick?' she said. 'Oh, the usual things. Home,

[22]

children, getting through college ... surviving. Just general surviving.'

He was expecting more and it wasn't fair. David had always
dictated topics of conversation he knew she could follow. His
questions had been straightforward. The only other man in her
life had been Steve, and they had shared misery and comforted
one another. This man was offering no comfort.

'Why have you stayed in Sunderland?' she said, suddenly determined to carry the war into the enemy's camp.

He grinned in appreciation of the ploy. 'I wanted to see you.'
And when she blushed – 'I like to see you go pink. You do it in
group discussion, every time I ask you to take up a point.'

Fran was nettled. 'So that's why you always pick on me.'

There was crisp dark hair in the open neck of his shirt and
along the backs of his hands. He reached out a forefinger and
momentarily touched her wrist. 'You shouldn't complain. I'm
bringing you out of your shell. And you still haven't told me
about yourself.'

She was into the game now. 'I live in a shell. I'm a single parent
of limited intelligence who had the temerity to think she could
cope with a teaching course. Correction, the entirely misplaced
temerity.'

He was laughing and it gave her confidence. 'I can't help getting myself into situations where men far cleverer than I ask me
impertinent and unanswerable questions, to which I can give
only the sketchiest of answers.'

'Men? So I'm one of a long line?' He had caught her.

'No, that's not what I mean ...'

He had very good teeth and he knew it, allowing his tongue to
touch against them when he smiled.

'So I'm the only man in your life?'

Careful, Frances. Don't say too much. 'The only clever man.
So please don't torment me.' She was useless at conversational
tilting. That was for the Germaine Greers of this world who were
born with a thesaurus in one hand and a lance in the other.

He didn't take her arm when they came out into the evening

[23]

air but his presence was all around her. He was sexy, she decided over her prawn and almond balls. Or rather, sexual. And sensual. Sometimes he laid one fingertip on her upturned wrist to emphasize a point, and afterwards she looked down, convinced she would find a burn mark.

His mood changed abruptly with the lychees. 'What made you go in for teaching?'

She chewed for a moment, trying to gain time. She could hardly tell him she had chosen teacher training because it seemed to postpone taking an actual job, or because she could just manage to live on the grant and, most importantly, the hours co-incided with Martin's school times. Besides, it was no longer true. In the beginning she had felt no great calling, but things had changed. With each spell of teaching practice she felt more involved. Perhaps she might make a teacher after all.

'I always wanted to do it but David ... my husband was called David ... wanted to get married as soon as we could and it didn't seem worth training if I was never going to teach. So I worked in a bank, just marking time.'

'Your husband didn't believe in working women, then?'

She couldn't resist a smile. 'I don't think he ever thought of me as a working woman.' She felt suddenly disloyal. 'No, that's not quite true. I never saw *myself* as a career woman. I wanted to be David's wife. From the first, that was all I wanted; and then Martin came along and we were very happy until...'

He filled her glass and then his own and showed no sign of wanting further information. Fran was first grateful and then piqued. His interest didn't last for long.

'What about you?'

He was smiling again. 'What about me? You know it all. I'm an open book. I'm thirty-seven years old, I teach sociology and I read the *Guardian*. I have two homes, a rather poky flat in Sunderland for term time and a house in Yorkshire for off-duty ... not that there's much of that.'

Fran was not to be fobbed off. 'You've never married?'

His smile deepened. 'There's no Mrs Lund.'

Fran felt her cheeks burn. 'I wasn't meaning that.'

They talked of the course, then, of students and lecturers and the possibility of a job at the end of it all, but the uncomfortable flush still mantled Fran's cheek. He must think her a complete square.

She had parked the car underneath a tree in a well-lit side street. He walked her back to it and waited while she fumbled for her keys. When the door opened she moved inside but he reached out a hand. 'Whoa. I don't bite.' He was holding her lightly and she could move away if she chose, but she was power-less to pull away and they both knew it.

He kissed her lightly on the forehead, then on each closed eye. His lips barely touched her but she found herself stirred out of all proportion. 'I'll ring you,' he said, suddenly distancing himself. She wanted more. She kept her eyes lowered, willing him to move back and uncomfortably aware that if she looked up, his eyes would be amused. She felt like a naughty child now, anxious to be away and yet incapable of moving.

He made it easy for her, opening the door wider and holding her elbow lightly to turn her car-wards. 'Sleep well.'

She was out on the Belgate road before she realized she had not said thank-you. It was a fresh embarrassment to add to the rest. She couldn't handle him, that was sure, and yet he turned her on in a way that was new to her. He had made none of the usual moves and yet she was hooked. She *wanted* him or, rather, the unknown quantity in him. Sex with David had been warm and comfortable. Sex with Steve had been an act of mercy, giving rather than receiving. Sex with Tony Lund would be – ? She thought about it for more than a mile without finding a single suitable adjective, but that there would be sex with him she had no doubt.

She felt distinctly sinful as she let herself into the house. 'Not a word out of either of them,' Bethel said. In his basket Nee-wan lifted an ear, then half-rolled on to his back in the hope of a tickled belly. 'Good night?' Bethel asked.

She knows, Fran thought, busying herself with the kettle. She knows I'm having randy thoughts. 'It was all right. He's just one of my lecturers.'

Bethel nodded. 'So you've been having a night class. By, it's nice to see someone dedicated to their work.'

They were both laughing now, sitting down at the table to share coffee and sympathy. 'Anyway, he's probably got someone else.' She was thinking over Tony Lund's words: *'There's no Mrs Lund.'* That meant he had no wife. It didn't mean he was unattached.

Bethel blew out smoke. 'If he is, drop him. If they'll play away once, they'll play away twice. All these lasses nowadays, snaffling other folks' husbands. Proud of it, some of them. Beats me why they can't see it. On the other hand, he might be a single feller. If he's been at college he might not have had a chance to meet a lass.'

Fran considered explaining the sexual mores of university life and decided against it. 'Well, we'll soon know for sure.' The possibility that he might be living with someone had obviously never entered Bethel's head and Fran was glad.

She put Nee-wan on his lead and set Bethel to her gate. The July sky was still tinged with pink and there was night-scented stock in someone's garden. Fires burned in the grates of Belgate in spite of summer and smoke rose into the air from several chimneys. 'Watch what you're doing, lass,' Bethel said as they parted. 'You're enough to drive a body up the wall but I wouldn't like to see you come to harm.'

'I'll be careful.' Fran felt good now, at peace with the world as the adrenalin subsided. He might ring tomorrow and if he did she would handle it better. He was attractive and he knew it, but that was not a crime. If all he wanted was sex, there were others in the class who would be happy to oblige and much better at it than she. 'Perhaps he's after my mind,' she said aloud. 'In which case he'd better bring a magnifying glass.' She was still chuckling when she was safe inside and bolting the door.

[26]

4

She was out in the garden before 8 a.m., gathering up weeds by the handful and piling them neatly in a corner. It was the height of summer and couch grass tickled her bare legs and poked through the crevices of her sandals. Nee-wan had trotted after her at first. Now he lost interest and lay, belly upwards, in the sun.

Ever since end of term she had felt guilty about the garden which David had planted and she had let run to seed. Coming to grips with it was a tremendous relief – and enjoyable! She had not realized how satisfying it would be to rescue a clump of iris from encroaching weeds, trowel the hard-baked earth until it was black and moist, and leave the green spears standing proud.

She would garden a lot more now that she knew she could do it. That was her trouble: she shirked because she feared her own inadequacy and other people's competence. Having discovered a Titchmarsh-like talent, she would be at it all the time, hoeing, pruning, tying up with twine. She tried to straighten her back and found herself doing a Richard-the-Third hobble. Time for breakfast!

She poured water into the dog's bowl and he lapped noisily, droplets leaping from the bowl and spattering the floor. At last he looked up and turned expectantly towards the biscuit cupboard. 'Just one, then.' To think she had gone thirty-two years of her life without knowing the love of a dog! She had taken the puppy to comfort Martin for the loss of his father, and had found endless comfort for herself. She bent to fondle the silky head. They had named him Nee-wan because no-one (as 'nee-wan' as her neighbour had put it) knew his breed, but he was a noble dog, whatever his genes.

She was still enjoying a flush of emotion when the phone rang.

It was Min. 'You're OK, aren't you?' She was making rapid calculations about dates. It couldn't be the baby, not yet!

'I can't talk, Fran ... not now. But I've got to see you!' Though Min was usually impassioned when she wanted something, this sounded different.

'I could come over about seven; I'm coming in to Sunderland then, in any case.'

'No, that's no good. You've got to come now! Dennis is out ... I don't know how long for, but I've got to talk to someone.'

Fran's heart thudded towards her boots. 'Oh Min ... it's not Hindson-Evans again?' It was Min's affair with a surgeon of that name which had almost wrecked her marriage.

'Are you mad? I can hardly cope with one man at the moment – I can't see my feet ... No, this is serious, Fran. Too serious to talk about on the phone – you must come over. Now!' If Fran hadn't known that Min never cried she would have thought she detected tears.

'I've promised to take Martin to Seaham. He's not going to fish, thank God, but he wants to watch. I'll come to you first. Martin can play with the kids ...'

Min's tone was flat. 'They're not here.'

Now Fran was really alarmed. 'OK. Let's not go on about it. I'll be with you as soon as I can.'

Martin was mutinous when she suggested a change of plans. 'I don't want to go. You promised we'd go to Seaham.'

In the end Fran compromised. 'I'll drop you off there, but you're not to go near the water.' Martin's eyes rolled heavenwards. 'All right, I know you're eleven but that doesn't mean I don't want you to make twelve! Stay where it's safe and I'll get back as soon as I can.'

She was getting out the car when Terry Malone came into view. At a distance he looked remarkably like Brian, his dead brother, but as he drew close the tilt of his chin, the direct gaze was his own. Brian had been as easy as an old shoe; Terry was made of sterner stuff. In the strike he had been for Scargill, his father for a ballot. When his father returned to work, Terry had

[28]

moved out so as not to share a roof with a scab. Though the strike had been over for more than a year, still he had not gone home.

'Hallo, Terry. I was going to pop round to your mam's in the hope that I'd catch you.'

He was bending to fondle the dog. 'Good lad . . . all right now, no need to jump up. What can I do for you, Mrs Drummond?'

She wanted him to baby-sit. 'Bethel's got a chance of the holiday flyer, so she's Bingo bound tonight – though what she'll do with a package holiday abroad I do not know.'

Terry was more knowledgeable. 'They sell them. There's always someone wants it. You get half-price, mebbe a bit more if it's a fancy place.'

The mysteries of the holiday flyer had only recently been explained to Fran – every Bingo winner received a ticket entitling them to take part in a special game whose prize was a package holiday. 'Treesa goes to Bingo, doesn't she?' Fran asked. 'It'd be nice if she won a holiday. You could go with her and take the baby.'

She had made the remark innocently enough but he blushed to the roots of his hair. She was about to make some mollifying remark when she changed her mind and opted for defiance. 'I know you're fond of her, Terry. A blind man could see that. She hasn't said anything but I'm certain she feels the same. So why shouldn't you go on holiday together?'

He shook his red head. 'Don't ask me, Mrs Drummond. I'm not the one with the mucky mind. It's all the tongues round here, that's what's got Treesa scared.'

Aloud, Fran made light of public opinion. Privately, she conceded Treesa had a point. Belgate was like any other place, full of sympathy for a widow unless, and until, she decided to retire from the widowed state. It had taken them a while to concede to Treesa the status of widow. Having given her a grudged respectability, many would disapprove if she took up with another man, especially if that man was her dead lover's brother.

Terry was willing, even eager, to sit with Martin and Fran finished getting out the car. Martin appeared before she could shout. 'Come on, let's get going.' His tone was imperious and he fastened himself into the passenger seat with aplomb.

'What are your orders, sir?' she said once she was behind the wheel.

'Drive on,' he said, waving a lordly hand, and shaking out his comic.

'Yes, sir,' she said and let out the clutch.

They had left Belgate behind and were driving between fields when she saw a familiar figure in the distance. It was Fenwick, the miner who had been the first to break the strike. She was used to seeing him alone now, wearing the aura of the outcast. Damn the strike.

She cheered herself up by remembering that she had two cans of lager at the back of the fridge. She would put them out for Terry tonight. He was still short of money, still repaying debts incurred during a year without work. What spare money he had went on Treesa's baby so he would appreciate a drink.

'Wake up, mam. You'll miss the turning.' She swung the wheel and left the A19. 'The sooner I'm old enough to drive the better,' Martin said smugly and returned to his comic.

She left him at the harbour, urging him to stay away from anything that might be in the least dangerous. He nodded reassuringly, spitting on his hand to reinforce his promise, but she was still anxious as she walked back to the car.

'I see he hasn't brought the rod today.' It was the man who had helped them on the pier.

'No. I think one day was enough.'

He was tapping out his pipe on a stone wall and he caught her looking at it. 'That's all I seem to do with this thing. Fill it up, have a dozen goes at lighting it, and then knock it out.' He shook his head ruefully. 'Cigarettes were so much easier.'

Fran felt the instant sympathy of the fellow nicotine addict. 'Have you just given up? Stick it out ... I gave them up a while ago and it was hell at first. Now I'm glad I did.'

Suddenly she remembered Min and was guilt-stricken. 'I'll have to go. A friend of mine is in some sort of trouble ...' She looked back towards the harbour, searching for Martin, and he followed her eyes.

'Are you leaving him? Don't worry, I'll be hanging around for a while. I won't let him fall in.'

She was grateful and then suddenly afraid. A man wandering about? He looked respectable, but who said psychopaths had to dress in rags? As if he had read her mind he fished in his pocket. The wallet was shabby and bulging and opened to reveal a photograph of two children, boy and girl, a small picture of a woman superimposed. As she admired them, he fished in his wallet for a business card. 'There you are: my bona fides. I'll be down here for an hour or so, I've nothing else to do. So off you go!'

Fran felt suddenly ashamed of her doubts. 'I didn't need your card . . .' she said, and was fumbling for the right words when he cut her short.

'Don't apologize. It pays to be careful.'

As she let out the clutch and moved back on to the road, his face was in her mind. A nice face, even good-looking. But not her type. She could be on a desert island with him for ten years and feel not a flicker. The pier man faded and Tony Lund took his place. That was different. Last night he had fingered the nape of her neck and she had felt her vaginal muscles contract. It was crazy but it was true. Just like that – a reflex action but quite devastating.

She looked up and caught her own eyes in the rear-view mirror. Guilty eyes. She tried to banish randy thoughts and fixed her mind on Min. What could it be? Surely Dennis had not strayed from the straight and narrow? Lots of men did when their wives were pregnant. On the other hand, Dennis's delight in the coming baby was genuine enough – she would bet on it. She was still conjecturing when Min's driveway loomed up, and the car ground to a halt in the gravel.

Min's eyes were huge in a white face. 'She's got no make-up on,' Fran thought, and knew that whatever was wrong must be very wrong indeed.

'We've gone bust,' Min said when they were sitting at the kit-

[31]

chen table. 'Finished. Kaput. Not a penny!'

Fran's first reaction was relief. So it was only the money! Then she thought again: Money was life-blood to Min. What did you say to someone when their life collapsed like a pack of cards?

'I'll make us a nice cup of tea,' she suggested.

'It can't have *all* gone,' she ventured later, when they were supping the tea.

'All,' Min replied flatly. 'Shops, houses, cars – they're all company property. Some nasty little man from the Official Receiver's office came round this morning and immobilized the cars. He says the Receiver will take everything. The kids will even have to leave their schools ... my God, I could weep when I think of it.'

Fran tried to marshal her thoughts. 'I thought Fellowes was a limited company, and that meant they couldn't touch your possessions?'

Min's tone was bitter. 'That's what I thought. But Fellowes got into deep water during the strike – you know all their business was in mining areas. There was stock unsold, no one paying their HP ... The business needed cash to keep going, so they put up our houses as security.'

'Your in-laws' too?' Fran asked.

Min nodded. 'I can't help feeling sorry for them – awful to build up a successful business and then see it pulled down by a bunch of shits.'

Fran couldn't let that pass. 'It wasn't as simple as that, Min. The miners didn't strike on purpose. They thought they had a cause.'

For once Min was not disposed to argue. 'Oh, all right. What does it matter, anyway? Whoever's to blame, it's done.' She put a hand on her swollen belly. 'I've got to keep calm for the sake of the baby. If it wasn't for that, I'd get in my car and drive it into the nearest wall ... just to stop them getting their thieving hands on it. I loved that car!'

Fran couldn't resist a smile. 'Oh, Min, trust you to think of your Capri.'

A ghost of a grin touched Min's face. 'I know. I'm upset about the whole thing, but the car really hurts. And the thought of Eve! She's going to *love* all this. Harold rang Dennis this morning to say he would help if he could. I should bloody well think so! He's been our accountant for the last ten years, he should've seen this coming. God knows what he's made out of us. Now we lose everything and he keeps the lot. It makes you sick!'

Fran listened while Min poured out her anger and fear for the future, but her mind kept straying to Martin and the North Sea, sucking greedily at the harbour walls. 'I'll have to go,' she said at last. 'But you know where I am. I'll do anything.' She hesitated, wanting to help and yet afraid of putting her foot in it. 'Remember, we've got heaps of room. If you and Dennis and the kids need a place – in between houses – Martin and I would be glad of the company.'

Min looked suddenly confused. 'I never thought of that. Where will we live?'

Suddenly Fran remembered her own fears after David's death. 'I'll tell you one thing,' she said firmly. 'However things turn out, it won't be nearly as bad as you think.'

In the hallway Min suddenly reached out. 'Oh, Franny, isn't it a bloody life?' She looked down at her bump. 'Still, we'll have to make the best of it! And Dennis, poor sod – I'll have to keep going for his sake.'

Fran smiled. 'You'll be all right, Min. It'd take more than liquidation to get you down.'

Martin was sitting on a wall when she got to Seaham, watching cranes swing backwards and forwards. The pier man was expounding about imports and exports. 'You're back,' he said, as Fran reached them. And then, seeing her face: 'Bad news?'

Fran shrugged. 'It could've been worse. All the same ...'

Martin looked suddenly perturbed and she hastened to calm his fears. 'No one's hurt, so it's not really bad. But Aunty Min's had a shock. Uncle Dennis's business will have to close.' She looked towards the pier man to explain. 'They're friends of ours, close friends. And she's expecting a baby soon.'

[33]

He had taken out his tobacco pouch. Now he put it away. 'I think you could do with a drink,' he said and, looking at Martin, 'Coke for you – or lime and lemon?'

As they walked up the bank towards the pub on the sea-front, she wondered how old he was. Late thirties? There was something careworn about him, a fatherly quality. And something else, less reassuring. They were almost at the door of the pub when she realized what it was: an air of defeat, as though he were coping with a terrible despair.

They chatted about Min and Dennis over the drinks. He didn't know their name or location, so it didn't seem disloyal to discuss them with a stranger. He was sympathetic and knowledgeable about the strike. 'We did quite well out of it,' he said. 'We brought in coal to some of the smaller harbours ... but it was different for other people.'

Fran remembered his card, still in her pocket. He was something to do with shipping.

He walked them back to the car and she thanked him. 'It was a great help, knowing you were there,' she said and he smiled.

'It was no trouble. That's a nice lad you've got there.'

She was driving away before she realized he had said nothing about seeing them again. 'Ships that pass in the night,' she thought.

'His name's Jim. He used to go to sea,' Martin said, turning back from waving. 'He's been to every continent. He says he'll show me some photographs next time.'

Fran nodded. 'That's nice.' All the same, she would have to check. You couldn't be too careful; he'd said that himself.

The phone was ringing when she got home. 'I thought it might be you, Eve,' she said, trying not to sound acid.

'Of course, they'll lose everything,' Eve said. 'I know she's brought it on herself – I mean, the mad extravagance! – but you can't help feeling sorry. Still, Harold will help. I've told him to pull out all the stops.'

Alone in the hall, Fran winced. When David had died she had been on the receiving end of help from Harold and Eve. Eve had

[34]

expected her to live like a pauper and Harold had tut-tutted over the least extravagance. Even bubble-bath had been forbidden – and all for her own sake. She was tempted to tell Eve to leave Min alone, but they had been friends since infants' school and it wasn't that simple.

'It may not be as bad as they think,' she said but Eve was not to be gainsaid.

'Harold says they'll lose everything, and are lucky to be in liquidation, rather than bankruptcy. *That* means they can take everything, down to your undies. They only need to leave you a bed and a chair. You can't even have an electricity bill when you're bankrupt.'

Fran tucked the telephone under her chin and began to push back her cuticles. In an hour or so she would be meeting Tony. They would go for a drink, perhaps a meal. Perhaps go back to his flat. She put up a hand and felt her hair. There would be time to wash it if Eve would just shut up.

Martin appeared from the kitchen and she began to signal. 'Who is it?' he mouthed, and she mouthed back, 'Aunty Eve!' and rolled her eyes to the door. He nodded and tiptoed away. The next moment the ring of the doorbell pierced the air. 'I'll have to go,' she told Eve, and then ran upstairs to get ready.

5

The smell of new-baked bread was like no other, Fran decided. 'Aye, they're not bad,' Bethel conceded when Fran showered praise on the plump rolls and crusty loaves that covered the kitchen table. Bethel had only lately agreed to bake in Fran's kitchen, declaring the electric oven a menace until she had mastered it.

Today Eve and Min were coming to tea. 'Min'll adore these,' Fran said, breaking off red-hot crust to reveal the steaming, doughy bread beneath.

'She'll be lucky to find any left,' Bethel said tartly. 'I'll be glad when you get back to that college of yours and let me have this kitchen again.'

Outside, the August sky was still blue but this morning Fran had seen a browning leaf. Autumn, autumn. Worse still, autumn term, the beginning of her final year. The thought was so frightening that she turned back to the bread.

When Min arrived she would ply her with hot rolls and butter. Actually, Min was being amazingly brave. Every night, or so it seemed, notices of Fellowes' liquidation appeared in the evening paper, alarming, official notices that made the whole thing seem to roll on remorselessly. In spite of all this, Min carried on, cheering Dennis, encouraging the dazed children, and preparing to give birth.

Eve was scathing each time she phoned. 'She won't stay. You wait till this baby's born. She'll be off! I mean, what will there be to stay for? You know Min, money mad! And the best Dennis can hope for is some sort of job in retail. Harold's always said you can't beat having a qualification. If Dennis had a few letters after his name, he'd be in a better position now.'

'What's the matter with you?' Bethel was glowering at her across the kitchen table. 'Your face is tripping you up.'

Fran nodded. 'I know. I was thinking about poor Min.' She was saved from Bethel's scorn by a knock at the yard door.

A man stood in the back lane, his bike loaded with bags of coal beside him. 'Need any coal, missus? It's proper coal, not duff.' That meant it was stolen, Fran thought.

'Thanks a lot but I've got plenty for the moment. I have it delivered.'

He nodded and turned away as though he had been expecting a refusal. If he had argued, pushed even a little, she could have closed the door but his resignation was harder to deal with. 'How much is it? Perhaps I could take a bag.'

The coal was £2 a bag: half-price. But what was a saving of £2 if you went to gaol?

'You know who that is?' Bethel was peering out at the man tipping the bag into the coal-house and her voice spoke volumes.

'No,' Fran said, raking through her purse for two pound coins. Bethel bridled. 'He's a right villain! You've done it now, miss, throwing in with the likes of him.'

Fran forbore to answer until the back door was safely rebolted and she was back at the kitchen table. 'I haven't thrown in with anybody, Bethel. I've bought a bag of coal, probably stolen, definitely cheap. I've told him I have it delivered so it's unlikely I'll see him again, and there's no need for you to get uptight. However, I can see from your face that you're going to give me chapter and verse, so let's get it over with.'

'You should've told him to hadaway to Hell, never mind getting it delivered. He's a real hard case, lives opposite Treesa. She wants to keep her doors locked. Lost his job for GBH – nearly maimed a man. And that's just what they can pin on him . . . God knows what the truth of it is.'

So he was the sacked miner Treesa had mentioned. That explained his downcast air. The coal would have come from the stockpile at the pit. Stealing was rife and the police seemed to do little about it. 'It hasn't been fair,' Fran said defiantly. 'If they really did wrong, they should lose their jobs but the policy hasn't been fair. You can't say it has, Bethel! They've been taken back in one place and left sacked in another, for the same offence. That can't be right?'

Bethel took refuge in a mighty sniff which meant she knew she was on shaky ground. Fran decided not to push her advantage and poured herself a second cup of tea.

The man hadn't looked like a villain, he'd looked like a confused boy. Technically he was a thief, but he was taking what he felt to be his due . . . the fruit of the Durham earth, hard, black, unyielding coal. He was a casualty of the strike, like Fenwick who had been left without friends, and Mrs Botcherby, who had begun the strike as a bubbly little blonde and ended it as a hollow-eyed patient in a psychiatric ward.

As if she had read Fran's mind, Bethel spoke. 'Botcherby's

lass's home.'

Fran was pleased. 'That's good. How is she now?' If she was home her husband might lose his haggard air and her little girl look like a child again, instead of a woman cut down.

'Not too bad, by all accounts. But you can't tell when they first come out. It's what they're like when they're under pressure that counts.' At the height of the strike, Mrs Botcherby had walked naked into the street to demonstrate her pain. *'It's the pressure,'* her husband had explained. *'She always liked to pay her way.'*

The front door banged and Martin appeared in the doorway, Mike Malone behind him. 'We want Penguins, or custard creams if you've got none, and Coke, and Mike's shoelace's broke. Can you put a knot in it?'

Fran hunted for a spare shoelace while Bethel told both boys what she would like to put a knot in. 'Aunty Eve and Aunty Min are coming to tea,' Fran said while they swilled biscuits and orange, the nearest thing she had to Coke.

'I'm off then,' Martin said and made for the back door.

'His manners don't improve,' Bethel said, oozing satisfaction. 'I warned you about bad company. Give your Martin a week or so, and he'll be worse than them he's learned it off.'

Fran smiled sweetly. 'That's why I love you, Bethel. You're such a ray of sunshine.'

Bethel grinned. 'I do my best.'

Eve and Min arrived at four, Eve fussing around Min like a mother hen. 'Watch that step. There you are, Fran, I brought you a jar of my lemon curd. I know you like it.' And then in a lower tone, 'I'm far too busy to take an afternoon off, but I couldn't let her come on the bus, could I?'

Fran groaned inwardly. So that was how it was going to be. They got the difficulties of dressing for so many functions with the bread buns, and the impossibility of finding decent domestic help with the Victoria sandwich. This was after Bethel had clumped in wielding a steaming kettle and topped up the teapot with a muttered aside about hollow legs.

Min's face was a mask of impassivity but Fran knew it must be irking her. Eve had taken Min's place at the top of the heap and was being none too subtle about it. Fran's thoughts wandered: if David had lived she would have continued to see Ladies Circle as the hub of the universe. She might even have been elected to office like Eve, and had a medallion on a ribbon to prove it.

At five to five the phone rang, and Eve jumped to her feet. 'It'll be for me. I left your number with the girl, I knew you wouldn't mind.' Eve's 'girl' was a wide-eyed Sunderland teenager, as near to an au pair as they could get.

'They pay her peanuts,' Min said as Eve rushed to answer. 'Sheer exploitation! It's enough to make you take out a Party Card.'

The idea of Eve's reaction to Min's joining the Labour Party struck them simultaneously and they had to stifle their laughter in case it percolated through to the hall. 'We're being hysterical,' Fran thought and was suddenly sober.

'Seriously, though,' Min said at last, wiping her eyes. 'Let's talk while she's out there.'

Fran took another slice of cake and pushed the plate towards Min. 'She'll be there for hours.'

Min nodded and fell into a passable imitation of Eve's voice. 'I'm doing my best for Min ... well, what are friends for? I drove all the way to Belgate in second gear in case I brought on premature labour and on the way home I'll help her to count her blessings.' Her merriment subsided. 'Not that that'll take long.'

'How are things?' Fran asked.

Min shifted her bulk into a more comfortable position. 'Fairly bloody. If only I could get out from behind this bump and get cracking!'

Fran was sympathetic. 'Not long now. Three weeks?'

'And two days ... and then we might see some progress. Dennis does his best but he's still punch-drunk. His father kept him in the dark about the money side. You know Dennis ran the shops ... he knew sales were down – God bless Scargill for that – but he didn't realize the cash position was so desperate.'

Fran was going to ask about the house but decided against it.

[39]

'Even when the house was put up to the bank, he didn't twig. His father had the deeds; he just said he needed a temporary guarantee, and Dennis signed. So did I, God help me. I'll read what I sign from now on. Not that it would have made any difference – if he'd said they needed the house to save the business, I'd have said "Go ahead."'

'So there's nothing left?' Fran said.

A ghost of a smile flitted across Min's face. 'Next to nothing but not actually nil.'

Fran was intrigued. Out in the hall Eve was beginning her good-byes. Fran leaned closer. 'What d'you mean, Min? Hurry up, we've only got a minute.'

Min glanced at the closed door and then wriggled around to bring her face close to Fran's. 'Well, you know how they take everything from the business' I mean, everything! Well, Dennis had this box of ornaments ... ghastly things, sort of cheap Capo di Monte imitations. Fellowes used them in window displays, but customers could buy them if they wanted to for thirty or forty quid. Anyway, the ornaments kept getting smashed in the warehouse, so he brought boxes of them home and stuck them in the garage. He was going to take them and give them to the liquidator! "Are you mad?" I said. So I've got them.'

Fran was puzzled. 'What will you do with them?' Min's home was stacked with *objets d'art*. Overstocked, by Fran's standards.

Min was looking at her with a jaundiced eye. 'Sometimes, Fran, I can't believe you did GCE! I'm going to flog them, of course. I'm going to flog everything I can get my hands on. We need a stake if we're going to get back in...'

She would have continued but there was a ping from the hall as Eve replaced the receiver, and both women sprang back into place. Min smiled angelically at Eve, but Fran could think only of what Min had told her. It was illegal, but was it immoral? Not that Min would care. Something had awakened in Min; a burning desire to protect her family.

They left at half-past five. 'Take care,' Fran said and gave Min a hug. It was difficult, the bulk of Min's swollen belly protruding and keeping them apart. Min's eyes rolled skywards. 'How long, Oh Lord? How long?'

She was trying to squeeze into the seat, where Eve was holding out the safety belt with an impatient hand. 'Sorry to rush you,' she said, 'but I've so much on.' Fran's eyes locked with Min's for a second and saw fleeting pain there. Once Min would have said 'Shut up, Eve,' and Eve would have obeyed. Once Eve would not have dared tell Min to hurry. Once Min would have had her own gleaming pink Capri and not have been dependent on Eve at all. As if Min had read her thoughts she smiled. 'How are the mighty fallen,' she said quietly, and closed the door.

Fran was still waving to the departing car when Walter's three-wheeled invalid car drew up at her side. 'Hello, Walter.'

He had wound down his window but made no move to get out. 'Hello, yourself. Never mind the hellos. I've come for me bread ... if Sally Bethel's going to keep a promise for once.' His tone implied this was unlikely but his eyes were twinkling.

He was dressed in his usual tweed jacket in spite of the summer's day, shirt-collar and tie immaculate, knees covered by a plaid rug bound with a leather strap. He had lost the use of his legs in the pit before Fran was born but his arms and hands were still strong and his shoulders massive.

'Well?' His eyebrows jutted. 'I know I'm a magnificent specimen but you should've seen enough of me by now. Hadaway in and get me a flat cake. Well done, mind. None of your pale imitations of a good stotty.'

Bethel carried the flat cake out herself, wrapped in a clean tea towel. 'Here it is, Walter, as promised.'

He unwrapped the bread and looked at it critically. It was perfectly baked to a rich golden brown lightening to cream at the edges, and still floury. 'Aye, it'll do. It's not what I'm used to, but I'm in no position to argue.' It was exactly what they had expected him to say.

'Bethel's sitting in for me tonight,' Fran said coaxingly. 'Why don't you come to supper? She'd be glad of some company.'

Bethel's snort was pure outrage. 'Company – him? I'd sooner

[41]

be put in a cageful of monkeys.'

Walter's voice was silky, his remark addressed to Fran. 'She plays hard to get but we all know she fancies me. Silly old moo.' Fran was giggling.

Bethel was less impressed. She pushed the stotty cake close to his chest and leaned in the window. 'You've got your stotty, Walter. Take it home and let your meat stop your mouth. And don't bother coming round tonight or you'll get a bucket of water over you.'

He had put the car into gear and was moving off. 'Will you be coming?' Fran called.

He was nearly at the corner when his reply came drifting back. 'I might ... if I've got nothing better on.'

She left Bethel in the kitchen, preparing Martin's tea, and ran upstairs to get ready. If Walter came round it would be nice. She could relax with Tony without guilt about Bethel sitting alone in Belgate. She tried not to think about the other guilts that might strike her tonight. 'Nothing to be gained by crossing bridges, Frances,' she said aloud to the mirror.

Her face looked back, thin still and pale but more resolute than it used to be. The red hair still curled but there were lines at the corners of her eyes and two distinct furrows between her brows. She would have to stop frowning.

She inspected her upper lip. Every magazine she picked up told you about the ageing upper lip which developed thousands of cracks into which your lipstick bled if you didn't watch out. Her upper lip bore even the most searching examination and she got down to basics, turning on the hot tap and fastening up her hair.

In the bath she thought about Tony Lund, acting out various scenarios in her mind. She was pleased about his interest in her, no two ways about it! When she thought of the beginning of term, the one bright spot in an otherwise gloomy picture was the prospect of telling Gwen ever so casually that she was in cahoots with a lecturer. Not just any lecturer, but the most personable of the lot. He would never marry her, he wasn't the marrying kind. All

[42]

the same she ran through the acceptable wedding colours and settled for cream.

As she rubbed herself dry she pondered the divisions of the mind. With one bit you could think something quite barmy – like believing you would ever be married to a handsome sociology tutor – with another bit you knew you were fantasizing, even despised yourself for doing it; and yet the two parts could co-exist quite happily.

The thought sustained her through two goes at getting her make-up right, telling Martin to go to bed when Bethel told him, bearing Bethel's disapproval of her slit skirt, and driving nine miles to Sunderland. She felt quite serene as she walked into the cocktail bar and accepted Tony's smile of appreciation as though it were her due.

They went back to his flat for a meal, and as she teased him about his culinary abilities, her mind was in a ferment. She knew what would happen. She was thirty-four years old, a married woman, not a novice. They would eat and drink, and they would make love. No big deal. She let out her breath in annoyance. Martin was always using that stupid Americanism; now she was doing it.

To take her mind off the evening ahead she looked around the flat. It was not what she had expected. She had had two distinct sets of expectations. In one daydream, he had been surrounded by Victoriana. Not expensive bits, but good. One or two rare prints, a worn but valuable Persian carpet, and shelf upon shelf of books. In the other setting it had all been high-tech: plate-glass and chrome, original cartoons on the walls and a cord carpet. The reality resembled neither.

It was shabby. Not nice shabby, like comfy old shoes that had once been expensive, but cheap shabby. Hardboard sides and wafer thin veneers, a shag-pile carpet and rampant tigers in lacquered frames. 'Don't blame me for this,' he said, catching her unawares. 'It's rented and, as I don't use it except to sleep and work, I've refrained from imposing my personality.'

[43]

Fran doubted if you could impose much personality on shag pile and jungle prints, but there were other things to worry about. He had planted a dish in front of her. 'Crudités,' he said. The dish was piled with strips of raw vegetable: carrot, cauliflower, celery, marrow, and a couple of things she couldn't identify. There was a bowl beside it, containing what looked like speckled mayonnaise.

'Tuck in,' he said, gathering a handful of strips. His fingers were lean and brown, and his nails immaculate but a trifle long. He was dipping a strip of carrot into the bowl and munching. His teeth were his best feature. She bit on a piece of dipped marrow and found it delicious. She was going to enjoy this after all!

They had lasagne to follow ... Marks and Sparks, from a microwave she guessed ... and then cheese and biscuits. He served things, leaving her to eat what she chose. She liked that.

He was in the kitchen, collecting coffee, when the phone rang. She waited for him to hurry through the door but the ringing ceased and she heard him talking. There must be an extension in the kitchen. She couldn't hear exactly what he was saying but it sounded like a casual conversation. He gave no explanation when he came back, simply put down the coffee and slid easily to the floor to pour.

There was a tape playing in the background, a piano trio making pleasant but unrecognizable music. 'Loussier,' he said, and Fran nodded sagely, although she hadn't the faintest idea what he meant. The coffee was strong and dark and good, the perfect finish to a meal. He patted the floor beside him. 'Come here.'

She said, 'Yes, lord and master,' but she went just the same.

He was touching her mouth, her neck, her breasts with the one gentle tracing finger. 'Funny Fran.' He was lifting her chin so that their eyes would meet but she struggled, unwilling to look at him. 'Are you scared?' His tone suggested that if she were scared it was for nothing, and yet his finger undid the buttons of her blouse and pulled it free of her skirt. 'I want to love you, Fran.'

She put her face into the hollow of his neck. 'I know.'

[44]

His hand was running gently up her spine, unfastening her bra. 'Can I? Is it all right.'

There was nothing to be afraid of, after all. He was letting her decide. She could call a halt and he would not be angry, nor contemptuous. Not even defeated, as Steve had been. 'Yes,' she said and began to get to her feet.

'Where are you going?' He was holding her arm, drawing her back.

'To the bedroom.'

He laughed gently, pulling her against him and rocking her gently to and fro. 'Oh Fran, what a baby you are. Haven't you done it anywhere else but in bed?'

He didn't expect an answer and she gave none. Instead she concentrated on the parchment shade of the ceiling light and the single burning bulb, trying not to mind about the indignity of shedding shirt and tights. He was holding her head in the hollow of his hand, murmuring encouragement, and she was suddenly grateful. She must pretend it was good. Perhaps it would be, if only she weren't so aware of the lights, the open kitchen door, the bentwood chair legs only inches from her eyes.

'It's all right isn't it, Fran darling?' She was forced to meet his gaze, not comprehending the question. His eyes were light blue, almost turquoise, flecked with green around hard, dark pupils. 'You are on the pill? We don't want you preggers in your final year.'

She nodded and nuzzled his neck again. No point in explaining she was safe as the rock of Gibraltar inside her infertility. ' It's all right,' she said and gave herself up to pleasing him.

6

The stamp of Tony's personality was more evident in the bedroom. Black sheets with tiny coloured diamonds here and there to match the duvet; two pairs of slacks hung neatly on the wardrobe front; paperbacks and folders everywhere, as in the living-room; a diverse and rather touching jumble on the ghastly, glass-topped dressing-table. Perhaps, after all, he was an ordinary man. Fran closed her eyes and snuggled down. It was five weeks since the first time they had made love but she still felt the original excitement and the same post-coital inertia.

Tony was in the shower. He always showered after making love, emerging clean and pressed and totally asexual. Which was strange, because beforehand he was totally the opposite.

She was finding it difficult to define her relationship with Tony. He came and went between his homes, and when he was in Sunderland he wanted her in his bed. No, that was not strictly true. He wanted her. The bed was at her insistence, which caused him to call her 'a complete pleb'. He had smiled when he said it and seemed not to mind, but she was left with an aftertaste of guilt, as though she were hanging on to some outmoded convention. Everyone she knew made love in bed. Or did they? Most of the pillars on which life was based were assumptions. You thought you knew what went on behind the closed doors of your friends, your colleagues, your bank manager, but in reality you never did.

The thought of her bank manager orgiastic on the hearthrug was so delicious that she laughed out loud, but cut it short in case Tony overheard and thought she was laughing at his performance. Which would have been unfair, because he was good at making love, leaving her at peace. She moved her legs in the bed and remembered him inside her.

[46]

She was roused from a pleasant rerun of the last hour by the shrilling of the bedside phone. In the kitchen there was a faint echoing peep-peep and in the living-room too. When she found he had two extensions she had thought it the ultimate extravagance; now it seemed a good idea. She waited for him to pick the phone up but it rang on. He must still be in the shower. She looked at her watch: four-fifteen in the afternoon. It was OK for her to be there. She picked up the phone.

'Tony, the kettle's on the blink. Bring the Russell Hobbs with you. Don't forget ... and remember we're out to dinner.' There was a pause and then, *'Tony?'*

Fran moistened her lips. 'I'm afraid he's not here at the moment.' She was prepared to stammer out some explanation of her own presence, but the caller seemed not to need one. *'Oh ... all right. Tell him about the kettle. Boiling pans is bloody and I haven't time to shop for a new one. He'll have to do that at the week-end.'*

When Fran had replaced the receiver she lay still. At the sound of the woman's voice she had wanted to put down the phone but you couldn't do that. So he was married, after all! Such a domestic message could have come from no one else but a wife. Which made him a liar.

He came through the bedroom door just as she had pictured him: clean and shining and precise, all the langorous, teasing quality of his pre-coital performance gone.

'Someone rang,' she said, sitting up, hugging duvet and sheets to her breasts. 'They didn't give a name, but they want you to take the kettle with you. The other kettle's gone wrong.' He didn't answer, forcing her to add, 'It's terribly important. And you're to remember you're out to dinner.'

He was nodding, shovelling change and other paraphernalia from the dressing-table into his trouser pockets. 'Are you getting up? Otherwise, I'll have to leave you here, I'm afraid.'

She tried to wriggle into her clothes under cover of the sheet. She knew it was crazy after such uninhibited love-making, but she couldn't help it. Her modesty was superfluous. When she looked in the mirror he was busy filling a leather grip, quite ob-

[47]

livious of her presence.

They went out to their cars together, his arms full of files and loose-leaf folders. 'Don't forget the kettle,' she said as she climbed into her car.

For a moment his old teasing manner returned. 'I won't forget, Miss Nags. Can't get it out of your mind, can you? It was just a friend. We share things. If she needs a kettle she shall have one. Now go home and forget it. You've got four more days of freedom, so enjoy them!'

She went up to the bathroom when she got home and stepped out of her clothes. At the beginning he had offered her the use of his shower, but when she had refused she could see he was relieved. He liked to keep his shower to himself, which was exactly the way she felt about her bathroom. It wasn't just that, though; it was that he wanted rid of her afterwards. She was trying not to mind, to get it into perspective, but it wasn't easy.

She lowered herself into the warm water. Four more days to relax, and then she must work hard. In less than a year she would be a fully fledged teacher – if she passed. He *wasn't* married: no wife would be so offhand about a strange woman answering her husband's phone. Outside she could hear Martin shouting. Shouting gleefully, which was all right. She sank lower into the water and gave herself up to luxury.

She was trying to pretend that the water was not cooling when she heard the phone ring. Still smarting from effects of the call at Tony's flat, she decided to let it ring, but the impulse was short-lived: if it stopped ringing she would spend the rest of the day imagining the worst. Better get it over with. In the end she half leaped, half stumbled down the stairs, clad in towels.

It was Dennis. 'She's started, Fran. She wanted you to know.' He sounded less than jubilant.

'Has she gone in?' Fran was making rapid calculations.

'Not yet. We thought it'd be best to hang on . . .' Min's bed in an expensive nursing-home had been cancelled when the money ran out. She was having the baby on the NHS and Dennis's sombre tones said it all.

'She'll be all right, Dennis. It's terribly efficient in the District General. That's where I had Martin.' She stopped then, anxious not to labour the point and worried that her towel would slip and leave her naked in the hall. She felt uneasy, just like she did in communal changing-rooms: you were defenceless without the clothes and jewellery that were your identity. She cut Dennis short. 'Look, I'm coming over. Tell her to hang on.'

As she struggled into the first garments that came to hand, she pondered the unfairness of life. She had wanted another child so much, had sat through endless sessions at the infertility clinic to achieve it. All in vain. Now it seemed her life revolved around other people giving birth.

No one had asked her to go to Min, but it was obvious where her duty lay. 'Oh God,' she said aloud, 'I sound just like Eve.' Should she ring Eve? There would be hell to pay if she didn't, but worse if she did and Min didn't want it. She decided to be cautious.

It was Wednesday, Bethel's Bingo night. She would forgo it if Fran asked, but it wasn't fair. It would have to be Terry and if he failed, Martin would have to go to Treesa's. Except that she couldn't be sure how long she would be away. Some babies took hours. She would have to explain to Martin and then seek out Terry.

He was in when she called at his lodgings, coming to the door in his stockinged feet. His T-shirt was old and shabby but his arms were amazingly strong and muscled. She had noticed that about young miners ... their faces were the faces of children, their hands were huge and powerful, almost out of place.

'Why aye, I'll watch him, Mrs Drummond. It's nee bother.' He nodded towards the living-room door behind him. 'They'll be glad of the place to themselves for a while.' At the height of the strike he had left his parents' home, and since then he had lodged with a young miner and his wife, both as militant as Terry and glad to give him a home. All the same, it must be difficult at times.

'Martin was over the moon when I said you might come round. Can you stay if I don't get back in time? You never can tell with babies.' Terry assured her that she could stay away for a week, and watched as she went down the front path. 'Leave it all to me,' he called as she got into the car.

Driving towards Sunderland, she thought about Min and Dennis. At the moment they were both bearing up, Min better than Dennis. This baby would tip the scales one way or another, would be a millstone or a blessing, depending on their attitude.

The H of the hospital sign came into view and she shuddered. Till the end of her days that sign would remind her of David, strapped to the stretcher, lying grey and quiet as the ambulance skidded and swerved to get him there on time. *'He'll be all right now,'* the driver had said when they got there, but he had still died. She shook her head to banish morbid thoughts and took the turning for Min's. At least she lived near to the hospital; that would make it easier for everyone.

Dennis was in the hall when she got there, with Anthea, Peter and James, all unnaturally solemn and clad in their outdoor clothes. 'Dad's coming for them,' Dennis explained. 'If they're round there, it leaves me free.' The three little faces were tense. Poor kids, Fran thought. They must have been aware of the business collapse. A *'For Sale'* board stood in the garden, and now they were being shipped to their grandparents.

'You'll have a new baby by tomorrow,' she said. 'Do you want a boy or a girl?'

The reply was unanimous. 'A boy!' 'We don't want another girl,' James said and gave Anthea a look of scorn.

Usually Dennis was good with his children. Today he seemed not to care. 'Go in,' he urged Fran. 'I'll take the kids down to the gate. Dad should be here any moment.' She was moving away before she realized he didn't want her to meet his father. She had known Mr Fellowes all her life, had watched him grow from a one-windowed shop proprietor to the owner of a chain of stores. He had gloried in his increasing wealth and new-found status.

Now it was gone, he was probably anxious to avoid prying eyes.

'Thank God you've come,' Min said. And then, suddenly anxious, 'You didn't ring Eve, did you?'

Fran shook her head. 'No, I'll ring her when it's over. How do you feel?'

Min's face gleamed with sweat as she pushed down with her arms and tried to shift her body into a more comfortable position. 'Bloody ... but I don't care. As long as I get it over with, that's all that matters. Do you want tea?'

'No, but I'll get you a cup.'

Min shook her head. 'I'll only want the loo if I drink and I can't face getting up. I feel as though I'm coming adrift.'

A spasm of pain crossed her face and she started to pant short breaths. 'I don't know if this stuff helps, but might as well try it.' Her breathing slowed and she relaxed. 'That's it for a while ... about twenty minutes, I think. When it gets to ten-minute intervals, we'll go.' She licked her lips. 'I'd love a gin.'

Fran was alarmed. 'You can't drink, Min. Not now. It's dangerous.'

Min threw back her head to laugh. 'It's bleeding impossible, darlin, 'cos we haven't got none. Just another of life's little luxuries gone down the plughole. Still, I've always got Eve to comfort me. She rang yesterday. "Don't worry about going NHS," she said. "It's not quite the same, but as long as you both survive it doesn't matter, does it?"'

Fran giggled. 'She didn't say that?'

Min's nod was emphatic. 'She did. The inference being that we'd be lucky if we did survive.'

Fran shook her head. 'She's wrong, Min. The treatment's the same, the standards are just as high. There are two differences: you don't get the etceteras like tea for visitors and Laura Ashley curtains; and they treat you with less respect.' She had never realized that until now, but it was true. Martin had been born in a NHS maternity ward. Most of her friends, apart from Treesa, had given birth in private wards. The only difference in attitude had been that the nurses in the public wards told you what to do, whereas in the private ward they asked. And yet you paid for medical treatment, no matter where you got it. By cheque or by taxes, you paid just the same.

Min was grimacing. 'I think it's another, Fran.'

Fran took her hand. 'Are you sure?' It was a labour pain all right. Min's knuckles showed white, and where she had gripped Fran's hand there were red marks.

'I'll ring for a taxi,' Dennis said, coming back into the room.

'Don't be stupid.' Fran was fumbling for her keys. 'Take the Mini.'

They half-carried, half-bundled Min into the car. 'Stay with him, Fran, when he comes back. I don't want him sitting around the hospital, feeling sorry for himself. See if you can get him to eat something. They'll ring when there's any action!'

Dennis was harder to persuade.

'I don't want you there, Dennis,' Min said. 'I absolutely, positively want to do this on my own. You won't help, you'll just divert everybody's attention from me. I want you to come back to Franny, and come in again when it's all over and there's a wizened little red thing with a big mouth for you to admire.'

She's trying to protect him, Fran thought. It isn't that she doesn't want him there, it's that she doesn't think it'll be good for him. 'Go and get on with it, kid,' she said, patting Min's arm. 'I'll see to everything here.'

Dennis was still dubious when he returned. 'I should've stayed.' Fran had tea ready on a tray, and they carried it through to the living-room. 'Do you want the fire switched on?' he asked. She shook her head, remembering the days when Min's central heating, thermostatically controlled, had run round the clock. Now, like the almost empty fridge, it was in retirement.

'I don't expect it'll be long,' she said, handing him tea.

'They're going to ring when she goes into the delivery room. Then I'm going back.'

Fran raised her eyebrows. 'Does she want you to do that?'

He shook his head. 'No, but I'm going anyway.'

Fran smiled. 'Trust Min to be different. It's the fashion now-

[52]

adays to have your husband in at the birth, but she has to do it her way.' Her tone was affectionate and he took it as it was intended.

'She's never run true to form ... not even now. I used to think all she cared about was the goodies – you know, clothes, jewellery...' His voice faltered a little. 'That bloody awful pink car of hers. I thought she'd take it badly when everything went but no... "We'll start again," she said. That's all.'

'And will you?'

He shook his head. 'No way, Fran. If we get this baby safely into the world, we'll sell the house so the bank stops moaning, find somewhere we can afford on a mortgage, and I'll get a job flogging something. We'll manage.' Fran would have changed the subject but he seemed anxious to go on.

'I should've seen it coming. I thought once the strike was over, things would pick up but I was wrong. It's been worse since the miners went back. They suddenly realized they had huge debts – debts they could never repay, in some cases. No one dunned them while the strike was on – you can't get blood out of a stone. But once it was over, everyone wanted their dues. The miners thought once the strike ended, everything would be roses. They were wrong.'

Fran knew what he meant. In Belgate the mood had changed completely since the strike. Even the perception of how the strike began was different. They did not see Scargill as the cause of their troubles, now – that had changed on the day he was defeated and became the underdog.

'I wish I could offer you a drink, Fran, but the cupboard's bare.' Fran wondered if she dared suggest nipping out to an off-licence. She had the milk money in her purse, and cheering Dennis was a good cause. She was saved from decision by the phone.

'That's it, Fran. Can you drop me off?' Dennis was moving for the door as he replaced the receiver.

'I'll come in with you ... just till I know everything's OK.'

He made no move to drive and she got behind the wheel. Dennis's long legs looked incongruous shoved up against the dashboard. His own car had been a sleek Mercedes, and now he had no car at all.

'It's a girl,' the nurse said, when they arrived. 'You can look in the nursery window when they come out of delivery, and hubby can have a few words with mum. Only a few words. We don't want the ward disturbed at this time of night.' It was nine o'clock and the TV was still blaring, but there was no mistaking that the nurse meant what she said.

Min came past them on a trolley. Dennis seemed overcome at the sight of her and it was left to Fran to say, 'Well done!'

Min smiled. 'I really wanted another girl. Two of each. Have you seen her?'

Fran shook her head. 'I'm going to have a look now, but I bet she's gorgeous. I'll wait for Dennis and run him home.'

Dennis had to wait while Min was returned to her bed behind drawn curtains. At last they were pulled back and the staff nurse gave an imperious nod. 'Off you go,' Fran said and turned towards the nursery. A midwife pointed out the right cot but Fran would have known it anyway. The baby was dark like Min, black hair, moist now but with a trace of curl, eyelashes fanned on cheeks. She's going to be a beauty, Fran thought, and was pleased.

It was a minute or two before she realized that it didn't hurt any more. She could look at babies and not feel anything except a surge of goodwill. The baby was not hers, never would be, but it had come safe into the world and that was cause for rejoicing.

She looked down the ward. Dennis was bending by the bed, kissing Min's cheek, and her hand was cradling his head. It was the first time she had seen Min show Dennis affection. So good could come out of bad, she thought – another old wives' tale proved true.

She turned away, a little ashamed of watching their intimacy and waited while Dennis looked at his daughter. 'She's lovely, isn't she?'

He nodded. 'A proper little Frances.'

She looked at him. 'What do you mean?'

He was smiling. 'She's going to be Frances Mary.'

'Oh Dennis ... there's no need. It's such an old-fashioned name!'

He turned to wave to his wife. 'No use arguing, Franny, it's the boss's idea. You'll just have to put up with it.' Far down the ward, Min lay back on her pillows but her eyes were expectant. 'Tell her you're pleased,' Dennis said, and Fran mouthed her delight.

'We're going to be OK,' Dennis said suddenly as they drove home.

'I'm sure you are,' Fran said, and meant it. There was nothing like a baby for giving you a boost.

She felt tired but peaceful as she made for the Belgate road. The night sky was pink in the west, blue mother-of-pearl above her, and there was a bottle of white wine in the larder, a gift from Tony. As soon as she got home she was going to have a drink. She bloody well deserved it.

7

Fran opened the car boot and reached inside. 'Take these, and keep them off your shirt.' Martin gave her a pitying look and held the tray of sausage rolls with one hand. 'I can take the vollies as well.' Fran give him the tray of vol-au-vents as Min appeared in the doorway.

'Can I help?' Fran handed over the tin containing the cheese-cake and looked her up and down. 'You look smashing, Min.' Min had regained her figure, and her face, always attractive, was more interesting now that faint lines of worry punctuated her brow.

'It's an ancient suit,' Min said, 'but it's crêpe de Chine. You can't beat silk.' The suit was black and white, sashed with a broad red leather belt. Shoes and tights were black and Dallas-style earrings bright red. 'You've got style, Min,' Fran said.

Min was turning away. 'It's about all I have got at the moment, darling. But at least we've got some booze.' Fran gathered up the last of the food and slammed the Mini's boot.

The kitchen was awash with food but it was mostly home baking, not the extravagant cream- and sauce-smothered creations of Min's former days. The booze stood on the freezer, an impressive array. 'Where did you get it?' Fran said in awe.

Min tried to look enigmatic. 'Balloon seller with dog.' Fran was uncomprehending. 'Talk sense.'

Min shook her head. 'I am. That's how I did it. I sold one of the ghastly Capo de Monti fakes ... "Balloon seller with dog". I went into the wine shop with "Girl with umbrella" under my arm, pretending I daren't leave it in the car in case it got nicked. I know the owner's wife – if someone else has something, she has to have one too. You know the type?'

'*Indeed I do,*' Fran thought but said nothing. This was a changed Min; no point in reminding her of the past. Min was continuing, 'I knew she'd be all eyes, so I said I'd been able to get it half-price, forty quid. Could I get her one? she said. I said probably not because they were supposed to be one-offs, and in the meantime could she take my booze order? Then I rang the next day and said she couldn't have one like mine because they were all unique, but she *could* have "Balloon seller with dog". Except that it was more expensive, so she probably couldn't afford it. Of course that clinched it! "Name your price," she said, so I said sixty pounds, which covered the bill.'

Fran was lost in admiration. 'You must be pleased with yourself.' Min looked at her for a moment. 'Pleased? Yes I suppose so. If only I can keep Dennis up. He's got to deal with all these ghastly official things like the winding-up process. Which really means grovelling to a bunch of supercilious accountants who have no real ability except that they can bear to make a living out of battening on other people's misfortunes.'

Fran knew she meant Harold. He was not the accountant charged with liquidating Fellowes Furniture Limited, but in Min's eyes he personified all liquidators. Perhaps it was time for a change of subject. 'Are you going to have enough food?'

They spent the next ten minutes setting out the buffet and fending off hungry children who all wanted Bethel's bread buns. 'She's an old cow but she can bake bread,' Min said, looking at the high-piled basket. There had been a rapport between Min and Bethel since Min had come to Brian Malone's funeral but each of them would die before admitting it. '*Take her these,*' Bethel had said, '*and tell her she's lucky to get them. I'm past baking for all and sundry.*'

Eve arrived as they were finishing. 'Very nice,' she said, handing over her own contribution and eyeing the table. The words 'in the circumstances' were not said but hung in the air. When she turned to go back to the living-room Min stuck out her tongue and jerked index and middle fingers upwards in a rude gesture.

'She means well,' Fran said, but her tone was uncertain.

Min put both hands on the kitchen table and leaned forward. 'Fran, we've all been kidding ourselves for years. I've had time to think during the last few months. Nobody's "friends for life". You say that at school and you mean it – but people change. Life changes them. And if you're honest you have to face facts. I've had to face the fact that for most of my life I've been an empty bitch. No, don't go po-faced and embarrassed. I was a shit to Dennis for most of our marriage, and I filled the kids' heads with a load of pseudo-upper class rubbish. Well, the boys are too young to have taken it in but Anthea has the makings of a right little pain if we don't watch out. I came from nothing and it didn't hurt me. We were as poor as church-mice. I've faced all this, and a few other things too, and I'll tell you this: I don't like Eve!'

Fran was groping for words. If she was honest, she didn't like Eve much either. Half of her did, clinging to the memories of schooldays and shared confidences. The other half of her sometimes wanted to smack her old friend right between her neat, blue eyes. On the other hand, she remembered the time after David's death, the terrible anger she had felt at everyone – particularly Min, if she was honest. Bereavement did that to you.

[57]

Min had been bereaved, shorn of her lifestyle overnight. Perhaps her anger, too, was temporary. 'Well, we can't talk about it now,' she said at last. 'This is supposed to be a happy day.'

She carried the baby down from its cot, blue eyes startling between dark lashes. 'She may be your namesake but she's all Min, isn't she?' Dennis said, gazing fondly at his daughter.

'She's Min's image,' Fran agreed.

Dennis looked forlorn. His cheeks were hollowed and his hair, once so well cut, straggled his collar. He was offering the baby his finger and the tiny fingers curled and gripped. He smiled, and would have gone on smiling had not Harold appeared in the hall.

'We'll take the proud parents. No offence, Fran, but a Mini's hardly the thing for a state occasion, is it? You can fit in Dennis's folks. Everyone else has wheels.'

Dennis disentangled his fingers from the baby. 'OK, Harold,' he said. 'Lead on ... you seem to have everything organized.'

One day, Fran thought, as they made their way out to the cars, she would take a large pin and puncture Harold, so that all the self-importance oozed out of him.

The church was crowded, the christening a bit incomprehensible. It would no doubt be followed by the inevitable handshaking that seemed to be part of services now. It was all right, but it was no substitute for real brotherly love, which often seemed in short supply among church-goers.

The words of the christening ceremony flowed over her but she was thinking about her role as godmother. People took it so lightly, regarding it almost as a social cachet to have been asked. Eve had expressed relief at not being chosen. '*I'd have done it, of course, but I have so much on it wouldn't have been easy.*' Privately, Fran was sure she was choked.

'You're being bitchy again,' Fran told herself, and then offered swift mental apologies for thinking a dubious word in church. They filed back to their seats and sang 'The King of Love my Shepherd is' and then, as she had predicted, the people turned to each other and the handshaking began.

[58]

Outside, the baby was admired and pieces of silver pressed upon it. 'Everyone likes new babies,' James said. He sounded forlorn.

'Poor thing,' Fran thought, 'he's been the baby until now, and he feels pushed aside.'

But Dennis was scooping his younger son into his arms. 'I like new babies,' he said in a stage whisper, 'but I like four-year-olds better.'

Back at the house food and wine flowed. Everyone did their best but no one could forget the '*For Sale*' board at the bottom of the drive or the grandparents, shadows of their former selves, sitting quietly in the corner. Mrs Fellowes had been a pack-leader in Inner Wheel, a golf-fanatic, a fierce worker for the more fashionable charities. Once, long ago, Min had referred to her mother-in-law's middle-aged spread as 'committee woman's arse'. What would she do now? Remain a committee leader or seek a blessed obscurity?

Fran was clearing plates and stacking them in the dishwasher when Harold came into the kitchen. 'This is the last of the plates, I think. Where d'you want them?' She made room on the draining-board and he took a tea-towel. 'I'll dry some of these while we chat. I've been meaning to look you up for weeks. It's just that we have so much on, Eve and I. But you must come over soon.'

'How's business?' Fran asked, and immediately regretted it. Once launched on his favourite subject, Harold was unstoppable.

'Too good, Fran. There aren't enough hours in the day. Not that I have much to do with winding up ... we specialize, you know, and taxation's my forte. But the firm's burdened down with liquidations, and the workload spills over. Well, you know how it is.'

Fran nodded. 'I see it in the paper every night.'

Harold was shaking out his towel and folding it neatly over the rail. 'That friend of yours has had it. That motor salesman.'

Fran tried to look nonchalant. 'You mean Steve?'

Harold nodded. 'Yes, that's the guy. I told you we did his business. We tried to help, but it was useless. Stock he couldn't sell, a mountain of bad debt. The Inland Revenue applied for the order, but there'd've been others.'

'Has he lost everything?' Fran asked.

'Afraid so.' There was regret in Harold's voice. 'Not that there was much to lose, in the end. We'll be out of pocket, I should think. It isn't as though he had a house to sell – that went to the wife when they split, and she made sure that he had no claim on it when they were reconciled. She's quite a tough cookie, by all accounts.' Fran dried her hands. Though Steve had been her lover until he went back to his wife, now she could barely remember his face.

Harold had turned to the miners' strike. 'That's what caused it, of course. All his trade was with the mining community – like Fellowes, but on a smaller scale. We haven't seen the last of the repercussions round here, Fran, I'll tell you that. I was in a warehouse this week piled to the roof with TV sets. Not old models, decent colour jobs. The miners packed them in during the strike, to save the rental and the colour licence. They made do with old black-and-white sets. Anyway, when the strike was over they wanted to begin hiring again ... but they didn't want the sets they'd given back. Oh no! They wanted brand-new sets, never seen a plug. So this chap – my client – he's left with hundreds of nearly new sets that he can't hire at any price. He'll be lucky to give them away. I don't know about closing pits, but friend Scargill's closed down quite a few firms round here. I was talking to a credit bookmaker. All his business is done by phone, but half his clients gave up their phones during the strike, so he's lost out to the corner betting-shop. I tell you, it's endless.'

As she drove past the *'For Sale'* board on Min's drive, Fran thought over what Harold had said. Poor Steve. Jean, his wife, had been hard enough to handle when he had money; she would be a poor companion in poverty. Except that you never could tell.

She'd've said that about Min three months before, and look how that was turning out! As they had made their good-byes, Min had asked if she could borrow the car next weekend to join in a boot sale. 'Of course you can,' Fran had said. 'I'll help any way I can.'

It would be no great sacrifice. If Tony was staying in Sunderland for the weekend he would pick her up, and if he was away she would work, work, work.

'It was a good christening,' Martin said from the passenger seat. 'Can I go out when we get back?'

Fran looked at her watch. Six-fifteen. 'Well, for a bit, but there's school tomorrow, don't forget.'

He groaned. 'Wish I could.'

Ahead Belgate appeared, the sea foaming beneath. 'You like school, don't you?'

'It's OK. Bit boring. I like English, that's about all.' There was a pause and then . . . 'You won't teach at my school when you're done, will you?'

Fran giggled. 'You make me sound like a side of beef. No, I won't teach at your school when I'm done. Wouldn't you want me?'

His reply was fervent. 'No fear. You get bashed up in the bog if your ma's a teacher. I'll probably get it a bit, anyway, even if you're somewhere else.'

She wanted to chide his language but the thought of his being bullied was dreadful. 'They wouldn't really hurt you, would they?'

'They might try, but Mike sticks by me and I stick by him, so they lay off.' Solidarity, Fran thought. The secret of the universe.

8

Outside, the November drizzle was so fine she had to cross to the window and look at the wet yard to decide whether or not it was raining. She had an old T-shirt under a blouse and cardigan, but still she was cold. Time to light the fire! She was buying cut-price coal from the sacked miner, so she could afford a blaze.

As flames devoured paper and licked round sticks, she squatted by the fire. The coal was stolen property; she was an accessory before the fact because she knew he had pinched, was pinching and would pinch in the future. She was suddenly taken up by the word 'pinch'. It was a euphemism, an acceptable way of saying 'steal'. She was an honest woman and wouldn't steal or have any part in a theft, but 'pinching' was slightly different.

The sacked miner was called Dave, and increasingly she saw him as a Robin Hood figure. The NCB was rich, it had mountains of coal on the ground, not to mention stocks yet unmined. Dave stole from the rich to help the poor. He was out of work and therefore skint, and God knows she was poor. Thoughts of Christmas and present-giving slid into view and were shouldered aside. Don't think of Christmas, think of sacked miners. No greater balm for your own misery than to see the other fellow worse off.

Dave was thirty-two and had been a miner since his sixteenth birthday. He had four kids, twin girls of eight, a boy of five, and another just two years old. He had told her about the strike and the loss of his job, and Treesa had filled in the domestic details. He had been on a picket line in Yorkshire when he had seized a working miner by the lapels and butted him in the face, breaking his nose. There had been no satisfaction in his voice when he told her this; if there had been she would have been repelled. Instead she had listened, amazed by the violent details emerging from the mouth of this mild-mannered man.

'We'd had this clash with the police, you see. Me dander was up and then, there he was in front of me, bloody well grinning. Well, I thought he was grinning. Maybe he was just shit-scared like me. Anyroad, I butted him and there was blood coming out his nose and his mouth, and I just felt sick. It was like I'd taken it out of him for everything, no work, no money, our lass taking on so much. I knew I'd be clobbered in the court. I was fined £100 and got a twelve-months suspended sentence. The next week I got a letter from the pit – sacked on the grounds of misconduct. No appeal. Sacked just like that, after sixteen years.'

She had tried to cheer him up but there wasn't much she could say. He had little or no hope of a job, not in this area. There was no work for men even with clean records, so a conviction for GBH would be the bitter end.

'I thought there'd be an amnesty once it was over,' he had said last time. 'And then some of the men sacked for taking coal got took back and I thought, "Maybe me next time." Now I think I'll be pushing this bike around for ever. And I never even wanted a strike, I only came out to please the other lads.'

The fire was burning now, the coal consumed by flame. She put Dave and his troubles aside and sat down to her books. A buckshee day off always made her feel guilty. If she caught up on all her essays she wouldn't feel so bad.

She looked at the blank page and drew a female profile in the top right-hand corner. They said that if you doodled faces it meant you weren't satisfied with your own. Well, that was true. In seven months' time, if she worked, she could be a fully fledged teacher. Her name would be pinned on the wall – providing she'd passed the medical – and she'd be sent a scroll during the holidays. She put the blemished sheet aside for scrap and tried to begin.

She wanted a cigarette! It was months since she'd given up smoking but every time she sat down to work she wanted a smoke. She wrote a neat heading – '*Environmental Studies*' – and then her name – '*Frances Drummond*.' The trouble with ball-

[63]

points was they didn't need sharpening. If she'd been working in pencil she could have taken a knife and carved off satisfying bits of wood tipped with lead.

The clock showed nine-twenty and suddenly she was galvanized into action. Tony was coming for a meal at seven-thirty, the first she had cooked for him. If she didn't get a move on it would have to be takeaway. Fear oiled her pen, and once she was halfway down the page she knew it was going to be all right. She had finished '*Environmental Studies*' and was on to the first of her psychology essays when the phone rang. It was Eve.

'They've sold it. £90,000, but Harold says it'll all go to the bank.' So Min's beloved house was gone. 'Heaven knows where they'll live now. Harold says they should apply for a council house. Can you imagine ... after all that ostentation over the years? Min used to say their garage was bigger than a council house. Well, it goes to show...'

She had no sooner put down the phone than it rang again. It was Min. 'We've got a buyer!' Fran feigned surprise. 'They're coming here from the north. He's some sort of big wheel with that American factory at Peterlee. Oodles of money. Anyway, we got the asking price.'

'Where will you go?' Fran said tentatively. 'You know what I said about moving in here.'

Min sighed. 'It's lovely to know you're there in the background, and we're both grateful, but I hope it won't come to that. What you can do is lend me the car again.'

'Another boot sale?' If Min took the car every weekend, how would she cope? On the other hand, how could she say no in such circumstances?

'No, it's not a sale this time. I've sorted out some of my clothes and there's this marvellous woman in Newcastle who sells second-hand models, only the best mind, and gets you the most marvellous prices. Dennis has borrowed a pick-up from someone in Round Table ... so he can get backwards and forwards and try to get work. Some people stick by you, isn't it funny? Anyway, I could ask him but I don't want him to see me flogging

[64]

my clothes. He's down in the mouth as it is. I don't mind, I'm glad to be rid of most of them, and when I'm rich again I'll stock up with new things – but if you could lend me the Mini he doesn't need to know. I'll pay the petrol. We got a lovely Giro today so I'm feeling flush.'

When Fran came off the phone she sat down. She was non-plussed, but she couldn't decide whether it was the idea of Min on Social Security that floored her, or what Min had said about getting rich again. In the end she decided that the most remark-able thing about the conversation had been the sensitivity Min had displayed towards Dennis's feelings. In the old days she would have not given a fig for them.

Martin came in at lunch-time and they shared their beefbur-gers and beans at the kitchen table. 'Before you ask,' he said, sit-ting down, 'school was OK.'

Fran was affronted. 'What do you mean, "before I ask"?'

He grinned. 'You always say, "How was school?" every time. As soon as I get in.'

'OK, cleverclogs. So you've got a predictable mother.' Round one to him, she thought, but at least he looked pleased.

'Are we going to Seaham this Saturday?' he asked. Most week-ends now they went to Seaham. If she had given him a good day it made her feel less guilty about leaving him at night to see Tony.

'Do you want to?'

He shrugged. 'Don't mind.' This was something new.

'Have you gone off Seaham?'

His shake of the head was emphatic. 'No way. But Jim won't be there this weekend.'

She chewed carefully on her beefburger. Quite often they saw the pier man ... she must remember his name was Jim ... when they went to Seaham. He was good with Martin, but she hadn't realized how attached to him Martin was becoming. She would have to be careful.

However kind he was to Martin, he had a family of his own in London. There would be a limit somewhere, and Martin was probably too young to realize that. She had seen a spasm of sympathy cross the man's face when she mentioned that David was dead, but sympathy only went so far.

'We might do some Christmas shopping,' she said. 'It's getting too late in the year for Seaham harbour, anyway.'

She would have gone on worrying about Martin's possible emotional entanglements if Bethel had not arrived with momentous news. The portents were there as she walked through the door. Usually she crossed to the sink and filled the kettle before shrugging out of her outdoor clothes. When she had *big* news she followed a precise ritual, unpinning her hat and sticking in the hat-pins before laying it upside down on the dresser. Her silk scarf came off next, to be placed, carefully folded, inside the hat. After that came gloves, if the weather required them, and then her coat. After that she would fill the kettle. Then, and only then, would she give vent to the bombshell. And if you tried to hurry her, she became even slower, much more precise in her movements, to teach you a lesson.

Patience paid off. 'They're closing Belgate!'

Fran usually registered enough amazement to keep Bethel happy, but this time it was real. '*Belgate Pit*?'

Bethel's scorn was boundless. 'No, Belgate Opera House. My God, no wonder bairns is getting dafter if you're a sample of what's let loose on teaching them. Belgate pit. P.I.T.'

Fran couldn't take it in. Belgate to close? It was unthinkable. They were on to their second cups, and steeped in gloom, when a car horn sounded outside. 'That's Walter,' Fran said. 'Shall I go out?'

'Just possess your soul in patience,' Bethel said, rising to refill the kettle. 'If you go rushing out, he'll feel he has to drive off so you won't take him for granted. I keep telling you that but you never listen.'

So they sat until Walter's outraged bellow permeated the kitchen. 'Howay, howay, give a feller a hand. I bet you're in there, Sally Bethel, stuffing tea while I bloody well struggle with these steps. I've said it before, I'll say it again. The feller that built this house was a step-fanatic. *Sally*?'

[66]

The rising tone of his voice prompted action. Fran sprang to empty the teapot and Bethel armed the wheelchair into the kitchen.

'You've heard then?' he said, when a cup of fresh tea had been pressed on him.

'Heard what?' Bethel said.

'About the pit! About your friend Mrs Thatcher and her pal MacGregor. I told you they'd shut this village down, but you wouldn't have it.'

'I've heard,' Bethel said. A moment before she had been calling down curses on the government in general and their hatchet-man, MacGregor, in particular. Now, things were different. 'Well, it's Scargill we can thank for this. It was losing money before the strike, so it was hanging by a thread. Now he's finished it off.'

'You won't catch me with that one, Sally. You know how I feel about that shower. Belgate'd have a better chance if we had a united union. I'll never forgive him for what he's done to the NUM.'

'Do you think the pit'll close?' Fran asked.

The massive shoulders raised and then slumped. 'All I know, bonny lass, is that it'll stay open or close according to the powers that be. Little minions like you, me and the rest of Belgate'll have as much effect on the outcome as fluff.'

Fran was not in the mood for controversy but she couldn't resist the question. 'Well, was Scargill right about his hit-list of pits?'

The next moment the argument was away. Bethel and Walter enjoyed a verbal scrap and Fran adored seeing them at it. It was love-play: she had decided that a long time ago. Insults would emerge from either mouth and land on target, but the general effect was to bring the two even closer, where they would have driven any other couple apart.

In spite of the disturbing news it was a blissful afternoon. A good fire, toasted tea-cakes, two people she loved, and stimulating conversation. She didn't think about Tony and the evening

[67]

ahead until Martin came home from school.

'Hallo, Walter,' he said. Nee-wan was leaping up to lick his face, and Walter scowled.

'Who trained that dog? If your mam does as good a job on her scholars as she's done on you and that dog, she'll be getting paid for nothing.'

Martin was grinning. 'I'm all right, aren't I, Bethel?'

Fran had to struggle not to chortle aloud. The little monkey! He had Bethel on toast now. She either must say he was a good boy or side with Walter, something she never did on principle.

She had underestimated Bethel, who took a third option and completely ignored the question. 'You've got company tonight, miss. It's time you got on with it, if you ask me.'

'I didn't half best her, didn't I?' Martin said when they were alone. And then the question she dreaded. 'What did she mean about company?' He didn't like Tony and he made it obvious. They had spent an agonizing afternoon at the Leisure Centre and only Tony's forbearance had stopped an explosion.

'Tony's coming to supper,' she said and adopted Bethel's strategy of ignoring his theatrical groan.

He went off to bed early because there was nothing on TV and he had two library books he wanted to read. They were both Goodies books. 'Very educational,' she said, secretly pleased at the innocuous nature of his reading. 'I'll bring you some supper up,' she promised and then, on impulse, sat down on his bed.

'I know you don't like Tony much, but he is my friend. I like him. You're growing up and one day you'll go away. I want you to go. Not because I don't love you, but because I do. I want you to make a life of your own and get married and be happy like daddy and I were. So I have to make a life of my own, so that I'll be all right when I'm on my own. Do you understand?'

He was wearing his man-of-the-world expression. 'I don't know what you're going on about. It's no big deal.' She was half-way downstairs before she realized he had not made his usual statement about never getting married. So he was growing up after all.

She had prepared lasagne and bought an expensive bottle of wine. Whether or not it was good wine she had no idea, but the price had been mind-numbing. Bloody standards! That was the cause of half the trouble in the world. You couldn't ask anyone to a meal now unless you provided wine, whether or not you could afford it – which she certainly couldn't. Once you'd met that standard, there was the next hurdle: good wine versus bad wine. Hell, hell, bloody hell.

In the end she had worried for nothing. Tony arrived with a bottle of wine. Its label was not brilliantly patterned and it looked uniform and cheap, but she knew it was good. As Bethel would have said, she could feel it in her water. She put her own bottle in the larder and was about to put his in the fridge when he took it from her. 'Not red wine,' he said. 'It needs room temperature.' He took the sting from his words by stroking her hair behind her ears.

She felt the old familiar earthquake in her pelvic region but willed it to subside. She was not having sex here, in her own house, with David's child asleep in bed. Or not asleep, depending on how long she could avoid the subject.

The lasagne was OK except for the top bits which had the consistency of steel sheeting. She kept those bits for herself and gave him the soft underbelly of the dish. That was a woman's lot, to eat up the undesirables.

It was the most domestic situation they had enjoyed. They often had meals at his place, very nice meals but eaten in an impromptu fashion. They had never sat either side of a table with white cloth and table mats and a cruet in the middle. 'Very nice,' he said, smiling at her. 'It's nice to be civilized occasionally.'

It was one of those remarks, inconsequential in themselves, which pack the punch of a nuclear warhead. '*This is not for me,*' he was saying; warning, even. It was funny because she hadn't invited him in order to demonstrate domesticity or draw him further into her net. With another man that might have been her

[69]

intention, but not Tony. She had invited him here because for once she wanted to have the upper hand, and by golly she'd got it. He was running scared. She was so pleased that she allowed him to top up her glass so that there was hardly enough left for him – and she didn't even like red wine. 'Here's to crime,' she said, and this time laughed aloud at her own words.

9

The air outside the bedclothes was as good as any calendar. Three weeks to Christmas, and ten degrees below zero by the feel of it. She snuggled down for her Saturday lie-in. Before long Nee-wan would make his presence felt and she'd have to get up and let him out, but for now enjoy, enjoy!

Thinking of Nee-wan lead to thoughts of Brian Malone, whose dog he had been originally. Next week would be the second anniversary of his death in the pit, the pit that now was hanging between life and death. The NCB was waffling, and nothing was yet definite, but she had an uneasy feeling that Belgate was doomed. The pit would close. The younger miners, Terry Malone among them, would be bussed away to other pits and the older men would take their redundancy and haunt the street corners.

Fenwick came into her mind. Gaunt Fenwick, the strike-breaker, who spoke to no one now. Before the strike he had been a cheerful man, devoted to his prize pigeons. Their necks had been wrung to punish their owner for strike-breaking and with their death the heart had seemed to go out of Fenwick. Fran doubted whether he would care if the pit lived or died.

Downstairs there was a thump and a scrabbling sound. Nee-wan was giving warning of an impending flood. 'I'm coming,' she said resignedly, and leaped out of bed.

The boiler was alight and the house warming up when the

doorbell rang. Min stood on the step. 'I had to come through. I know it's daft to use petrol when I could have phoned, but I wanted you to be the first to see it – after Dennis – and I've got *piles* to tell you.'

'It' was a car, a battered Ford Fiesta sporting a Y registration.

'What d'you think?' Min asked. 'It's only done 45,000, and they threw in two new tyres.' There was oil on her right cheek and lipstick on her teeth, but pride of ownership glowed from every pore.

'It's marvellous,' Fran said, averting her eyes from the bubbling paintwork of the wings.

'No,' Min said graciously, 'it's not marvellous, but it's mine. Well, mine and Dennis's. It's a start, Fran. We are back on the road. Now, where's the coffee. I can't stay but I must fill you in.'

'I can see you're pleased with it,' Fran said as she filled the kettle.

'Pleased?' Min said solemnly. 'Fran, I never knew what satisfaction was until now.'

Over coffee she imparted the rest of her news. 'You're not going to believe this. I only half-believe it myself. You know we need somewhere to live? Well, the outlook was grim: two rooms above a butcher's shop, or a council house in an area no one else would touch. I said to Dennis, "We'll take anything . . . it doesn't matter because we won't be there long." But you know what men are like: he saw it as the end of the world. Anyway, he was seeing our solicitor about the sale of the house and everything, and he asked where we were going. Dennis said the street probably, or words to that effect, and then the solicitor came up with this marvellous offer.'

'What? Get to the point!' Fran could hardly contain herself.

'OK,' Min said, 'I'm getting to it. There's this family . . . he's a civil engineer and works abroad. The wife's a bit fed up and wants to join him. The kids are just at the right age to change schools for a while . . . anyway, they have this super home . . . it's even got a pool. It's in one of the best areas, quite near to Eve and Harold. These people daren't leave it empty for a year, so they want to rent, but they want someone they can trust because they're leaving absolutely everything behind. A Bendix and a double split-level gas and electric; two bathrooms ... and all for a peppercorn rent!' She paused for a moment, her jubilation subsiding. 'We'll have to find the rates, of course, and it's oil-fired heating ... but I expect we'll manage.' She brightened again. 'At least it's a roof of our own, and a posh one!'

Fran felt as though she were going to cry. 'It's too good to be true, Min. But you deserve it. You've been so brave!'

Eve did not share her enthusiasm when she rang shortly after Min's departure. 'Of course, I'm pleased. I mean, no one wanted to see them on the street. But you can't help wondering how she managed it. If it had been Harold and I, we'd have wound up in a hostel. There's no justice. I knew Min would fall on her feet.'

Fran was dying to rub Eve's nose in the double hobs and the gold bathroom taps, but she refrained. Better to leave well alone. Besides, Eve had found a fly in the ointment. 'What will they do with all their stuff? If it's a fully furnished house, they'll have a problem.' In fact, Min was going to sell the entire contents of the house, and hoped to make a tidy sum. She had told Fran yesterday. '*They can't touch it, you see. They can take everything that belongs to the business; that's how I lost my car. But the goods and chattels are mine.*'

Eve was coming to an end. 'Well, I'll have to go. I've so much on. All I can say is, I wish them well. A house of that size and no income ... and she's just making light of it. She doesn't seem to care.'

This was too much. 'I think she's been jolly brave, Eve. In fact, I admire her.' When Fran put down the phone, she felt satisfied. She had spoken her mind. She could have added that the crash was probably the best thing that could've happened to Min, who had been bored, and now was discovering what life could be when it had a purpose other than party-giving and trips to Tenerife. All the same, the outlook for them was still far from rosy.

They set out for Seaham at two, well wrapped against the cold. 'We can't stay long,' she warned. 'We'll freeze if we do, and Treesa's expecting us for tea.'

Martin was belting himself into the passenger seat. 'I just want to see Jim. He's got a book about artics, and he said I could borrow it.'

She changed gear to gain time. 'Jim? And what on earth are artics?'

He heaved a sigh. 'Articulated lorries. You wouldn't understand.'

She understood only too well. 'Jim' seemed to be the most important thing in Martin's life now and it would have to stop, before he got hurt.

They had left the car and were walking down towards the harbour when they saw him. He was watching a ship easing through the harbour entrance but he turned at their approach. 'She's a timber ship – from Sweden.'

Martin nodded. 'She's not light-ship,' he said solemnly.

Jim was smiling. 'That's right. She's down at the head.'

They're shutting me out, Fran thought. They're in their male world of technical jargon, and I'm not considered fit to take part. As if he had read her thoughts Jim turned. 'Are you freezing?'

She nodded. 'Just about.'

He looked down at Martin. 'I think we ought to consider your mum today. What about coming up to the hotel for a drink?' He looked at his watch and then at Fran. 'We've just got time ... if it's all right with you.'

Fran nodded. 'If you let me pay. No, I won't come unless you do. You've been very kind.'

The pub was unbelievably warm and cosy after the cold outside. He ordered the drinks but accepted her five-pound note and handed over the change. 'I'll not be a moment,' he said and vanished through the residents' door. When he returned he was carrying a book and an oblong parcel in Christmas wrapping. 'There's the book I promised you, and a little something for

Christmas. Not to be opened now.'

Martin was glowing. 'I got something for you.' The parcel was small and probably contained the tobacco which Jim used. He was looking from her to Martin and she shook her head.

'Don't look at me. I knew nothing about it.' It was true. The parcel was a complete surprise. So was the fact that her son was now capable of conducting his own affairs. She felt both proud and put out at the same time.

Martin went off to play the Quiz machine and Jim leaned closer. 'I think it's time for a few explanations. I can see you worry ... no, I understand, honestly. I know what it's like to be a single parent: you do nothing else but worry. But I'm not some sort of pervert setting my cap for your lad. I have two kids of my own, as you know. They're with my mum in London. That's where I belong, as you may have guessed from the twang. I used to be in the Merchant Navy – navigating officer. Then my wife died ... she had cancer ... so I came ashore. If you're an engineer you can always pick up work, but a master's ticket fits you for nothing. My wife's brother had a shipping agency – that's how I met her. He offered me the north-east area, and I took it. It means I don't see much of the kids. I'm up here almost every week. I was used to being away from them when Dorothy was alive, but it's different now.'

'And Martin fills a gap?'

He nodded. 'He's a great kid.'

Fran smiled. 'I won't argue about that. He amazed me just now. He must think an awful lot of you.'

Jim looked across to where Martin was manipulating the machine. 'It's mutual, and I won't let him down. When he told me about his dad it seemed to click.'

'What was in the parcel?' she asked Martin as they drove back towards Belgate. It was getting dark now, dusk settling on the landscape like grey chiffon.

'St Bruno. It's the sort he likes.' There was uncertainty in his voice.

'Well done,' she said firmly and sensed him relax.

Treesa was waiting in the open doorway. 'I heard the car. Come on in, you must be frozen.' Treesa's living-room was already dressed for Christmas. A brand new silver tree stood ceiling high, laden with baubles. Every ornament and protrusion was garlanded with tinsel, and jovial Santa Clauses leered down from vantage points.

'I know it's early,' Treesa apologized, 'but I did it for the bairn.' She looked little more than a bairn herself and Fran could imagine how decorating the room had eased her boredom. Living alone with a fifteen-month-old baby would leave acres of silence.

While Treesa scalded the tea Fran thought about her own tree. She had put it up each year since David died, but it wasn't the same. Now she would have to bring it out once again. On the floor Martin was playing with the baby, building a tower with blocks and grinning at the baby's renewed delight when it tumbled. Fran put the tree out of her mind and enjoyed the spectacle.

They were gorging on hot sausage rolls and two kinds of quiche, with Black Forest gateau to come, when Terry arrived. That he had not been expected was manifest from Treesa's agitation. 'What are you doing here?' she said.

Fran's heart sank. 'I'm pleased to see you, Terry,' she said to mitigate his embarrassment and his grin faded.

'I'll get a cup,' Treesa said and dived for the kitchen. Fran made room on the settee and beckoned Terry to sit down.

'What do you think of the bairn?' he said. Proud parenthood was in his voice.

'I think he's wonderful,' she said, 'and a proper Malone.'

Martin looked up. 'I expect he'll be just like Mike when he grows up.'

Terry's retort was fervent. 'I hope not. Our Mike's a cheeky little b... so and so!'

Tomorrow, Fran thought, or as soon as she could, she would sit down with Treesa and talk. About love and death and love after death and what right you had to make a new life when you were left behind. Except that she had never managed to work those things out for herself, so how would she convince someone else?

That evening she wore a red wool dress she had not worn for years. It had been David's favourite and she had not had the heart to wear it until now. Tonight she needed it for courage. Since the day Min had told her she didn't like Eve, Fran had been thinking hard. '*We've all been fooling ourselves,*' Min had said, '*but sooner or later you have to face facts.*' Fran put in her Dallas earrings and took a final look. Not bad.

At her suggestion she and Tony went to the Mohti Raj. She ordered Kashmiri chicken and managed to eat it all, although the sausage rolls were reluctant to give way. 'I wanted to talk and it's easier on neutral ground.'

He raised his brows. 'That sounds ominous.'

She smiled and shook her head. 'Not really.'

She had seen a fleeting anxiety in his eyes: perhaps he thought she was going to tell him she was pregnant! It was tempting to give it a whirl and send him home with a king-sized worry, but she decided against it. She was not a child, she was a grown woman.

'You've always said you weren't married, but there's someone, isn't there? I know you said you shared, but it's more than that.' Her question had turned into a statement and he didn't argue. 'Anyway, I've been thinking. I'm not the kind of woman who believes in threesomes.' Too late she remembered that meant three in a bed.

'Hardly that!' He was back to his mocking self now he knew she wasn't in the club, and it made her angry.

'Anyway, like I said, I've been thinking. We've had a fling, Tony: no big deal, as Martin would say. I'm not so naïve as to imagine I mean anything to you, or that not seeing me again will even ruffle your surface. It won't mean much to me either. I got a buzz out of going out with a lecturer. I should have known better at my age, but it's true. And you're good in bed, I don't need to tell you that. But I've realized that I prefer my men to be sincere. It may be frustrating at times but it's better than feeling like something that's just passed through a photocopier!'

Her fingers closed around a note inside her purse. Please God, let it be a fiver; she couldn't afford a tenner, and there was no way she could ask for change. 'That's my share of the meal. Thanks for everything. See you in class.'

He rose to his feet as she swept off, out of politeness not shock. She might have known she couldn't faze him, but she was glad she had done it all the same, and choosing the restaurant had made sense. No need to be polite when you were neither guest nor host.

As she drove home she felt free. She would be alone again at Christmas, but that was no big deal. She looked for the Christmas star and found it, just where she had expected it to be.

10

The kitchen had taken on a look of shell-shock. Dishes, tins, opened packs of butter and marge, a pile of chestnut peel, a bowl redolent of sage and onion. 'Well to be seen you were born a lady,' Bethel said, eyeing the mess. 'The sooner you're out of my way the better.' She started to clear up, putting lids back on jars and sweeping flour from the table-top into her outstretched palm.

'I'll tidy up in a minute,' Fran said placatingly. It was two o'clock on Christmas Eve afternoon, still time, if she wished, to hurry through to town for last-minute shopping. It was always a temptation, to join the jostling crowd and be part of it all, but if you did you found it an empty exercise. Far better to be at home.

'How many's coming?' Bethel asked.

Fran smiled. 'You know very well. You and Walter, me and

Martin.'

Bethel was running hot water into the washing-up bowl.
'That's who I thought was coming. When I saw the mess I
thought you'd invited the Russian army. Don't expect me to stuff
meself, mind. I don't know about Walter.'

She was taking the dirty dishes in precise order, clean things
first so as not to sully the water, then the slightly dirtier things. If
they were bad enough, they were first rinsed under the tap.
Gradually the kitchen was clearing. This was Bethel's gift, the
ability to restore order. 'I love you, Bethel,' Fran said, suddenly
overcome with gratitude and Christmas.

'Get off.' Bethel was fending off her hug with one hand and
washing up with the other. 'Put all that energy into something
useful like making tea.'

They were seated at the kitchen table when Walter's horn
sounded in the street. 'He smells tea,' Bethel said. 'If you brewed
up under a blanket, he'd be there.' They went through the ritual
of ignoring his presence until he was on the step, and then wel-
comed him in.

'Is it still on then, tomorrow?' He was dipping his biscuit into
his tea and scooping the damp bits into his mouth.

'You know it is, Walter. You were properly asked and you said
yes, so it's on.'

His eyes were twinkling. 'All right, Sally, all right. No need to
take an old man's head off.' He sighed. 'Aye, it'll be a funny
Christmas for some in Belgate. And a poor one next year if the
pit's gone.'

'Do you think they'll really close it?' Fran asked. 'I thought it
was a good pit.' Years ago, or so it seemed, Brian Malone had
said, *'They'll never close Belgate, a canny little pit like that.'* Yesterday she had taken sponge cakes from the freezer to make the
Christmas trifle base. Since she had started her teacher course
there was never time to make things, but previously she had been
precise. *'Sponge 21st December, 1983.'* it was labelled: the day
they'd buried Brian Malone. 'I must go round to Treesa's later
on,' she said, 'to take the baby's presents.'

[78]

The phone sounded in the hall; it was Eve, ringing to repeat her lukewarm invitation for Christmas. 'Oh well, as long as you're fixed up. We didn't like to think of you and Martin alone. Put the 8th in your diary; that's two weeks on Wednesday. The girls are coming and we'll have a super do.'

Another ghastly girls' night, Fran thought, as she put down the phone. They would all moan about the weight they'd put on over Christmas but it wouldn't stop them eating themselves silly. Vivienne would have news of someone's infidelity and at least one of them would be pregnant. Oh, well, it would have to be endured. If she cried off, Eve would summon a doctor. No one turned down a girls' night unless for birth or death.

They walked round to Treesa's as soon as Martin arrived, treading gingerly on the iced pavements. 'It's nearly dark,' Martin said, 'and it's only three o'clock.'

In almost every window a Christmas tree glittered, festooned with lights. There were no children on the streets but here and there a small face peered between curtains, watching for parents home from last-minute shopping. Martin had insisted on carrying all the gifts, and from time to time he took her elbow to help her along. She was about to say, 'I'm not ancient,' when she remembered how little chivalry there was nowadays. No need to kill it at birth.

'Do you like Christmas?' she asked.

His face gleamed in the light of a street-lamp. 'Yeah, it's good. It's a bit miserable after, that's the only trouble. You've played with everything and read all the books and there's only school to look forward to. Ugh!'

She offered up a swift prayer that soon he would start to appreciate the joys of learning, and opened Treesa's gate. This was probably the last Christmas of Martin's childhood. Next year he would want clothes or a proper watch. And after that, aftershave and cigars; but it was silly to worry. Martin's childhood had really finished when David died. After that things could never be the

[79]

same. She raised her hand and tapped on Treesa's door.

'Come in, Mrs Drummond.' Treesa's face was alight at the prospect of company.

'It's Frances,' Fran said. 'I've told you before … call me Frances or Fran. We've been friends long enough for that.'

Treesa smiled. 'I'll try, Frances, but I'm that used with saying Mrs Drummond it just slips out.'

Martin piled the gifts beneath the tree and then settled down to amuse the baby.

'He likes bairns, doesn't he?' Treesa said, eyeing Martin fondly.

'He'd have been a big brother if things had worked out as I intended,' Fran said. 'I always wanted four children, two of each. Now he's got Christopher … so it's all worked out in the end.'

They had a sumptuous tea, baby included. 'Should he have fresh cream?' Fran queried.

'He loves it,' Treesa said, expertly scooping melba from the baby's chin to his mouth. The question of vitamins hovered on Fran's lip, but she bit it back. The legs and bare feet kicking beneath the tray of the high chair were rounded and sturdy. Treesa was doing all right without advice.

'What are you doing tomorrow?' Fran asked when Martin had carried the baby off to its 'lobster pot' and she and Treesa settled with a third cup of tea.

'We're going to Brian's mam for dinner and my mam for tea. It seemed the fairest way.'

Fran nodded. 'Keep everyone happy. What does your mother think of the baby? It's her first grandchild, isn't it?'

Treesa was slow to reply, and when she did it was not a direct answer to Fran's question. 'She's very set in her ways, me mam. Once she gets an idea, she doesn't let go. She never liked Brian. He was a Malone, that was enough for her. Anyroad, she doesn't like them seeing the bairn so much, specially Terry.' She was seeking for words and Fran came to her aid.

'Does she think he's round here too much?'

Treesa nodded. 'She says people'll talk. She says he's got his eye on the compen. money. I know she's wrong, but she keeps on about it.'

Fran was shocked. 'I think that's wicked, Treesa. Terry's the last person to care about money; he'd cut off his arm for a principle. And he idolizes that baby ... and you.'

There was no answer.

'What about you?' Fran said gently. 'Sometimes I think you're fond of Terry, and other times you're quite short with him.'

'I do like him, Mrs Drummond ... I mean, Frances. Well, I could hardly help it, he's that kind. But ... you were happy once, weren't you? You know how it leaves you. You can't just put it all behind you.'

'*You were happy once.*' The phrase was chilling. As she and Martin walked home, arm in arm under cover of darkness, Fran thought about the words. '*Happy once*' – as though it could never come again. And yet she *was* happy sometimes. Quite often, in fact, if you didn't count the times when she worried over money, or college, or things like that.

She couldn't resist broaching the subject with Bethel when she got home. 'How long have you been on your own, Bethel?'

The old woman blew a smoke ring. 'Thirty-six years. No, thirty-seven.'

Fran poured the tea that always lubricated conversation between them. 'You've never thought about re-marrying? I know I pull your leg about Walter but, in a way, I'm serious. You're so fond of one another, it would make sense.'

Bethel blew more smoke. 'Not now, at my age. I'd lay down my life for Walter, God forbid he should hear me say that. I'd do any mortal thing for him except marry him. Not that's he's asked, mind. He's got more sense.'

She gave Fran a sharp look. 'You're not leading up to something, are you, miss? Come straight out with it if you are. No need to go all round the houses with me.'

Fran smiled. 'If I'm ever contemplating remarriage, Bethel, you'll be the first to know. No, it's not me, but I sometimes wonder about Treesa? Terry's very fond of her but something holds her back.'

Bethel gave a snort. 'I should hope so. They want to call that house where he lives Little Moscow. He's left of Mao Tse-tung. I'm not saying I want to see the lass live alone, but there's a happy medium and he's not it.'

Fran would have flown to Terry's defence if the phone had not summoned her to the hall. 'I'll be on me way,' Bethel said as Fran left the kitchen. 'I'll be round first thing to give you a hand.'

It was Min on the phone. 'You're sure you won't change your mind? You're more than welcome. It's not our usual thrilling repast, but there's plenty of it.' She assured Min that she was all fixed up for Christmas, and referred to Eve's invitation for the 8th.

'Oh God. She hasn't asked me yet but I expect she will. Unless I've been struck off the social register.' No chance of that, Fran thought. Min would stay on Eve's list for one good reason, so that she could see how Eve was occupying her former place as queen of the heap.

'I thought you used to enjoy girls' nights?' Fran said, to cover her thinking.

'I suppose I did. I mean, it was a chance to dress up and show off and return hospitality. No one asks us out now ... well, hardly anyone ... so I suppose I don't have to have do's any more.'

There was an uncertain note in her voice, as though she couldn't decide whether to be pleased or vexed. Fran sought for a way of diverting her. 'D'you know what I used to call them last year, when I felt bad? Another ghastly girls' night, I used to think.'

Min's tone was almost incredulous. 'Even *mine?*'

Fran laughed. 'Sometimes even yours, Min.'

They said good-bye, promising to meet up on Boxing Day. As Fran went back into the empty kitchen faint sounds of canned laughter came from the living-room and occasionally Martin's added chortle. She crossed the hall and pushed open the door. Martin was stretched out in one chair, Mike Malone in the other.

Both of them had their shoes on the upholstery, but it was Christmas Eve after all.

'Want some supper?' she said, and then: 'Does your mum know you're here, Mike?'

Martin's reply was swift. 'His mother doesn't worry. She knows he's all right.' The inference was plain.

'Well, I'm sorry but I do worry. And so does Mrs Malone, whatever you may say, so if she doesn't know where Mike is, go round and tell her. Then I'll make you sausage and chips.'

Mike's legs were already swinging to the ground.

'With gravy?' Martin asked.

'Buckets of it,' she said, and let them scamper past.

When supper had been made and consumed and cleared away, she sent Mike on his way. 'Now we work,' she said. They sat either side of the kitchen table, wrapping, sellotaping, writing tags. 'It's good, this,' Martin said. They were trying to make the paper meet round Bethel's boxed teapot set when the phone rang.

'Not again,' Fran groaned. It was ten o'clock. Who would call at that hour?

'I thought I'd just give you a ring, season's greetings and that sort of thing.' It was the pier man, sounding as though he were already regretting the call. 'It's Jim,' he said before she could reply. 'You know, from the harbour.'

She had collected her wits now. 'Of course, I recognized your voice. How is London?'

His reply was rueful. 'I wouldn't know. I've hardly had my nose outside the door since I got back. Well, you know how it is ... a lot to do ... and I can't ask my mother to see to everything.'

They swapped stories and sympathy for a while, and then she said, 'I expect you'd like to say Happy Christmas to Martin?'

'If it's no trouble. He's not in bed, is he?'

She laughed. 'I haven't suggested it. Besides, he's helping with the gift-wrapping. Wait till yours are that age.'

He groaned. 'I can't imagine them helping. Hindering, yes, that I can conceive. But helping...'

[83]

She was about to hand over the phone when she heard him clear his throat. 'I'll be back in the north-east the week after next, if things go according to plan. Anyway, I just thought, if you're free one night … you know I know you're tied … but if you could get a sitter…'

She had had stranger invitations but never more tentative ones. 'That would be lovely. Ring me when you're up here. Now I'll get Martin – and a very happy Christmas.'

While she piled up the wrapped gifts and put them ready for the tree she could hear Martin's excited chatter. 'That's long-distance,' she mouthed as she passed through the hall.

Martin pretended to ignore her but he wound up the conversation just the same. 'See you then, Jim. And I hope you have a good time.' She was reflecting on the propriety of his calling a man old enough to be his father by his Christian name when he came into the kitchen. 'I knew he'd ring,' he said. 'That's why I stopped up.'

Long after he had gone to bed she sat, staring through the gurgling television, reflecting on the ironies of life. If only she could be as enthusiastic about Jim as her son was, there were all the makings of a happy ending. Unfortunately, there was no X factor there, no weakening of the knees, no drying of the vocal chords. She wouldn't marry him in a million years. 'It's manners to wait till you're asked, miss,' she said aloud in a fair imitation of Bethel's tartest tones.

She poured herself a glass of Christmas booze and watched as the fire turned to ash and dropped, piece by piece, through the grate. Was she like that, a burned-out case? Perhaps she should feel something for Jim, some response. She was capable of love; why not with him? Inevitably, David came into her mind as she always saw him now, coming through the doorway smiling. She felt her own lips curl in sympathy but there were no tears. It was pleasant to think of David now, without pain, remembering only what was good.

But had she loved him? The thought was disloyal and she was tempted to put it aside, but it persisted. Had it been love or had she been swept along in the wake of other teenage pairings? Had she chosen David, or accepted his choosing her? She had never loved Steve; impossible now to believe she had shared his bed. He was someone remote, like a figure on a platform glimpsed from a moving train. She could remember Tony well enough, even without his presence at college to remind her. Why had she done it? Animal lust or a desire to be well in with authority? People fantasized about figures of authority, policemen, teachers, even Water Board men. She started to laugh out loud. The booze was making its mark: time for bed.

Upstairs she drew back the curtains and looked out on Belgate. Frost gleamed on the eaves of the houses and tinselled the gardens. Last Christmas Belgate had been torn apart by the strike, this Christmas it was under sentence of death. Last Christmas she had been alone, this Christmas she was still alone, and she would probably be alone next Christmas, too.

Perhaps she would never be loved again. At least it would do away with the hassle of second relationships that was plaguing Treesa now. And you could live without a man; that much she had learned in the years since David's death. Once she'd believed you needed a man for almost everything. Now she could do most things for herself.

Suddenly, she felt chilled and twitching the curtains back into place made her feel no warmer. '*Into my heart an air that kills ...*' It was ages since she had read any poetry. She went back downstairs for her shabby volume of Housman and read until the distant church clock told her that Christmas Day was come.

11

She drove through the trough of darkness between Belgate and Sunderland but tonight that darkness was relieved by banks of snow on either side of a road whose surface sparkled like marcasite.

She felt the car skid slightly and eased her foot from the accelerator. Mustn't speed! Mustn't slow and change down, though. If you did that you could be left slithering in the road, your wheels unable to get a purchase on the ice. With roads like this she would have a good excuse for leaving Eve's at a reasonable hour, and she gave thanks for frost and small mercies.

If she was going to leave early she'd have to get there on time. Perhaps arranging to see Jim beforehand had been a mistake? You could hardly throw back your drink in one gulp and say thanks very much and ta-ta. He had been so good to Martin that she had felt under an obligation, which was why she had agreed to meet him. '*I'm going to a friend's house. It's been arranged since before Christmas. But we could have a drink beforehand, if you'd like?*' She had sensed a certain relief in him, as though a brief first meeting was not altogether undesirable, and had been faintly piqued.

The first lights of Sunderland loomed up, and after that she was too busy halting at junctions to worry about anything else. He was waiting in the foyer of the hotel. 'Hello,' she said and was struck once more by his aura of despair.

They carried their drinks to a corner table. 'What time do you want to be away?' he said. 'I don't want to spoil your night.'

She was suddenly filled with a desire to comfort him. 'Don't worry about it. I've got heaps and heaps of time,' and to prove it she took off her coat and scarf.

'Tell me how you wound up in the Merchant Navy and you a

London boy.'

He was smiling. 'I'd never seen the sea till I was twelve. Then we went to Southampton for a family wedding, and I saw the big ships in the harbour. "That's for me," I thought, and after that there was plenty in London to fuel the flame. Stand on a London bridge at night and hear the hooting of the sirens down the river – that can get up a wanderlust on its own.'

'You sound as though you miss the sea?'

He raised his brows. 'Sometimes. Yes, I do miss it. Ireland like a jewel; going up the Rhine at Christmas with a lighted tree on your mast; coming into port just before dawn and seeing a city waken ... But it's a young man's life. I'd have come ashore anyway, sooner or later, but when Dorothy died, that changed everything. I couldn't let the kids grow up without either of us. They were pretty cut up, and I wanted to be around. I had this idea I could start up in marine paints. I had a few contacts, in the Southampton area, but you can't chance things when you're on your own. You must know that. So I settled for what I could get. Dorothy's brother had this shipping agency. They were twins, and very close. He more or less took it for granted I'd come in with him.'

Fran smiled. 'I know what you mean. I chose teacher training when David died because it seemed so safe. I'd never even thought about teaching before. But it seemed a good idea: the hours were the same as Martin's, and so were the holidays. I'm lucky, really, because now I'm actually doing it I quite enjoy it. How do you feel about your job?'

He shrugged. 'It pays the bills. I'm not mad about the paper-work, but I can cope. It's better than being out of work.'

This time her nod was fervent. Yesterday Min had told her about Dennis's fortnightly visits to sign on. '*There's a little bitch there who ticks him off if he's early and makes him wait till the end if he's a minute late. As though he were a little boy – a man who ran a company.*' There had been tears in Min's eyes, tears of rage and humiliation.

'Yes,' she said aloud. 'Anything's better than being out of

work. Unemployment's nineteen per cent in Belgate, and it's changed everything. Miners used to scheme to keep their sons out of the pit. Now they're mad keen to get them in because there's nothing else.'

'Tell me about the pit,' he said, leaning forward. His amazement at finding she was a newcomer to Belgate was only equalled by his interest in her tales of mining life. 'I'll have to meet this Walter,' he said as they got up to leave. And Walter gave the excuse for an easy leave-taking.

'You must come to supper with him. And Bethel. Martin would love it if you did. Give me a ring.' A moment later she was in the car and away, congratulating herself that, for a while at least, while he had talked about the sea, he had looked no more than his age.

Eve was flushed when she opened the door, but it was the glow of triumph, not exertion. Through the open kitchen door Fran could see 'the girl' toiling at the sink, rinsing glasses. She looked all of fifteen. Any day soon Eve would have her decked out in cap and frilly apron like 'Upstairs Downstairs'.

'Everyone's here.' Fran was tempted to say, 'Even Diana and Charles?' but the sarcasm would have been wasted on Eve, who for years had fretted in Min's shadow.

'Come and meet the poor relation,' Min murmured in her ear. And then, flopping her skirts, 'Unclean! Unclean!'

Fran looked around uneasily. 'She'll hear you, Min.'

Min's eyes widened. 'I don't care. She makes me feel like a leper, so I'm acting the part.'

Now that Min could no longer afford to have her black hair cut every second week it hung in wings on either side of her head, and the longer length suited her. But it was her face that had changed most. It was thinner and the eyes were a little shadowed, but the mouth had softened and the old, bored pout was gone. 'You look a million dollars, Min,' Fran said.

They walked together into the room and the flow of gossip

engulfed them. 'She said it was a model ... model Marks and Sparks, more like. I don't know why she does it.' 'Well, Geoff says he's had Tenerife ... never again.' 'Roger says protein balsam's the answer ... he won't perm it till it's in condition anyway. You know what he's like when he puts his foot down. So he took the ends off and I had it lamp dried.'

One or two acknowledged Fran and gave Min a beaming smile. 'All right?' they asked brightly, and she replied, 'Fine! Marvellous!' in equally bright tones. 'Let's get another drink and get out of here,' she whispered at last.

Eve was circulating madly between the living-room and the hall, with frequent trips to the kitchen to check on 'the girl'. 'She won't miss us for ages,' Min said as they climbed to the landing. 'We're not VIPs any more.'

They settled on the top stair and were about to chat when an upstairs door creaked and there was a subdued giggle.

'Who's that?' Min said, peering through the banisters.

'Me,' came the answer.

'Me who?' There was silence, then, 'Is that Aunty Min?'

Min started to climb the remaining stairs. 'No, it's the Big Bad Wolf and she's coming to eat you up!'

There was another giggle, a scampering of feet, and the sound of bodies hurtling on to beds.

'Shut up and give us peace, and I'll smuggle you some eats up when I go down again,' Min said, and shut the bedroom door.

'Eve won't approve of you feeding them,' Fran said.

'All the more reason for doing it, then,' was the reply.

'Hey, I've got something to tell you.' Min settled her back against the wall and sipped her drink. 'Remember Margot? Manky Margot we went to school with, who went all left wing and peculiar?'

Fran remembered Margot. 'She's hard to forget,' she said. Last year, during the strike, Margot had haunted Belgate, expressing solidarity with the miners and getting on Fran's nerves. In the end she had told her to scram in no uncertain terms, and could still blush at the memory of Margot's astonished face.

'She's shacked up with an anarchist,' Min said. 'According to Vivienne, he plants bombs and poisons Mars bars.' Given Vivienne's propensity for exaggeration and Min's own tendency to hyperbole, this probably meant he was an active member of the SDP, but Fran expressed suitable surprise.

'How's life?' she said, when Margot had been laid to rest.

'So so,' Min said. 'I mean, it's not as bad as I feared and it's not as good as I hoped. Does that make sense?'

It made eminent sense. 'That's how I felt,' Fran said. 'After David died, when I had to start again, I was really frightened. But I always managed. Except that I always seemed to be up against it at the same time, so I know what you mean. Have you decided yet what you're going to do?'

Min shrugged. 'Not really. It's a relief to be getting the house, but that's just half of it. We've got to get an income but there's no work to be had. We'll have to start something of our own; it's the only way. We toss ideas around, but Dennis is just shit-scared, if you'll forgive the forthright language. I never realized what it meant to a man to lose his livelihood. It's far more than a job, it's his whole purpose.'

Yesterday Dave had said much the same as he tipped coal into Fran's bunker. 'There's nee point in life since I got sacked. Nee bloody point at all.' She was about to tell Min of the plight of sacked miners when she realized that Min's sympathies were all with MacGregor and Thatcher.

'Something will turn up,' she said, trying not to sound complacent. 'When you least expect it, something will click.'

Min drained her glass. 'I hope it does. I've flogged those bloody ornaments to everyone short of the Lord Lieutenant. They've made the difference between living and existing. When they're gone, we've had it.'

They went down to supper and filled a plate for the kids. 'Poor little buggers,' Min said as they sneaked upstairs. 'Fancy facing adolescence with Eve and Harold for support.'

Downstairs again they tucked in to an array of meats and

salads, asparagus rolled in brown bread, Continental sausage and tiny kebabs on cocktail sticks. 'You know what's paying for this lot, don't you?' Min said, wrinkling her nose. 'All the poor shits who've gone into liquidation. The more of us down the drain, the fatter accountants get! Bugger them!'

Memories were stirring for Fran. In her own trauma after David's death, she had discovered the relief of using oaths. Admittedly she had done it under her breath, whereas Min said them aloud, but it was the same syndrome: the relief of anger and grief. Under the bold exterior and the constant quips, Min was afraid. 'Tell me about my namesake,' Fran said, steering her on to happier topics.

After supper they collapsed into chairs or sat on the floor, elegant legs tucked under expensive skirts. 'Oh God,' Vivienne said. 'I'll have to stop eating so much. I'm like a house-end.'

Pam was unrepentant. 'Well, I don't care. It was absolutely sumptuous, Eve and I'm not ashamed to say I pigged myself.'

They talked about losing weight and the Princess of Wales and how Mrs Thatcher was saving or ruining the country, with the weight of the argument in favour of the former. 'You can't keep on supporting lame ducks,' one girl said. She had huge pearls in her ears and obviously believed she resembled Joan Collins. 'If a firm can't make it, it ought to go to the wall.'

There was a sudden uneasy silence as one or two eyes flicked to Min and back again. This is history repeating itself, Fran thought. Two years ago she had been the spectre at the feast, causing everyone to watch their tongues. Now it was Min's turn.

The penny had dropped for Joan Collins. 'Well,' she said desperately, trying to extricate herself, 'they can always start again. I mean, there's heaps of incentives, government help and everything. And there should be ... I mean, I'm all in favour.'

Min was sitting with her back to the stone fireplace wall, her face bland. Eve was perched on the arm of a chair and looked as though she was about to give birth. 'Goodness, this conversation's getting serious,' she said at last. Any moment she'll rise to her feet and do her head-girl act, Fran thought. '*Parents, staff and fellow-pupils, I am here tonight to demand we change the subject...'*

'It's OK, Eve,' Min said suddenly. 'It doesn't upset me. We went bust – so what? Actually, it was the best thing that could've happened. Dennis's always been the office boy as far as his parents were concerned. Now we're branching out on our own, and I'm going in with him. I can't say too much at the moment, but watch this space!'

A relieved hum of congratulation and encouragement engulfed her. Min was not going to let the side down after all, and wasn't that splendid! Only Fran was puzzled. A moment before Min had been talking about the vague hope of something turning up; now she was hinting at something of Tiny Rowland proportions.

'What was all that about?' she whispered, as they collected their coats.

'Don't ask me,' Min said, a note of desperation in her voice. 'But I wasn't going to sit there and say nothing, was I? I'll just have to think of something.' The next moment someone called out that the Mini was blocking them in, and Fran had to rush down the drive.

All the way home to Belgate she thought about Min. Something had better turn up before the last of the fake Capo di Montes was gone, or Min's plight would indeed be desperate. Losing your home was one thing, losing face was another. She was sure Min could cope with the first. She was not so sure about the second.

12

She was applying eye-liner when the phone rang. 'Can you get that, Martin?' She had managed to finish the left eye and was stretching the lid of the right to match up when his face appeared in the bathroom door. 'It was Aunty Min. She says its nothing special if you're going out. She'll ring another time.'

He was half-way back down the stairs when Fran called out, 'How did she know I was going out?'

He kept on descending. 'I told her. I said was it important 'cos you were busy, and she said "no". It's all right ... I'd have got you if she'd said yes.'

'I wish you'd asked me first,' she said, glaring as fiercely as she could with one made-up eye. 'I don't mind you answering the phone, but I'd like to take my own calls.'

Martin had tired of the subject. 'Drop dead,' he said, *sotto voce*. She felt her lips twitch but pulled herself together before she spoke. 'What did you say?'

His reply was conciliatory. 'Nothing. I was just mumbling.'

She went back to the mirror to apply the rest of her make-up. Martin was becoming quite single-minded lately. Jim's phone-calls took precedence over everything; her going out with Jim was of paramount importance. He would kill to ensure their meeting, let alone get rid of Min. Sooner or later she would have to sit down and tell him the facts of life. Jim was nice, very nice, in fact. But if Martin had any rosy ideas of romance he would have to think again.

Last week she had invited Jim to supper with Bethel and Walter, and the evening had been a great success. 'He's all right,' Bethel had said, which was praise indeed. Tonight he was taking her out for a meal as a way of saying thank you. It was no big deal. She grimaced into the mirror: she really must stop using that stupid phrase. She would be saying it to her class at Broad Street if she wasn't careful.

While she slipped into the navy suit she thought about her teaching practice. The best one so far! She knew what she was doing now and it was a good feeling. This morning a small boy had taken her hand as she walked across the yard, and the touch of the small fingers in hers had been suddenly thrilling. 'He likes me,' she'd thought, and had had to restrain herself from grinning like a fool.

[93]

When she was ready she dialled Min's number. 'Hi . . . sorry I was upstairs when you rang. Is everything OK?'

There was a moment's silence and then, 'Which do you want first, the good news or the bad news?'

Fran felt behind her for the second stair and lowered herself to a sitting position. 'The bad news.' Always get the worst over first.

'I've finally flipped my lid, Fran. Gone bonkers, berserk, etc, etc. The good news is I'm going into business. In a small way, no big overheads and that sort of thing.'

Fran drew breath. 'Is that all? I thought something was wrong.'

Outrage came down the line. 'Is that *all*? I like that. Here I am chancing my arm, and all my best friend can say is "Is that all?"'

Fran smiled. 'No, I didn't mean that. I'm impressed. Very impressed, but I wish you'd tell me what you're on about.' The clock was moving forward remorselessly, and while Jim might not be the love of her life she didn't want to keep him waiting.

'Well, you know those ghastly Capo di Monte fakes I pinched from under the liquidator's nose? I sold the last of them last week at the boot sale, and I was just getting ready to clear up and come home when the woman who'd bought it came back and said did I have another because her friend was going mad for one. I said no, that was the last – and then I started to think. "Can you go back to the warehouse?" I said to Dennis, and he hummed and ha-ed a bit, but he said he could if we had cash because all the firm's accounts were closed and no one would give him credit any more. So I took the woman's name, and I raked up every spare cent. It was Giro week, and I'd just got a cheque from that woman in Newcastle for all the clobber she sold for me. So we went to the warehouse. Fran, I kid you not, it was Aladdin's cave. Pure kitsch. I wouldn't have given it house-room. Anyway, we got another piece . . . it was the Pied Piper . . . but there were heaps of them, a lot cheaper. Dennis used to buy top of the market for the windows, but some of those things were only a couple of quid. So I sold the woman the piece she wanted and she . . . Oh God, this story's getting longer and longer. Fran, the fact is, I've taken a stall with Gamma Fairs . . . you know, they run the antiques fairs, but bric-à-brac's included. I start this weekend. I'll have to wrap up because the woman who runs it says you can freeze, but the main thing is, I'm in business. What d'you think about that?'

The idea of Min as a fairground barker was mind-boggling.

'What did Aunty Min want?' Martin said when she came off the phone. He was developing a nose for anything out of the ordinary and knew something was up.

'She's starting a business,' Fran said. 'A market stall.'

Martin's eyes widened. 'Selling what?' The news that Min would be flogging china damped his enthusiasm. 'Can I have cod and chips for supper?' he said and brightened visibly when she fished in her bag for the money. There was cod in the freezer and frozen chips, but nothing home-made equalled the magic of that vinegar-soaked, newspaper-wrapped bundle. Not in Martin's eyes, anyway.

She was half-way through the door when the phone rang again, and she could never walk away from a beckoning phone. When she saw people do it in TV plays she always knew it was a poor script. Real people were compelled to come back and pick the damned thing up!

'Fran? I've just had Min on the phone ... she says you already know and you approve. Surely, you can't be in favour of this crazy scheme? I've only had time to mention it to Harold, but he thinks they've gone mad. As if they're not in enough trouble already ... Fran, are you there?'

She could put the phone down and pretend they'd been cut off, but Eve would only ring back and hassle Bethel. 'Yes, I'm here, Eve. Actually, I think it's quite a good idea. Better than just sitting around.'

The chill in Eve's voice was almost tangible. 'Oh, well ... I suppose everyone's entitled to an opinion – ' Before Eve rang Fran had been nursing grave doubts about Min's latest enterprise, but she was not about to admit it to Eve.

As she drove into Sunderland Fran was uncomfortably aware that she would have to re-assess her friendships before too long.

[95]

But not tonight. Tonight she was eating out with Jim and she meant to enjoy it.

A faint doubt stirred: was she leading him on? He liked her; more than liked. She liked him, too, but not in the same way. Perhaps she was presuming too much; perhaps he saw her not as a woman but as a mother figure? He was certainly fond of Martin. The chess set he had given him for Christmas was Martin's most prized possession and hadn't been cheap. As the lights of the town appeared ahead she tried to still her faint unease. It was only a meal, after all, not a nuptial mass.

They dined in a newly opened Chinese restaurant and she was amazed at the confident way he negotiated the menu and dealt with the waiter, until she remembered he had been at sea for fifteen years. He was wearing a dark grey suit and a patterned silk tie, and it made a difference. He caught her looking him over and gave an embarrassed half-laugh. 'Thought I might as well dress up.'

She knew enough about his job to know that suits were not *de rigueur*. He must have brought it from London in the hope of taking her out. A tiny bowl of fragrant soup was in front of her and he was waiting for her to start. 'Um, lovely,' she said, and gave herself up to eating.

In the end it was easy. They talked about food around the world, and then the difficulties of feeding families. 'I never cooked after David died. Well, not properly cooked. I'd fry something for Martin or do him something from the freezer but I lived on cottage cheese.'

Jim had been more ambitious. 'I tried to carry on. Dorothy was a good cook, so I tried pastry, all that sort of thing.' He grinned. 'It was pretty disastrous. I could roll the stuff out all right, but when I put it over the pie-dish it would tear, and if I gathered it up again it'd have bits of pie filling in, so in the end it looked like a mosaic ... and tasted worse.'

The thought of him struggling with a rolling pin was not unpleasant. 'I like him,' Fran thought. 'No violins, no knee tremors, it's just nice.'

[96]

'Was your wife ill for long?'

Dorothy had died of cancer after a four-month illness. 'I know it's selfish,' Fran said, trying to find the right words. 'I'm only thinking of myself, because it was better for David that he died so quickly, but I sometimes wish he'd been ill for a while so that I could have prepared. As it is, one minute he was there, the next he was gone. I kept feeling unreal, as though if I gave a really good shake of my head it would all dissolve and we'd be happy again.'

An enigmatic Chinese appeared for their plates. 'Coffee?' Jim said, and then when the waiter had gone. 'It doesn't work like that. You don't prepare. I knew practically from the beginning. Just by little things at first ... sensing that they were sounding me out, seeing how much I could take. And then they said the surgeon wanted to see me. He sat there, just a little chap, very ordinary. He sat there toying with the notes and he said, "Three months." I argued. I remember I wanted to punch him because he was talking life and death and he didn't seem involved. I suppose dispassionate's the word. Anyway, I said no, it can't be like that, there are things you can do! But I think I knew, really. She was standing in the ward in her dressing-gown when I came out of the Sister's Office. I looked along and saw her and she was laughing and I thought I'd never seen her look so well.'

He looked down at his plate. 'I'm sorry, Frances. I don't know why I did that. I've never talked about it, not to anyone. And then I ask you out for a meal and spoil it all. I can only say I'm sorry.'

She tried to coax him to continue but he was adamant. Instead they talked about recent films and what he liked on telly. 'I'm in my room most of the time. I pick small homely hotels, like the Harbour View ... places where you're made welcome. And I like a pint. But you can't spend all your time drinking, so I watch TV and ring the kids. They like that. Kevin's quite good with the phone now. He's four. And Barbara's like a little old woman. "This is the Seymour residence," she says. It always creases me, the self-possessed little voice. Just like ...'

He stopped then, before he mentioned Dorothy again. Fran

[97]

would have put out her hand and covered his as it lay on the table but it would have been presumptuous. He had rather nice hands; she hadn't noticed that before but it was true.

She started to tell him about college then, deliberately choosing safe waters. 'When I look back I can't believe I did it. I must've been on automatic pilot because I have no recollection of applying and I only dimly remember the interview.' David had been dead for four weeks when she went for the interview and she had wandered, zombie-like, around a dress shop before she went in, but she decided to keep this to herself. 'The bonus is that I really enjoy it.'

He was smiling. 'Are you any good at it?'

She rolled her eyes. 'That remains to be seen.'

He laughed when she told him about teaching practice, and expressed a wish to meet Gwen one day, and then the inscrutable Chinese was presenting the bill and they were out in the cold night air.

'I'll pick you up next time,' he said, taking her elbow to cross the road. 'It's silly to bring two cars.' A little frisson of unease came and went. He was taking 'next time' for granted, and although she would be happy to see him again she wanted to be the one holding the reins.

'I've enjoyed tonight.' She opened the car door and threw her bag across into the passenger seat.

'So have I.' The street lamp shone on his hair and threw his face into shadow, so that she could not make out his expression. He was thirty-nine years old; she had worked that out by simple addition. Thirty when he married, married for seven years and widowed for two. Or was it widowered? Whatever the name, the pain was the same.

'Good night, Frances.' In another moment he would incline his head and kiss her, and, even if she was quick to turn away her mouth, it would still imply a degree of intimacy. She put out her hand. 'Thanks for a lovely meal. I enjoyed it.' The next moment she was safe in the driving seat. He shut the door and, more forthcoming now that danger was past, she wound down the window. 'See you soon, Jim.'

He nodded and was about to stand clear when he changed his mind. 'I hope I didn't upset you, talking like that about Dorothy? I don't know what came over me. I'm not usually a blabber-mouth.'

She leaned close to the open window and smiled up at him. 'I took it as a compliment. So don't be sorry.'

As she was driving away she looked in the rear-view mirror. He was standing there, hands in the pockets of the grey tweed coat, watching the retreating car. She would have to be careful not to hurt him. He was much too nice for that. And that was not the only complication: unless she was much mistaken Martin would be lurking on the landing, all agog to know how things had gone. 'Oh Frances,' she said aloud, as the street lamps fell away and darkness engulfed her, 'oh Frances, what have you got yourself into now?'

13

'For God's sake Fran, don't look so guilty. We're two grown women, not little kids.'

Fran was unconvinced. 'We're still playing hookey.'

Gwen shook her head. 'It's not hookey when students do it: it's exercising judgement. If you don't think a lecturer's worth listening to, do something else instead.'

Fran quickened her pace. 'Well, I'll still be glad when we're out of here. I keep expecting to hear Ogilvie behind me, saying, "And where do you think you're going, Mrs Drummond?"'

'Don't look now, but that's him over there.'

Fran shot a guilty glance right and left for the principal before she realized Gwen was fooling.

'Honestly, Fran, it's a good job you didn't opt for a life of crime. One sniff of the policeman's armpit, and you'd've coughed the lot. I can honestly say I don't have a single qualm about taking this afternoon off. I've worked damned hard, my notes are up to date and I shall spend the next four hours wallowing in idleness. Besides, I'm tired of friend Lund and his teaching methods. He's so laid back . . . or so he wants you to believe. He's a real phoney.'

The car-park was in sight and Fran was relieved. She had never told Gwen she was seeing Tony Lund, much less sleeping with him, but she felt bound to defend him. 'He's no worse than the others. I think he just wants us to feel his equals . . . I mean, not student and master.'

Gwen snorted. 'He needn't worry. I feel absolutely his equal, if not his superior. And I know you had a little fling with him, Fran. If I hadn't known before, I would now. Your neck's doing a litmus.'

It was useless to say, 'I don't know what you mean.' Gwen was far too shrewd. 'It was nothing, really, just a couple of dates.' She could have added 'and a clutch of orgasms and a phone call from his lover' but left well alone. 'How did you know?'

They had reached Gwen's car and she was scrabbling wildly inside her massive handbag. 'I'll clear this damn thing out tonight, God help me, I will. How did I know? You were seen. Jenny saw you, or Geoff, or somebody. And then of course we recognized signs: he'd throw questions your way and flirt with you when you answered. Then there was your term exam mark. If I'd had lingering doubts, that did away with them.' She reached out and pulled Fran's arm. 'Cheer up. It wasn't illegal. It might've been immoral. I hope it was, a little bit, but there's no need to look like the scarlet woman.'

'I wish I'd told you, Gwen. I don't know why I didn't. It was fairly awful, really. He has a woman – they're not married . . .'

To her surprise Gwen was nodding. 'I thought you knew. Everyone else does. They've been together for years. She's quite famous, older than him, and they have a child. A boy, I think. She's on the box sometimes. Very arty, long dresses and brooches like foundry off-cuts. Deirdre Paul, her name is.'

[100]

As she drove towards Belgate Fran tried to build a mental picture of the woman in Tony Lund's life, but it was useless. What kind of woman could hold him for years and years? And, more intriguing, what kind of woman would wish to do so? When she looked at him now she was amazed she had ever fancied him. It had been a schoolgirl crush; but she was no wide-eyed schoolgirl, she was a mature student who should have known better. It was embarrassing to be taught by him, remembering what had gone before, which meant that she could not concentrate. She tried to avoid his eye in class discussion but on the odd occasion that she did contribute he would listen gravely and then pass immediately to the next speaker as though her contribution was not worth comment. It was the perfect put-down, a favourite device of Robin Day, and at first it had stung. Now she didn't care, and that said a lot about Tony Lund. His impact, in bed or lecturing, was only transient. So why did Deirdre Paul put up with him?

The enigma of Tony Lund's love-life quickly palled. There were more important things to worry about. Today the review board would pronounce on the future of Belgate. Fran had only the dimmest idea of what happened when a pit closed. The colliery yard would be empty and barred, miners' buses would thread the streets carrying Belgate men away; but what would happen to the heart of Belgate? With a shiver she realized she was already assuming that the pit would be condemned. That was the kind of feeble acceptance that had landed the North in its present mess. Belgate would survive, and so would the pit! She put down her foot and watched the needle climb to eighty just to emphasize her point.

It was half-past one when she got home, time for her to take Nee-wan out before it got dark. Walks with the dog were great treats and she was in the mood for goodies of some sort. She kept him on the lead until they were on the old stagecoach road that ran above and behind Belgate. He was always overjoyed to be off the lead, running backwards and forwards in a frenzy of delight. 'Go on, daft dog. I'll be tripping over you in a moment.'

The path was scarred by tractor wheels, and here and there the imprint of a horse's hoofs. On either side the fields were black and rich with tiny pockets of snow in sheltered corners. Ice had formed in the tractor furrows, and cracked at the impact of her booted feet. Ahead, the trees of the copse were winter black, but up close she would see buds pressing against the bark, ready to burst forth at the coming of spring.

Then fields would be filled with fragile green shoots that would turn into sturdy corn almost before her eyes, and the hedgerows, brittle and grey now that the hips were gone, would blossom with old man's beard and willow herb and beautiful, starry dog-daisies. Her eye was caught by a single leaf turned red and clinging to its stem in spite of winter winds. The sight cheered her out of all proportion, as though she had found a jewel.

She reached the top of the track and turned to look down on Belgate. Far off, the A19 stretched like a toy track with tiny Matchbox cars and buses speeding north and south. Below the road, the roofs of Belgate ran down to meet the coastline. There was the inevitable ship on the horizon, the familiar dark band where sky met sea. Somewhere to the west lay Durham city with its cathedral tower. South was the smoke of Middlesbrough, a sleeping giant waiting for jobs that never seemed to come. She bent down and touched the cold earth. Durham earth. Rich earth, that would bring forth good crops in the fullness of time. Rich earth covering even richer seams of coal.

Her eyes were pricking with tears, sentimental tears. It was a good job no one could see her. On her left winter sun glinted off window glass but the nearest house must be half a mile away, or more. Besides, who cared? Suddenly she remembered the time after David's death when she had been afraid to walk in the park and cry because someone was sure to be watching her. And now she dared weep at will and shout out loud and even take a precious half-day off. She had come a long way.

A yard off, the dog watched her, hoping for a stick or a stone. Instead she threw up her arms and opened her mouth. 'Race you to the bottom,' she yelled, and began to run.

She had sobered up by the time she reached home. Bethel was sure to be there and would take a dim view of truancy for truancy's sake. She would have to invent a plausible reason for being home on a college afternoon.

She was spared interrogation for Bethel had news to impart. 'The NCB's decided.' Fran looked suitably impressed but kept her mouth shut. 'They've set a target: 5,000 tons a day, or else!'

Fran let out a slow whistle. 'Can it be done?'

Bethel shrugged. 'It'll have to be, won't it? That pit's losing best part of a million pounds every few weeks. How long can that go on?'

'Yes, but 5,000 tons. It sounds huge.' She thought for a moment and then decided to cheer up. 'Still, I expect it'll be all right. They'll never shut Belgate. It's a good little pit.'

Bethel was warming the pot, swilling it round and round against her bosom. 'By, you're green. You get older but you don't improve. "A good little pit?" It's losing millions, but it's a good little pit? Keep it open, God. We don't know where the wages is coming from but keep it open just the same.'

Fran was stung. 'What about the social consequences if it closes? There's no work in Belgate. They're paying off at David's old factory, and small firms don't take apprentices any more. Where are people going to work, Bethel?'

Bethel sighed deeply. 'That's not the point, is it? I never said put the lot on the dole. What I'm saying is that keeping a clapped-out pit open never solved anything.'

They were on to tea by now, elbows on table, Bethel's packet of No. 6 between them. 'I'd love a cigarette,' Fran thought and turned away her eyes. 'Well, what does solve it? I mean, whose responsibility is it? It's the government, they're responsible.'

Bethel shook her head. 'See what I mean: green as grass. The government's puppets, no more no less. Someone else has his hand up their jackets' ... she gestured with her hand right and left ... 'Yes sir, no sir, three bags full, sir.'

[103]

A delicious idea was forming in Fran's mind, a mental picture of someone trying to get his hand up Margaret Thatcher's frock. 'What about the Prime Minister? You don't think she's a puppet, do you?'

Bethel considered. 'No. She's a woman so she's not so easily led. And she's sincere, I'll give her that. She means what she says and she stands up for what she believes in.'

Fran was about to fall off her chair at this political conversion when the punchline came.

'The only trouble is, she gets everything wrong bar the date. We're saddled with one job-lot, and the alternative is worse, and you clap-trap on about it being logical. Get that dog some water and leave the thinking to folks that have the equipment for it.'

Fran was trying to decide whether or not Bethel was an anarchist when Walter's horn sounded. They sat still until they heard him fretting and fuming on the steps. 'Oh God, if ever a feller had a bunch of duds for friends ... wouldn't even help a cripple up a lighthouse ... hell and damnation. I'll best these bloody steps ...'

'I ought to go,' Fran said, feeling guilty.

Bethel shook her head. 'Let the bairn play. It's the breath of life to him to complain. Don't spoil his pleasure.'

When Walter was safely in, he looked around. 'Well, I can see I'm going to be offered neither bite nor sup in this house, so I'd best get back on the road.' He spun his chair and then, as both women sprang into action, swung back and settled himself.

Terry arrived as they were drinking the tea. 'I've brought you some logs, Mrs Drummond. I thought you could use them.' He looked around. 'Sally. Walter. I haven't seen you for a bit.'

One of the things Fran loved about Belgate life was the absence of a generation gap. Terry was twenty-three, Walter perhaps three times that. And still Terry could address him as an equal. In her middle-class suburb of Sunderland a twenty-three year old would have been tongue-tied in the presence of his elders, or so deferential as to make normal conversation difficult. Here, there was no such bar.

'I'm all right.' Walter's eyebrows were bristling. 'Except for worrying over what you lot'll do next.'

Terry grinned. 'What've I done now, Walter? I'm always glad to hear the latest episode.' He turned to Fran. 'It's nice when you can keep up with your own activities. I mean, I always seem to be the last to know.'

Bethel was scalding fresh tea at the sink but her eyes were on the two men.

'I hear you're talking strike again?'

Terry pursed his lips and considered. 'If you mean the lodge committee, Walter, we have discussed it. It's a legitimate working-class weapon. And there's never been a greater need for struggle – not even a die-hard like you can deny that.'

Walter fingered the arms of his chair. 'Aye, lad, you've got a bonny tongue on you. You dress it all up nice and you sound like butter wouldn't melt, but you're a bloody little agitator all the same. My union split down the middle, it'll never recover ... there's a dozen homes I could mention that'll never be the same again. The last strike was a bloody disaster, and you're talking strike again. God forgive you.'

Terry was shaking his head. 'The NUM's not split down the middle, Walter, not anything like it. There's a tiny fraction, a *tiny* fraction, split away and formed the UDM. They have no standing, legal or moral. We'll snuff them out and nee trouble. We'll see victimized men back to work, every man jack of them. And we'll keep this pit open. The strike wasn't a disaster, it was a breakthrough. We're politically aware now, Walter. We can't be pushed around any more. We've realized our power.'

Long after they had gone and she was preparing for her evening out, Fran was remembering Terry's words. They were chillingly reminiscent of something she had read in the paper weeks ago and cut out to show Gwen.

While her Carmen rollers heated she went in search of it. The cutting was from the evening paper of 28 March and contained a quote from Arthur Scargill, talking to a Russian newspaper. '*The most important achievement, the brilliant victory in this production conflict, was the struggle itself. In the course of twelve months many thousands of young men and women were politicized to a degree that seemed incredible just two or three years ago.'*

So Scargill had won after all, at least in his own eyes, in spite of the general opinion that he had suffered defeat.

She sat on the edge of the bath to put in her Carmens. A few hours ago she had been happy, perhaps as happy as she had been in a long time. Now it was spoiled. Damn Terry! And yet she liked him, with his cheerful, freckled face and willingness to do a good turn. And when he wasn't spouting Trotskyist rubbish, he could be good company. She was suddenly seized with curiosity about the word Trotskyist. She had been quick to use it but she hadn't a clue what it stood for. All she knew about Trotsky was that he'd been done in with an ice-pick. She offered up a brief prayer for Treesa to marry Terry and make an honest man of him, and vowed to look up Trotsky the next time she was in the college library.

She was meeting Jim at his Seaham hotel that night. They hadn't seen one another for nearly two weeks, so she was looking forward to it. 'Come here for a meal,' he'd said. 'I've brought those photographs I told you about.'

Martin had been all bright-eyed and bushy-tailed at the thought of her seeing Jim. 'I hope he stays till the weekend. I've missed him.' She had wondered if he might suggest coming with her but he seemed happy enough for her to go on her own. He was too young to be a matchmaker, really, but he was showing all the signs.

As Jim and Fran drank a fruity white wine in the bar, she felt her spirits rise. To hell with Terry and pit closures and the impossibility of her ever passing philosophy. Next birthday she'd be thirty-five: half her lifespan over. If she didn't start enjoying life soon it'd be too late. 'I'd love a rum baba,' she said when Jim asked about dessert. 'I'm full to the brim but I'm in the mood for going over the top.'

Afterwards, she would ponder her choice of words but as she uttered them she deliberately refrained from analysis. She had been on a seesaw of emotions all day. Now she was just glad to be here with Jim. He was nice – that much underrated adjective which teachers said meant nothing but really meant everything.

When Jim suggested going up to get the photographs she shook her head. 'I'll come up with you. We'll go out and come in again by the side door if that makes you feel better. No one will see.'

When they reached his room she could see he was both elated and uneasy. He rushed to tidy a clutter of socks and underpants and scooped his spare shoes under the bed.

'Sit down. There's only one chair but I'll squat down beside you in a minute!' He passed her the album. 'I've got a bottle of scotch here, if you'd like some?'

They had scotch and water in tooth-glasses, and turned the pages of the album. His children were lovely, a pert little girl and a camera-shy little boy who felt obliged to make faces at the lens. 'Your wife was very pretty.' A look of proprietorial pride touched his face and Fran felt an irrational hurt. She skipped through the last few pages and handed back the album.

Jim got to his feet and went to sit on the bed, looking first at his glass and then at his hands. After a moment he switched on the bedside radio and began to twiddle the tuner.

'This is crazy,' Fran thought. She put down her glass and stood up. 'Do you want to make love to me?' she said and waited until he was forced to meet her eye.

'Yes,' he answered. She put out a hand and felt his arm quiver at her touch.

'It's all right,' she said, drawing him to her. 'It'll be all right.' She held his head to her breast and soothed him, thinking all the while of the girl she had been who had always been afraid, and wondering from whence her present boldness sprang.

At last they drew apart, both calm. He got to his feet to put out the light, and she was glad. As her eyes grew accustomed to the dark she crossed to the window and drew back the curtains. A few hundred yards away a flat sea gleamed silver, only a faint booming betraying the force beneath it. 'Beautiful, isn't it?' Jim said, coming up behind her.

She turned into his arms and knew it was going to be all right. Funny, funny life, teasing and deceiving you so that you mistook sand for sugar and sugar for sand. He held her for a moment then turned her slightly so that once more she could see the sea.

'I spent half my life out there. It's strange to think of it now, that once it was my mistress ... and my comforter. There's a verse of John Betjeman's ...' He tilted his head, seeking the words, and then bent to recite for her.

'Here where the cliffs alone prevail
I stand exultant, neutral, free,
And from the cushion of the gale
Behold a huge consoling sea.'

She would never have guessed he loved poetry but the revelation was a welcome one. 'I like that,' she said. '*A huge consoling sea.* I always thought Betjeman wrote funny stuff – good, but light.'

His arms were like a shield around her. 'You'll have to read him again,' he said and touched her lips with his so that the last word was almost lost.

They undressed slowly, helping one another sometimes, neither of them afraid that the moment would slip away. 'Are you sure?' he said, when at last they stood naked together.

'This is comfortable,' Fran thought. Aloud she said, 'I'm sure.'

They took time, exploring, reassuring. 'Oh, my love,' Fran said at last and drew his body into hers. He took her with him, lifting her in arms that were surprisingly strong, cradling her head in one hand, touching her face with the other.

One tiny portion of her mind acknowledged his experience, resented it briefly, and ceased to care. All that mattered was that he was in her and around her and there was no possibility of failure.

14

'I've put in for Broad Street or High Barnes,' Gwen said. 'It'd be nice if we got on the same staff.'

Fran gave a hollow laugh. 'I just hope we both pass, Gwen. I'll worry about *where* I teach when I know they're going to let me teach at all.'

It was still winter but the earth was cracking to show impatient bulbs. They had almost reached the car-park when Gwen dropped her bombshell. 'I was told last night that you were courting. It's the first I knew of it, I said ... but when I thought it over I decided you'd been broody for a bit so it was possibly true.'

Fran felt guilty. 'I was going to tell you. It's not courting, not by a long chalk, but there is someone.'

Gwen's eyes were round with curiosity. 'Where did you meet him?'

'I picked him up on the dockside.' Fran said, and chuckled at the idea. 'It's true,' she said when Gwen expressed disbelief, and filled in the details while they stood at the car.

'He sounds nice,' Gwen said doubtfully. 'But with men who move around you can never be sure.'

'Sure of what?' Fran asked.

Gwen looked uneasy. 'Well, I mean, he says he's a widower but you only have his word for it ...'

Fran's smile was wry. If ever she had seen a man with the stamp of bereavement on him, it was Jim when she first met him. Now he looked better but there was still some way to go.

Bethel had the kettle on when she got home. 'I'm dying for a good cup of tea. The stuff we get at college is foul. I don't know how they can spoil tea but they seem to have the knack.'

Bethel pushed a mug towards her. 'Get that down you.' She sank into the opposite chair. 'I've bottomed your bedroom and tickled up the front room.' She looked around. 'We'll have to do this place when the weather picks up. It's getting like the black hole of Calcutta.' It was true; the once-white ceiling was yellow, and in one or two places the paper was coming away from the walls. 'It doesn't do to let a house slip,' Bethel said. 'Not if you're intending to stop in it.'

'*If you're intending to stop.*' Fran thought about those words as she cooked sausages for Martin's tea. Last night on the phone Jim had asked her a question: '*Could you ever imagine living anywhere else but the North?*'

'I suppose I could,' she'd said and changed the conversation, but really she couldn't imagine leaving her roots. Couldn't bear to leave Bethel. Couldn't leave this funny red house in this claustrophobic little Durham village, let alone move miles away. And that was what he had meant. He was saying, '*Have we a future, you and I?*' The trouble was that neither of them had the answer to the question.

Exploring John Betjeman's poetry, she had found a verse that summed it up. 'On leaving Wantage 1972', it had been called, and the last few lines had struck her as appropriate:

From this wide vale, where all our married lives
We two have lived, we now are whirled away
Momently clinging to the things we knew –
Friends, footpaths, hedges, house and animals –
Till, borne along like twigs and bits of straw,
We sink below the sliding stream of time.

She shivered, suddenly downcast. The poem was right about leaving your roots: once you did that you were nothing more than straw. It amazed her to realize that she had never felt for any man as she felt for Jim, not physically. She had never been more fulfilled or more a partner in the physical sense. If that was love, then she loved him. Remembering the early days when she had had difficulty in recalling his name let alone his presence, she could hardly believe her present feelings. To be in his arms was now everything, with none of the desire to please she had felt for David, no need to be the crutch she had been for Steve, and no sense of being used, which had neutralized all Tony's expertise. Just a feeling of total pleasure that was all the better for its mutuality. It was only when they drew apart that the doubts began. It was as though he donned his other hats with his clothes and became father, business man, grieving widower. And she returned to being foolish Frances, who was never sure of anything.

Martin was in a good mood at the tea-table. 'One more week and I'm free. I don't hate school, so you needn't make a face; it's just I like having freedom. We're going down the blast one day and Mike's making a go-cart. He's not half good with his hands, you know. I keep telling him he could be an apprentice, but he won't.'

'What does he want to do?' Fran asked.

Martin shrugged. 'Nothing much. I expect he'll be a dolie. There won't be a pit by the time he leaves school.' His world-weary tones suggested there wouldn't be much of anything in a year or two.

'You don't know that,' Fran said. 'They might hit the target and the pit might be reprieved. Anyway, there'll be other work by the time you grow up.' She tried to sound confident but he was not deceived.

'Like what? Unless we get more Japs, there won't be anything.'

He had a point. The Nissan car plant at Washington and NSK Bearings at Peterlee were giving jobs to Belgate men, but there was precious little else. 'Well, I still think there'll be other jobs before long,' she said.

'When we get rid of Thatcher?' he asked.

Fran grinned. 'I wish it was that simple.'

He had finished his sausage and chips and was on to cake. 'Anyway, I might not want a job here. I might go to sea.'

Fran's amazement was unfeigned. 'What put that in your head?' and then . . . 'I suppose it was Jim?'

'Not really,' Martin said. 'Well, not just him. I was already thinking I'd like to go round the world a lot ... like a pilot or something. Jim just said the sea was OK if you got all the tickets and everything and got good ships.'

Fran chose her words carefully. 'But wouldn't you mind leaving here? Leaving Mike and your other friends, and all the places you know?'

'Well, I'd rather not leave them but you have to sometimes. And anyway I could go backwards and forwards now. By myself. So I'd still be friends with him. Anyway, he might go in the army. He says he might do that if he doesn't go on the dole.'

Fran thought over their conversation as she washed up the tea things. A year ago, or little more, he had almost cried at the thought of having to change schools. Now he could contemplate a move with equanimity.

She had settled to her college work when Treesa arrived. 'Are you busy? Shall I go?' She looked miserable and Fran shoved her books aside.

'I should think not. I don't see half enough of you. Where's Christopher?'

Christopher was being put to bed by his Uncle Terry. 'It was Terry's idea I came round. "Go and see Mrs Drummond," he said. "She'll cheer you up."'

Fran settled Treesa by the fire and carried in instant coffee. 'Now, tell me what's wrong? It's not the baby, is it?'

Treesa shook her head. 'No, it's not us. But I'm that upset, it might as well be.'

In the hall the phone rang. 'I'll just let it ring,' Fran said. 'If it's important they'll ring back.'

Treesa's eyes widened. 'It might be trouble.'

It was Min. 'I'm just ringing to report on the first month's business. We've made a profit, Fran. But only just – not enough to live on.' She was trying to be cheerful but despair was in her voice. 'I'm learning, that's the important thing. There were one or two lines I simply loved but we couldn't shift them. So now I look for things in the worst possible taste and they go like a bomb.

Dennis says it's early days, and I suppose he's right.' Her voice softened. 'He's beginning to pick up, Fran. He actually took my head off this morning and I thought, "Thank God". I don't believe in tyrants but a man shouldn't be crushed, should he?'

Fran was dying to hear Treesa's story but Min couldn't be cut short. 'Well, I think you deserve to succeed, Min. You've been an absolute brick.'

'And you didn't think I had it in me?'

It was time for truth. 'No, Min. I knew you weren't completely empty and money-mad ...'

Min interrupted. 'Which is what Eve thinks.'

Fran ignored this and carried on ... 'but I didn't think you'd have the guts to start again so soon, especially when Frances is still a baby. It can't be easy.'

Min was regaining her confidence. 'I'm going to make it work, I promise you. The truth is, Fran, that I've been an under-achiever. That's why I was such a bitch; too much undischarged energy. Now I'm plugged in, you just watch me!'

Fran was smiling as she came back into the room. 'Good news?' Treesa asked.

'Yes,' Fran said, 'I suppose so. But it's not so much the good news, it's the way Min keeps up her end. I've never known anyone like her.' Treesa's brows were raised. 'It's Min. You know, that friend of mine with the very black hair. She came ...'

Fran suddenly realized what she was saying and stopped, but Treesa finished for her. 'She came to Brian's funeral. Yes, I remember her.'

'Now, tell me what's wrong?' Fran picked up her coffee. It was no longer hot but it would do.

'You know Dave, who brings your coal? Well, they've pinched him.'

Fran felt a jolt of alarm. 'For stealing coal?'

Treesa shook her head. 'No, much worse than that. They say ... well, he did do it. They say he broke into a deputy's house and took a video and some coins. He sold them in a shop in Sunderland and they traced them back. His wife's in a bad way – they were on the bottom, that's why he did it. Now she says he'll go up for a long time and she's beside herself.'

'Oh Treesa, I'm so sorry. And he'd never been in trouble before, had he, until the strike?'

Treesa was nodding. 'That's right. It makes you feel as though it'll never stop, all the trouble. Terry and his dad speak, you know, but it's not the same. I feel for his mam, I really do. I was feeling sorry for myself this afternoon, and then I heard about Dave and Audrey, and me own troubles just seemed nothing.'

'What troubles have you got, Treesa? I know you're on your own, but you have Terry. If only you wouldn't be silly and think you're being disloyal to Brian. I've told you before, he'd want you to be happy.'

Treesa's eyes were brimming and she twisted the sides of her cardigan. 'It's not that easy. I look at him sometimes and I think, yes, I do love him and we could work things out. And then it comes to it and I can't.'

Fran drew a breath and plunged. 'You mean you can't bear the thought of making love with him?' Treesa's down-bent head bobbed. 'I know how you feel. Brian was the only man you went with, wasn't he?' Again there was a nod, but the chin had come a little way from her chest. 'Well, it was the same for me. David and I fell in love at school, and after that I just never looked at anyone else. But I've had to make a new life.' Treesa's head came up, wearing an expression of shocked disapproval. 'Yes,' Fran said firmly. 'There has been someone else.' No need to say more than one: there was a limit to how much soul-baring people could expect.

'And it wasn't easy, Treesa, for all the reasons you know. But in my heart I know it's right to love again. Not to replace David; I wouldn't do that even if I could. Love isn't like that, something you give once and have to take away to give again. It's a growing thing and it expands for each new love you make. Each real love, anyway.' Treesa was still gazing at her, waiting to be convinced. 'Look, when you had Christopher you loved him, didn't you? And you didn't have to take love from Brian or your parents. You grew new love. You've already grown new love for Terry, whether or not you know it. I've known it for ages, since Christopher was ill. So why not let things be?'

Treesa was wiping her eyes. 'Well, put like that, I suppose it makes sense. But there's something else . . . it's not just me.'

'Does Terry feel it's disloyal to Brian?'

Treesa shook her head. 'I don't think so. It's the money, with Terry. I've got all that compen., and he's just a working miner, and he thinks it'd be sponging. I think he'd like me to lose it all overnight and then he'd be happy.'

Fran's patience was going. 'That's stupid. That really is stupid. Just let me catch him saying that and I'll tell him what's what. He's got so much stupid pride, has Terry – that's what caused the trouble with his dad. He'll have to curb it before he's much older.'

When at last she sent Treesa off, comforted, she thought how pat her arguments had been. Off with the old love and on with the new – except that the old love remained to haunt you, so that you could cry out one man's name in the arms of another, or murmur the other's name in sleep. And when there were two ghosts, one on each side, the difficulty was compounded.

She decided to work off her blues and went to collect the washing. She was feeding Martin's jeans into the tub when she felt the packet. King-size tipped. One whole cigarette, one fag-end. That was all she needed, a twelve-year-old heading for emphysema.

She was still feeling despondent when the phone rang. 'I've been thinking, Fran,' Jim said. 'I was going to try to get up to your end in the holidays and then I thought, why doesn't Fran come down here? You could meet the kids, and we could have a night out in London. How does that sound?'

She heard herself agree but her rush of joy soon subsided. London was a long way away and belonged to Dorothy. When was life going to be easy? When would problems have simple answers and not be so overhung with emotion that they defied solution? She put a hand behind her and lowered herself to the stairs. 'I'm glad you rang,' she said. 'It's been a lousy day.'

15

She felt better once they were actually on the road. Before that she had felt an almost physical pain at parting from Martin. 'It'll be all right, mam, honestly. I'll like sleeping at Treesa's. She's better than you about stopping up. And Bethel'll be there if I need anyone.'

She had decided not to take him on this first trip. It was a voyage into uncharted waters and he was better out of it. Now, though, she wavered. 'Let him come,' Jim had said, sensing her distress. It was Martin who'd vetoed the idea. 'Go on. I'm all right, mam. You're only going for two days.' His eyes said more: *'Have fun, mam. Like Jim. Sorry about the smoking.'* So she had climbed into the car for the journey to Twickenham, and waved and waved until the corner was turned and her son was out of sight.

'I'm soft,' she said, blowing her nose. 'It's crazy really.' He said nothing, simply smiled and kept his eyes on the road.

Peterlee came and the smoky blur of Middlesbrough appeared. 'I hope you know where we're going,' Jim said. He always used the A1, but she had suggested taking the A19 as far as Dishforth.

'I do and it's simpler. You'll see,' she said, regretting her cocksureness when they had to queue to get on to the A1 and lost all the time they had saved. But at least she had seen the hills, the blue, remembered Cleveland Hills. 'We used to have picnics there,' she said, and knew he understood.

Tonight she would ring Martin on Treesa's newly installed telephone. Tomorrow she would ring him again, and the next day. The day after, she would catch the three o'clock from Kings Cross and come home. As if he read her thoughts, Jim spoke.

'You must bring Martin next time. He'd get on well with Barb-ara, and Kevin would appreciate some male support. Barbara bosses him, I'm afraid. Well, she tries to mother him; I suppose it's understandable.'

They turned off at Newark and drove into the town to eat in an old, timbered pub. 'I used to use the M1 at the beginning, but it's so monotonous,' he said. 'I found myself falling asleep a few times and I thought, that's it.' She nodded and smiled, and he reached out and touched her hand. 'That's better. You looked a bit woebegone before.'

'I do feel better.' She had enjoyed her meal and was feeling distinctly relaxed.

'It's like that when you set out on a journey,' he said. 'I used to feel it on the ship. Ashore, you had a thousand worries; then you got aboard and you saw the ship leave the side, and suddenly there was nothing you could do about it until you were ashore again. So you stopped fretting.'

Fran smiled. 'The huge consoling sea,' she said and he nodded agreement.

She drove when they got back on to the A1. At first he demurred, then he accepted gratefully. 'I could do with a snooze.' A moment later he had tilted his seat and was asleep. She couldn't believe it. David had let her share drives but he had always stayed alert in case she missed turnings. She drove as far as the Peterborough junction and felt inordinately proud of the fifty-five miles on the clock. As she drove she watched his pro-file. He was handsome; why had she not seen it from the first? Or had he changed since they had been together, blossoming as women were said to blossom when they fell in love? Perhaps it was all in the eye of the beholder and she was seeing what she wished to see. It didn't matter. She stretched out a hand to his thigh and left it there as the miles fell away.

London appeared on a road sign. 'Almost there,' he said and she could tell he was glad to be coming home.

'Do you love London?'

'Yes, I love the old place all right. You can't help it. "Dull

[117]

would he be of soul," and all that.'

'"On Westminster Bridge",' she said.

He was pleased she recognized it. '"*This city now doth like a garment wear the beauty of the morning; silent, bare, ships, towers, domes, theatres and temples lie open unto the fields, and to the sky ... The river glideth at its own sweet will; Dear God! the very houses seem asleep; and all that mighty heart is lying still.*"' He recited simply and well.

'You know your poetry.'

He laughed. 'Some poetry. The bits I can understand. I used to read a lot at sea.'

'What about Housman?' Fran asked.

Jim shook his head. 'I don't think I've heard of him.'

She felt smug. 'You must have heard of *The Shropshire Lad*?'

He wrinkled his brow. 'I thought that was the name of a pub. Yes, I've heard of it but it sounds a bit ... bucolic?'

She let her enthusiasm show. 'Oh, it's not, it's lovely. You get the feeling of him being young and loving life and appreciating the things you appreciate. I won't go on about it, I'll lend you a copy when we get back. Then you'll see.'

As the outskirts of London began, she reflected that he was the first man she had talked poetry with. Real poetry, that is. David had liked the poems of John Lennon, but she wasn't sure they counted. Jim had introduced her to Betjeman and for that she was grateful.

They skirted central London and she didn't see a single familiar landmark. 'Never mind,' Jim consoled her, 'we'll go sightseeing tomorrow. There are things I've been meaning to show the kids ... if you live in London it's amazing what you miss. We'll go tomorrow. We could start with Hampton Court, that's practically on the doorstep.' He changed gear as the traffic thickened. 'You really must bring Martin next time. London's magic for kids, a living history lesson.'

There it was again, that acceptance of a shared future that filled her with delight and terror. He felt right; more than a lover ... he felt like a husband. Suddenly her happiness evaporated.

[118]

He wasn't like a husband, he was a husband. Dorothy's husband.

At once the remembrance of his loving her was shameful, so that she shut her eyes and squeezed her lids.

'OK?' His eyes were on her, anxious.

'Yes, fine. Just a little headache ... it's gone now.'

Twickenham was a town in itself. 'Lots of shops,' she said. It was half-past four and shoppers were still about.

'You can get anything here,' he said proudly. 'And there's a silversmith's down towards the river. Not many of them left. We're slap bang on the Thames, you know; you'll see tomorrow.' He was trying to sell the place to her and they both knew it. And they both knew that relocation would not be the only problem. '*That's just the beginning,*' Fran thought.

His house was old and roomy and pleasant. 'We bought it cheap,' he said, showing her round. 'It was in its original state ... stone sink, moulded arches. I kept what I could, but the plumbing's new, it's been rewired, that sort of thing. It's worth a lot more now, and it'll be mine in 1993!'

She asked about the children. 'I think Mother was taking them out after school. Just for an hour.' She could see he was on edge. 'I didn't want it to look like a reception committee ... they're all dying to meet you.' He went off to make tea and Fran sank into a chair.

The room was impressively tidy. There were toys in a corner, but all boxed and neatly piled. She rested her hands on the arms of the chair. They were slightly worn. Worn by whom? Jim's slippers were placed neatly on the opposite side of the hearth, his pipe-rack was nearby. That was his side, therefore this had been Dorothy's side. Remembering how she had hated alien hands on David's chair, she withdrew her own and folded them in her lap.

It was a woman's room – flowered carpet, flowered curtains, embroidered cushions and a photograph in a silver frame. Dorothy and the children, all squinting into the sun above holiday smiles. There was a box beside the photograph, hand-carved

[119]

with initials in mother-of-pearl: 'D.K.' D for Dorothy and K presumably for her maiden name. Fran was at once consumed with curiosity to see inside, and suffused with guilt at her own emotions. This was someone else's house. She moved her legs uneasily, tucking them neatly together. It was a pity he had kept the children away; they might have broken the ice.

'Do you need the loo?' He guided her to the upstairs landing and left her. 'Bathroom's on the right. I'll be in the kitchen.'

The bathroom was squeaking with Vim and elbow grease, and there was an embroidered guest-towel on the rail. On the way downstairs she passed an open bedroom door. There was a double bed and a man's jacket in a cleaner's bag hung on the wardrobe. This must be Jim's room, the bed he had shared with Dorothy. She sped down the rest of the stairs, praying for the front door to open and admit the children – anything to take her mind off things. Except that they, too, were Dorothy's, so there was no escape.

They came in when the tea had been drunk, their grandmother fussing over them and trying to make Fran welcome at the same time. 'Take your coat off, Kevin, there's a big boy. I do hope Jim made you some tea? We hurried back ... not there, Barbara, hang it up.'

Barbara was tall for her age, thin and intense. A freckled nose, hair scraped back into bunches in a style Fran remembered from childhood. They'd have trouble with her hairline in future if it continued to be pulled back like that. She would have to speak to Jim ... except that it was really none of her business. Barbara had seated herself close to her grandmother and bent periodically to pull up one sock or the other.

'Have you been somewhere nice?' The child shook her head and then decided some reply was necessary. 'We went to the library. Kevin's just joined. I've belonged for ages.' Kevin was eyeing the tea-tray and seemed disinclined to talk. He was more like his father, with a determined, if chubby, chin.

'This lady's a teacher, Kevin. Show her your books.'

Fran's heart sank. She was not sure that being introduced as a teacher was the best possible start. 'I'm not a proper teacher. Not yet.'

She looked round the room, trying to find a safe topic of conversation. 'I see you've got Mousetrap. My son likes playing that.'

Barbara spoke with all the assurance of a septuagenarian. 'We don't play that any more. It's a bit babyish.'

Kevin scowled. 'I don't think it's babyish, I think it's good. Anyway, it's mine.'

Jim had come back into the room and was beginning to look agitated. 'Who wants some tea? Proper tea.'

Barbara stood up. 'I'll make it, daddy. Tell me what you want.' She's demonstrating ownership, Fran thought and was struck by pity for the child. Second relationships were difficult for everyone, children most of all.

Jim's mother offered to take her upstairs. 'I've put you in my room. It overlooks the back garden, so you won't hear the traffic.' It was a typical spare room with a single bed and a narrow ash wardrobe.

'I haven't put you out by coming, have I? I could easily have used a hotel.'

The older woman sat down suddenly on the bed. 'To tell the truth, I'm looking forward to being in my own home for a few days. Jim's so good to me but I miss my own place ... well, you do after you've had it for forty years, don't you? Not that I mind. They're lovely children. You won't have a bit of trouble with them, and Barbara's getting very handy. The boy ... well, it's just high spirits ... you've got a boy of your own.'

Fran was dying to say, 'Don't worry, I'm predisposed to like them,' but it wouldn't have done. It was all getting too intense.

'Yes, I have a son,' she said instead. 'He's not a bad lad but he can be a bit of a handful at times.'

Jim's mother looked relieved and then at her wristwatch. 'There's a bus at six if I hurry. I don't want to take Jim away. It breaks my heart sometimes when I get home ... it smells so foisty. Of course, it's shut up all the time.'

The children were already at the kitchen table and Jim

motioned her to a chair. 'Sit down, Fran. I'll just see mother away.' He was flushed, and there were splashes of what Fran hoped was water but feared was fat on his trousers. Barbara was putting a plate in front of her. 'You can have beans as well, if you want them.'

Fran looked down at steak and mushrooms and chips. 'My, my. Your dad's a good cook. No beans, thank you.'

Barbara resumed her seat. 'Grandma cooked them. We just put them in the microwave.' There was a slight emphasis on the 'we' and Fran felt a spasm of irritation. '*All right, darling,*' she thought, '*we all know you're in charge.*'

The boy was easier ... or perhaps she was just used to boys. One of Fran's mushrooms slid from under her fork and she pretended to chase it round her plate. That made him laugh, so she did it again. '*Stop playing to the gallery, Frances,*' she told herself, and was glad when Jim came back to preside.

'Shall I wash up?' she asked when the meal was over. 'You two have worked hard. Let me clear up.'

Barbara was already piling plates. Jim had been right about her trying to replace her mother. 'You've marked the cloth,' she said accusingly when she moved Kevin's plate. He put a finger into the remains of his beans and made another smear to match the first. The little girl's face flushed. 'You're childish,' she said with contempt.

He put his fingers into his mouth and pulled the corners. 'Bugger,' he said, his eyes sliding towards his father.

Jim's expression was agonized. 'Kevin! That's naughty. Apologize to Frances. She didn't come here to hear that sort of thing.'

Barbara's eyes were on her, watching for the next move. 'What sort of thing?' Fran said, pushing back her chair. 'If Kevin and I give you a hand, Barbara, we could all have a game of something after.'

After that things were easier. Kevin, having been let off the hook, was disposed to be angelic, and Barbara was not displeased at the way things had turned out. '*She can tell him off but no one else should,*' Fran thought, and felt a faint warmth for the determined

[122]

little figure at the sink.

They played Mousetrap for Kevin and Trivial Pursuit for Barbara. Fran's eyes signalled, 'Intelligent, isn't she?' and Jim tried not to look overjoyed. They watched Russ Abbott and laughed at Kevin's uninhibited laughter more than the show itself.

'He's a happy little boy,' Fran said, when the children went up to the bath. '*What about her?*' Jim's eyes asked, and she hurried on. 'And Barbara's lovely. She adores you and Kevin, doesn't she?'

They came down, clean in cotton pyjamas, for milk and biscuits. Kevin climbed into the settee beside Fran and allowed her to put an arm round him for a story. *James and the Giant Peach* was his choice and she read his three favourite bits. Barbara listened gravely, giving the page numbers of the pieces he liked. 'You read it usually, don't you?' Fran asked and the child nodded.

'But you can do it. I don't mind.'

The atmosphere had undergone a remarkable thaw since teatime. 'We're like a family,' Fran thought, as they discussed the next day's sightseeing, and looked up to see the same thought on Jim's face.

Where would Martin fit in? How would he take to a small boy in her lap, which was where Kevin had wound up? If she was honest, he hadn't wanted to sit on her knee in years, so chances were he wouldn't mind. She was just about to suggest a pick-a-back to bed when the doorbell rang.

'Who can that be?' There was foreboding in Jim's voice and a weary acceptance of intrusion.

'It's just us!' The woman's voice was arch. They came into the room, giving false starts at the sight of a stranger. 'Oh, good Lord,' the man said, 'I'd completely forgotten you had a guest.'

'This is Desmond, Dorothy's brother,' Jim said. He didn't need to add, 'my boss'; Desmond's bearing said it for him. 'And Janet, his wife. This is Frances Drummond, a friend of mine. She's here for a few days.'

[123]

Desmond held out his hand. 'Jim did tell me. I'm afraid it slipped my mind.' If John Wayne had been there he'd have said, '*the Hell it did*'. All Fran said was, 'Hello.'

Janet's hand was warm and damp. 'Do you have a family, Mrs Drummond?' She didn't wait for an answer. 'We simply love the children. Desmond can't see enough of them. It's understandable; he and Dorothy were twins. Identical.'

Fran was aching to point out that identical twins of opposite sexes was a contradiction in terms, but decided against it. Jim was fussing around getting everyone seated, in spite of the new arrivals' vowing they hadn't come to stay.

'Oh God,' Fran thought, as Janet settled herself for what promised to be a long stay, 'I thought things were going too well.'

16

She was out of the house by seven-thirty and at the market by eight a.m. 'Fran, you're a brick. Now, it's perfectly simple ...' A moment later Min was gone, leaving Fran in charge.

She surveyed the stall: dainty ladies, pipe-playing urchins, bespectacled cobblers, all portrayed in china, and a crowd of pixies on spotted toadstools trailing electric flex. It would be awful if she sold nothing. People passing on their way to work did not spare a glance.

It had seemed quite simple last night when Min had telephoned. 'Fran? How was London?'

She had started to talk about London's parks and gardens being further on than the North's, but Min had cut her short. 'Stuff the shrubs and bulbs, Fran; get to the nitty-gritty. How did you get on with his kids?'

A man passed the stall, looking uncertainly at her. 'She away then, the usual one?'

Fran gave him what she hoped was an encouraging smile.

'Yes, she's got some business to attend to, but I'll help if I can.'

He leaned forward and lowered his voice. 'She was getting me something a bit special . . . to help with the wife.' He gave a wink and a nod of his head. Surely Min was not marketing sex-aids under the cover of a china stall?

The sex-aid turned out to be a porcelain poodle twelve inches high, with a jewel-studded collar and a wicked gleam to its eye. Fran found it, after a long search, tissue-wrapped in a box under the counter.

'I told her the wife was hard to please. "Leave it to me. What's her likes and dislikes?" she says, and I said she was mad gone on the dog. A poodle. Daft little beggar, has to have chicken breast. . . Any road, your friend says, "I can fix that," and by gum she has. I'll be well in when the wife sees this.' He parted with the £8.50 marked on the box, and went off satisfied. So that was Min's gimmick – giving each customer personal service!

Min could come back any time now that there was money in the till. Honour was satisfied. It was nine o'clock and the crowd of people going to work had dwindled. At Min's suggestion Fran had put on her sheepskin coat, but her legs and feet felt numb. She stood up to stamp them gently and tried to think of other things.

She had told Min that everything had gone well at the weekend, but that was only part of the truth. All the way home in the train she had wondered whether or not she loved Jim. They fitted together, each of them tongued and grooved by marriage so that they could slip into the roles of husband and wife at will. Except that there was that other husband and wife, ghostly and yet substantial, pushing up through the floorboards, widening the gaps.

She had refused to share Dorothy's bed. She would have said no anyway, because of the children, but the thought of sex in the bed they'd shared, with Dorothy's trinkets still on the dressing table, her clothes, for all Fran knew, still hanging in the closets . . . that was not to be contemplated.

They had made love once in the back of the car, giggling at behaving like seventeen-year-olds again. But the giggling had been uneasy. They were not seventeen and there was no escaping it. What was possible, even desirable, at seventeen was out of place at twice that age, when you were no longer green enough to bend, and valued your dignity.

A woman came up, enquiring about the pixie lamps, and although she bought nothing Fran was glad of the interruption. It was no good dwelling on things, especially emotional things. The practical problems were enough. Desmond and Janet had hovered over everything, present in spirit if not in body, and they had been there in body often enough.

'We wouldn't mind if Jim married again,' Janet had confided as they washed up together on Fran's last day. 'Well, a house needs a woman, doesn't it?' The word 'housekeeper' hung unspoken in the air.

'Of course, it can never be the same. You know that from your own experience, I'm sure. But companionship's valuable.'

Fran had wanted to hurl the plate she was drying against the wall and shout, 'Sod companionship. We fuck frequently,' but even saying the word in her mind was shame-making. She felt her cheeks flush at the remembrance of it, and decided to rearrange the stock.

She was putting a white-faced pierrot next to a street band on a flower-encrusted base, when she recognized the woman eyeing the display. 'Hello, I thought it was you.' She looked younger and prettier than the last time Fran had seen her, when she had been thin and strained, brown hair covered with a cotton scarf, eyes ringed with kohl in an otherwise white face. They had worked side by side in the woman's support group kitchen during the strike, and had struck up a kind of rapport. Now she was carefully made up, well-dressed and her hair was ash blonde. She smiled, seeing Fran's eyes widen. 'Yes ... I do look a bit different, thank God. I wouldn't want to go through that again.' She looked at the stall. 'I never knew you worked here. Somebody said you were a student.'

'I am,' Fran said. 'I'm just minding the stall for a friend.'

The woman leaned closer. 'What happened to that other

friend of yours? You know, Tokyo Rose?'

Fran smiled. 'You mean Margot. Well, last I heard she'd moved in with a terrorist.'

The woman's mouth opened and shut. 'You're having me on!'

Fran shook her head. 'That's what I was told.'

The woman looked at her watch. 'Do you get a dinner hour?'

Fran nodded. 'I hope so. I'll freeze to the spot if I don't. Shall we have a coffee or something? Then we can swop all the news.'

They arranged to meet in the Market Tavern at twelve-thirty. Surely Min would be back by then. Business was picking up; the pierrot went and a ghastly pot shell that might have contained a sea-monster. 'You put plants in them. Trailers. She suggested that, the woman what's on usually. I tried it and it looks lovely, so I'm having another. I'd buy one of those lamps, but you never know with electrics.'

Min and Dennis came back at noon. 'Well done, Franny. You've been an angel. I see you didn't shift those bloody pixies. I swear they're sneering at me. Now take this and buy lunch. No, I won't take no for an answer.' They had been for the final interview with the liquidator and relief showed on both their faces.

'I don't want anything, Min. It was fun.'

She had enjoyed selling. Perhaps there was more of the entrepreneur in her than she had thought. She went off with Min's fiver burning a guilty hole in her pocket, but there was no point in arguing when Min had made up her mind – Fran had known that since their schooldays.

The woman was waiting in a corner alcove. 'I got you half a lager,' she said. 'Is that all right?'

Fran carried the menu from the bar. 'Lovely,' she said. 'And lunch is on me. I got paid unexpectedly, so you can help me spend it.'

Over Cornish pasty and chips, they reminisced. 'Peeling onions and taties,' the woman said, 'that's what I remember. Hundreds and hundreds of taties and onions.'

Fran nodded sympathetically. 'I only came now and again, but I can remember how the onions made you cry. Still, it was worth it.'

The woman shrugged. 'Sometimes I wonder. We suffered, I mean, really suffered. I watched my bairns go without and if there's worse torture than that I'd like to see it. And where do we stand now? The pit has a chance to be shut by Christmas.'

Fran hastened to reassure. Terry had briefed her on the likely scenario, so she was well informed. 'The Coal Board has set a target, which the men might make. If they do, the pit's saved. If they don't, the Area Director will announce closure. The Union at area level will have counter proposals, and if the NCB doesn't accept them, it'll go to national appeal in London, and after that to the independent review body – that's a panel of six, and they're not all Coal Board men. So there's lots of ground to cover before the pit goes. And if it does, there'll be voluntary redundancy, and relocation money if you go to another pit. Fifteen hundred pounds if you've been a miner for ten years.'

The woman nodded. 'Yes. Very nice. My man'll get his fifteen hundred, and they'll bus him to Seaham or Murton. But what about my lads? I've got one fourteen, one eleven: where'll they go for work if there's no pit? You tell me, 'cos I don't know.'

Fran made no attempt to reply to her. There was nothing she could say. It was unthinkable to keep open pits whose losses regularly ran into millions, and equally unthinkable to present future generations with no occupation but the dole.

'Did you hear about Davy Sawyer? Him as got sacked for GBH? He's up for thieving. I'm not excusing it, but he'd never've done it if he'd still had his job.'

Fran nodded. 'I was talking to him yesterday.' He had staggered through her yard door, a sack on his back to be tipped into the coalhouse. *'This is the last you'll get. I reckon I'll be out of circulation for a bit...'* He had looked old and defeated, and she had been too tongue-tied to help.

'It's made me think,' the woman said. 'I blame Scargill, I still blame the sod. He's a proper First World War general, that one. Over the top, boys; lie down and die for the cause! But as long as the working man doesn't involve himself there'll be people like

Scargill to pull his strings. And people like Maggie to stamp him into the ground. We're on the bottom rung and we have to fight the system. I want power, not for power's sake but for the sake of my class.'

She was warming to her theme and Fran listened. 'The men don't like it, you know. The minute the strike was over they said, "That's it, canny lass – back to the kitchen sink." Well, bugger that. Ever since I got married I've conformed ... but now! I don't say "Can I?" I just go ahead. The strike made me political, which I never was before. Women have got to stick together. Mind you, I'm not anti-men – I love the sods!'

It was still light when Fran got back to Belgate. April was a lovely month. She thought of the evening ahead, of driving to Sunderland with a red glow in the western sky, Jim waiting for her and looking pleased to see her. That was the best bit of all. She was making him happy, so she could be happy herself, without guilt. 'I am entitled to this happiness,' she thought and went, smiling, into the house.

'Oh mind, that's a change. Something's pleased her.' Bethel was pretending to be sarcastic but it wouldn't wash.

'Hallo, lovely lovely Bethel. I've missed you, but I sold dozens of ornaments and earned a bomb and now I'd like a cup of tea.'

Bethel held her at arm's length. 'You've been drinking?'

Fran opened her mouth and blew. 'Yes. Alcohol. I'm under the affluence of incohol.'

She felt like being daft. She still felt like that when the tea was drunk and she was running upstairs to get ready. She didn't know why she was so euphoric, but no point in questioning a gift horse. She couldn't explain her present mood any more than she could explain the black moods that came for no apparent reason. Or why she had thrown herself at Jim, even suggested having sex when she considered such boldness unseemly.

She took her jewellery box and sat cross-legged on the bed to sort through it. She switched on the bedside radio and started to hand-jive to the beaty music. 'I'm being childish,' she thought, but carried on just the same. Lines from a poem by W. B. Yeats came into her mind:

> ...But lived as 'twere a king
> That packed his marriage-day
> With banneret and pennon,
> Trumpet and kettledrum
> And the outrageous cannon,
> To bundle time away,
> That the night come.

That was what she was doing ... bundling time away that the night come. 'I really want to see him,' she thought and went in search of the volume of Housman she had promised him. It was fun to share poetry with someone close. A new experience.

When she found it she carried it back upstairs and sat in the window, the book unopened in her hand. Could they be happy? Were they entitled to happiness the second time around? Could they take two different halves and make a whole? Would Barbara let them? Memories of Steve's daughter flooded back, the mutinous little face resenting her very presence. And Martin might be put out at no longer being an only child, in spite of liking Jim so much.

If they loved enough, surely anything was possible? Barbara and Kevin were Jim's flesh and, loving him, she must learn to love them too ... if she could. Or at least show affection.

They would have to take things slowly, one small step at a time. More trips to London, taking Martin with her; then a whole week with them up here. The kids would love Nee-wan. After that, a holiday together, somewhere in the sun. The book remained unopened as she indulged in day-dreams that might become plans if they were given half a chance.

17

'I'm taking the dog for a walk.' There was no response, so she called again. 'Did you hear me?'

Feet thudded to floor from arm of chair and the living-room door opened. 'Yeah. OK. I'll take him out tomorrow.'

She clipped on the dog's lead. 'Don't perjure yourself, Martin. And don't forget Terry's coming round tonight. Bethel's at Bingo. So no carry on.'

He went back to his television and she let herself out of the back door and made for the allotments. 'There now,' she said, unclipping the lead as soon as it was safe. The fences around the allotments always fascinated her – old doors, mostly, railway sleepers, corrugated iron sheets, even a metal advertising board bearing half a legend. Once upon a time hens had clucked, but there had been so much skulduggery lately that the hens had been taken away.

Between the cracks in the fence she could see colour. Belgate men loved flowers. They would come up from the pit and hover over roses or gladioli, carrying off prizes for chrysanthemums the size of tea-plates. And all that the South knew of the green-fingered North was its capacity for growing leeks! She smiled at her own fervour. She was becoming more northern as she grew older, or at least less ashamed of it.

She turned to look for Nee-wan as the alley to the main street came into view; he would have to be back on the lead before they encountered traffic. The alley had boasted a wooden fence once upon a time, but it had vanished during the strike, gone to fuel miners' fires like everything else that would burn. It had been replaced with metal-link fencing, but it was not the same and she was glad when she reached the brick wall.

Most of the graffiti from the strike was indecipherable now, but she could make out *Scabs are Shits* and one or two *Coal not Dole.*

A faint spasm of pain gripped her abdomen and she put up a hand to ease the top of her skirt. The curse must be on its way. She tried to remember the date of her last period: had it been early April or the end of March? Once she had counted the days of the month, hoping against hope that this time she would have conceived David's child; now she accepted her barrenness and the curse was just a nuisance. If she married Jim the yearning might return, except that he might think three children between them was more than enough.

She turned into the park and made for the beck. It was running clear today, leaping over stones and gurgling at its edges. She paused on the stone bridge, holding a twig she had picked up on her way. Years ago, when Martin was small, they had played on the bridge, dropping sticks in one side and rushing to see them emerge on the other. Sometimes they sank and never reached daylight, sometimes they re-surfaced and were whirled away. 'Borne along like twigs,' to slip below the sliding stream of time. As usual, when she thought far ahead, she felt afraid. There was no mistaking John Betjeman's meaning: he was talking of death. But she had never felt more alive. Never in her whole life.

She had the dog under control and was walking along Stafford Street when Walter's car pulled up alongside. 'I thought you'd had that dog put down?' Nee-wan stood on his hind legs and put his paws on the car door.

'He wants to give you a kiss, Walter,' Fran said, wondering, as she always did, why Walter's presence so lifted her spirits.

'Kiss? I'll kiss him. You want to get rid of him, he's ruined. You can blame Sally Bethel for that ... slop, slop, slop. It's not the dog's fault, poor beast.'

'Are you going to Bingo tonight?' That would guarantee an explosion, for he considered 'housey' to be a modern curse.

But with Walter nothing was guaranteed. 'Well,' he said, preparing to wind up his window, 'I might go. If Sally's going, I might force meself. Get her in the back row ... pop the question

[132]

between the Silver Chest and the Jackpot. She'll be all roused up by then, so you never know. Get your bridesmaid's dress out!' He was laughing so hugely he could barely steer, but Fran could only think how nice it would be if they did get together, in wedlock or out.

She was ready too early, but the pale, calm face in the bathroom mirror betrayed none of the doubts and fears behind. She knew tonight would be significant; she had sensed it in Jim's voice when he rang and suggested the meal. '*We can talk there,*' he'd said, naming a small Indian restaurant they'd used before. He was probably going to suggest marriage and if he did...

She came downstairs quietly and let herself into the front room. She could hear the television set on the other side of the wall, murmuring voices and studio laughter overlaid with Martin's constant chuckling. Thank God he had a sense of humour.

She sat on a high-backed chair, knees neatly together, hands on lap. She had sat like that on the day of David's funeral, all of the others watching her disintegrate. She had thought it the end of the world, but in a sense it had only been the beginning. She was stronger now, more grown up, more decisive.

In the wake of the self-congratulation came the terror. Could she mother another woman's children, take the place of a dead but still-loved wife? Could she flourish in the alien South if he asked her to move? Most important of all, how would it affect Martin? And Bethel, what would Bethel say?

A new, and niggling doubt surfaced: what about Jim's wedding ring? If he kept on wearing it, it would be a constant reminder. On the other hand, she could hardly suggest he take it off.

It was a relief when Terry arrived. 'I'm not late, am I?' He would have settled down beside Martin but she waved him into the kitchen. 'I want a word, Terry. I haven't much time so I'll get to the point. And don't waste time telling me it's not my business because it'll fall on deaf ears. Treesa is my business and so are you, whether or not you like it.'

He was holding up his hands. 'All right, all right. I'll surrender

[133]

now. I know when I'm beat.'

The smile left his face as she began, to be replaced by the look of resolution he had worn throughout the strike. '*It's hopeless*,' Fran thought but she ploughed on. 'Treesa's told me how you feel about her money, Terry, and I might have known you'd have some ridiculous notion like that. What the hell does it matter whose money it is? She knows you don't give a damn for money; so do I, and so does anyone else who knows you. So if you love Treesa, and I'm sure you do, you'll marry her as soon as possible and give her some happiness and security for a change.'

His expression said, '*Can I go now?*' but she had not finished. 'Brian gave his life for that money. He can't be replaced, but you can try to make sure that things turn out as he'd've wanted them. That's the least you can do. If you turn away from Treesa, you'll break her heart – and all over some bloody silly idea that the man should be the sole provider. You think you're such a man, Terry, a man of principle. But you're letting every little street-gossip carrier in Belgate run your life for you. You're running scared in case one of them says you've feathered your nest.'

She had one final shot. 'After David died I was scared if a man even knocked on my door. "What will they say?" I thought. "Mustn't upset them." And then I grew up. I do what I like now, not because I don't care but because I value my own opinion more than the say-so of Tom, Dick and Harry.'

She had run out of steam and they both knew it. She picked up her bag. 'I won't be too late. Martin knows what's for supper.'

She was almost out of the door when he spoke. 'Thanks for the telling off.' There was a rueful note in his voice that surprised her.

'Did it do any good, Terry, that's the point?'

He shrugged. 'We'll just have to wait and see.'

She felt excited as she drove into Sunderland. Perhaps she had had the desired effect? He and Treesa might be happy ever after, and tonight her own fate might be settled . . . if they could agree terms. Perhaps he would move North; you never knew.

Jim was standing at the bar and she thought once again how ordinary he was until he smiled. Then he was devastating. She sipped her sherry and wondered if the alcohol had gone straight to her brain. Still, he was special to Martin, that was for sure.

They talked of the children, of the fall in oil prices, the royal engagement, and a dozen other news items. Jim was quieter than usual, which increased her conviction that tonight was not purely a social occasion. She slipped her hand into his arm as they walked to the restaurant. 'We fit,' she thought again. 'It feels right.'

She ordered her favourite Kashmiri chicken, and ate it with gusto. She said no to dessert but accepted coffee. 'Fran,' he said, putting his coffeespoon carefully back in place. 'Fran. There's something I must say now, before I lose my nerve.'

She knew it was not a proposal. He had taken the old suede-backed volume of *A Shropshire Lad* from his pocket and was pushing it across the table. 'I brought that back. I knew it was precious.'

She knew, then, what he was going to say. That he couldn't go on without wanting to marry her, that he couldn't face marrying again.

'It's all right,' she said. 'I understand perfectly.'

'They've had so much upset, you see. I couldn't put them through another upheaval. Not just yet. I've got to think of them first; you read such terrible things about traumas in childhood. And we couldn't just marry – that would only be half of it. I'd have to leave Desmond or you'd never have a chance; he and Janet would see to that. I've thought and thought. I want you, Fran, but for your sake ... and the kids, all three of them ... I know how it has to be.'

He would have walked her back to the car but her refusal was firm. 'No thanks, Jim. If you don't mind...' She held out her hand. 'Good-bye. It's been really nice. I mean that. And thanks for all you've done for Martin.'

He was shaking his head. 'I'm sorry. Can I still keep in touch

[135]

. . . for the boy's sake?'

'Of course,' she said. 'I hope you will.'

She felt completely calm, almost as though it didn't matter. What was important was to get back into the car, that comforting haven on wheels, without losing dignity.

Driving back to Belgate she wondered what she would say to Martin. He would hang over the banister: *'Had a good time, mam?'* She could hardly tell him the evening had been dire. She decided to postpone her homecoming – if she left it long enough, he might be asleep. And Terry was babysitting: he wouldn't mind if she was late.

The car-park loomed up and she swung the wheel, coming to a halt facing the sea. She had come here often after David died. It was somewhere she could cry in secret, away from Martin's apprehensive eyes. She used to sit locked in the car, chain-smoking and trying to get a grip on her emotions. Tonight was different. She had grown up in the last few years, and felt calm, almost dispassionate. But she would still give anything for a cigarette!

To take her mind off nicotine she tried to marshal the facts. She had driven in to Sunderland expecting a proposal. Instead she had got the old heave-ho. Her lips curved in a grin. Perhaps she had BO – he was the third man she'd lost. Except that you couldn't count David, who had really loved her and would have stayed with her for ever if it had been allowed.

Steve had ditched her, though: he had sat on the side of the bed, head bowed, and said, 'I'm sorry, Fran. I'm going back to Jean.' Wives always won in the end – even dead wives like Dorothy. Her eyes pricked and she felt in her bag for a tissue. Instead, her fingers encountered the suede cover of the Housman. *'Into my heart an air that kills. . .'* She shut her mind resolutely on the rest of the poem. Poetry made you maudlin if you didn't watch out. Even Betjeman.

She went back to facts. He had said it was for the children's sake, but he had given himself away. His actual words had been, *'God knows I love you, Fran, but I can't face starting again.'* That was it: the crunch! Easier by far to cling to the wreckage of your first love than start, painstakingly, to build a new one. It was fear of the unknown. At first you were mad keen to fill the vacuum. You met someone and you thought, 'This is nice. This is lovely.' But that turned out to be just the beginning. It was afterwards that the doubts began.

He'd made excuses: *'Mother's brought them up so far. I couldn't take it out of her hands, just like that.'* She had wondered if she should tell him of the old lady's longing to get back to her own home, but decided against it. How terrible it would be to blow away his excuse and see desperation in his eyes as he sought another.

She turned on the engine and put the car into reverse. It was for the best. He might not have agreed to come north, and she could never have survived beyond the Cleveland Hills; not without Bethel. She was relieved, really, at escaping all the decisions, the traumas, the divided loyalties that would have beset them if they'd gone ahead. Yes, she was relieved. If she kept that in the front of her mind perhaps the pain of never seeing him again would go away.

18

'I'll be in touch.' The students kissed and hugged, making arrangements to meet to compare notes when they got their postings. Fran joined in, smiling, embracing, promising never to forget; but all she could think of was the train ride to Birmingham and what would come after it.

Gwen walked with her to the car-park. 'Did you say good-bye to Lund? That second-year was hanging around him ... the one who looks like Angela Rippon. Jenny says she's moved into his flat!'

Fran doubted that Tony would allow anything so restricting,

but kept a non-committal face.

'You can't really believe we did it, can you?' Gwen said, changing the subject.

'No, I can't believe it. At the beginning ... well, I don't know what I was playing at, but I never seriously thought I'd qualify.' Fran meant what she said.

They had reached the car and Gwen was fumbling for her keys. 'You were still in shock,' she said, 'poor little white-faced thing that you were. We all felt protective towards you ... and look how you've come on!'

Fran's smile was hollow. Gwen was suggesting that all was well, and all was far from well. It was simply that she had become a better liar. 'Let's hope we both get Broad Street.'

In a moment Gwen would drive away. 'Yes, that would be nice. I'll ring you as soon as I hear.'

Gwen's Ford reversed and then swung for the gates, but Fran kept her smile in place – you never knew about rear-view mirrors. Only when she was safe in her own car could the tears be allowed to flow, and then not for long. Martin would notice red eyes. If he didn't, Bethel would.

She had not been able to believe it at first. When it occurred to her that she might be pregnant she had laughed out loud at the absurdity of the idea. Not now! Not after all the years of trying! Not when it was utterly unacceptable that it should be so!

In the end, after lying dry-eyed and broad awake for three nights, she had driven to Middlesbrough to buy a pregnancy-testing kit in a back-street chemist, and had watched the yellow disc form on the surface with increasing incredulity. After that had come days of indecision. One night she had let herself out of the house and walked the dog down to the beach. It was three o'clock in the morning, and a cruising panda car passed her, circled, and returned to ask if all was well. She had chattered brightly about insomnia, and the driver had warned her of the dangers of deserted streets before driving away. At any other time she would have been frightened out of her wits. Then, compared to the enormity of what was happening inside her, danger

[138]

failed to register.

But the walk on the moonlit beach helped to clear her thoughts. The tide was coming in and foam edged gently further and further up towards the tide-line. The sea was calm but even so it looked remorseless. No longer the huge, consoling sea of which Jim had spoken. Almost defiantly, she picked up stones and threw them for a dog hardly able to believe his luck. One stone, flatter than the rest, skimmed across the surface, bouncing into the moon's track and out again. She could walk down that moonlit track, easily at first and then with difficulty as the water dragged at her clothes; but if she kept on walking and, once afloat, offered no resistance, it would soon be over.

And then Nee-wan had pawed at her leg for another stone, and she had looked down into the expectant face. He depended on her. So did Martin. She wanted this baby, but she must do what was best for Martin.

At eight o'clock that morning she had got the advert she had clipped from yesterday's paper and dialled the Birmingham number. Five minutes later it was all arranged. 'Termination' was never mentioned, let alone 'abortion'. She would be 'helped'. 'Try not to worry,' the voice said with professional smoothness. She didn't feel worried, she felt quite detached. She had got pad and ballpoint, and begun to make a list of what must be done.

Now, four days later, all was prepared. She had been 'summoned to the bedside of her aged Aunt Em in Hastings' and Martin was to stay with Treesa while she was away. In two days she would be back and it would be over. Something to be put behind her.

She had never seriously considered telling Jim. That he might have a right to know counted as nothing when set against the thought of what it would do to him. If she was tempted to shout for help she summoned up the thought of his careworn face the first time they had met, and temptation passed. She had allowed him to think she was on the pill, and he had been ready to accept it, as men were always ready to be relieved of responsibility. No, that wasn't fair – she hadn't given him the chance to take responsibility. Anyway, it was immaterial, now.

It was a tragic irony that a baby desperately sought with David had been conceived in a relationship destined to splutter out almost as soon as it had started. She couldn't keep the baby, not in Belgate, not and get a teaching post and explain to Martin and tell Bethel. She was not made of the same stuff as Treesa.

Belgate came into sight and she tried to put it out of her mind. She was going on a trip, then she was going to get a job at Broad Street and never think of the past. But she would have to be careful. Bethel was as sharp as a tack and already a little suspicious. So she must concentrate on the job of packing for herself and for Martin's stay with Treesa, and not think about things that could never be.

Bethel was warming the pot as Fran came into the kitchen. 'Sit down. We'll have five minutes, and then I'll have to get on.' The 'I'll' was accented to suggest the unlikelihood of Fran's getting on with anything of consequence, but Fran was too weary to rise to the bait.

They sat in silence for a while, Bethel occasionally rubbing her temple. 'Got a headache?' Fran asked. 'There's paracetamol in the larder.'

Bethel shook her head. 'I never take rubbish. It's only flitting anyway. It'll go.' She changed tack. 'You haven't seen that London feller lately!' It was an accusation, not a question. Did she guess?

'No. It was just a friendship. We didn't have much in common.' She was saved by Walter's horn sounding in the street. 'I'll get him,' she said, glad to escape.

Getting the wheelchair up the steps was always difficult. Today, as she felt the tug on her abdominal muscles, she hesitated: there was life there. Then she remembered the pointlessness of caution and tugged until Walter was safely in the kitchen.

'Aye ... where's the tea then? I'm not having a stewed pot.'

[140]

She smiled, waiting for him to work the old familiar magic, but today the mood was wrong. 'Lost a pound, found a penny?' he said, thrusting forward his head. She smiled more widely but it was useless.

'You're getting more like Sally Bethel every day. Sweet as a battleship.'

Bethel intervened. 'For God's sake, Walter, shut your mouth. The lass's just finished with that college of hers. It's only natural she's a bit upset.' The blue eyes were kind but shrewd as they rested on Fran's face. *Did* she know? Mercifully Walter was on to the subject of the pit, so Fran could pretend to give him her attention.

'Heard the latest? Output per man shift's up to 3.27 tonnes. Maggie must be rubbing her hands. More money to give to her rich friends.'

Bethel struck with lightning ferocity. 'They'll be the same ones that loaned her the £200 million?'

Walter's eyes flicked to Fran. 'What's she on about? £200 million. The poor old woman's wandering.'

He was not to be let off the hook. 'You know what I mean, Walter. The £200 million they lost in the Durham pits in the last two years. Who coughed up that lot?'

Walter decided to change the conversation. 'Did I ever tell you about the poor little trapper lad I started down the pit with?' he asked innocently. 'They set him to pull on the trap every time the ponies came through. Only they never told him the deputy'd fixed a bloody big hook on the back of it for his coat. So the first pony comes through ... wham ... hits the trap, sends it flying. The lad never came up at the end of his shift, and when they looked they found him stuck clean through with the hook, swinging backwards and forwards with the trap.' His look of pathos was a masterpiece.

'You've missed your vocation, Walter,' Bethel said. 'You're a better liar than Ananias. If the facts don't fit, make them up – and if you can't stand the facts, make up a fairy-tale. Very nice!'

On a normal day Fran would have been grinning by now, but it was not a normal day. Bethel passed a hand over her forehead and the smooth grey crown of her head, and Fran felt her own head ache in sympathy. She was about to suggest paracetamol again when the phone rang.

'It's me, Min. How was your last day?' Before Fran could tell her she was hurrying on. 'I'm ringing to tell you the good news. Remember that line in nursery lamps I couldn't shift? A pixie and a toadstool? They needed plugs and all the paraphernalia, and it put the punters off. So then Dennis got interested. He's decided to go in for electricals ... well, you know, he's good with his hands. He's going to take half the stall, just on a trial basis ... but it's a start, isn't it? And it's Dennis's thing, that's the best bit. He'll sell batteries, flex, adaptors – do on-the-spot repairs. I know he can make it work.'

Fran was genuinely pleased. 'It's lovely, Min. The best news I've heard today.' She ieaned her head against the wall. It was the *only* good news she'd had that today. 'By the way, Min, I'm going to Hastings for a couple of days. Aunt Em's not well...'

Min expressed sympathy and then talked of practicalities. 'What about Martin? Oh well, if he's going to Treesa he'll be all right. As long as she hasn't got that commie brother-in-law of hers around.' Walter appeared in the kitchen doorway and Fran bade Min a hasty good-bye.

'I'm off before that senile old rattletrap convinces me black's white.'

Fran was helping him negotiate the steps when Martin appeared. 'I hope tea's ready; I'm famished. Hi, Walter. Come to see Bethel?'

Walter reached the pavement. 'I've seen more than enough of her for one day, young sir. Put your shin-pads on if you're going in there. She's bowling bouncers this afternoon!'

Bethel was unexpectedly kind when they got back to the kitchen. 'You sit there, son, and I'll get your tea. And *you* get yersel upstairs and pack so you can have a bit time off tonight. You look washed-out.'

Bethel must know: that was the only thing that would explain her sudden mildness. But she *couldn't* know! It was only seven weeks, and she had watched herself carefully to give nothing away!

She was still speculating as she took down the tartan grip and began to pack. She had not reached any conclusion when Martin's voice rang out below. 'Mam. Mam. Come quickly. I'm frightened.' He was standing in the hall, his upturned face contorted with fear until it resembled a gargoyle.

'What is it, Martin? What is it – tell me!' Her own voice was rising, screeching in anger. Why was he doing this to her? It wasn't fair!

'It's Bethel, mam. I didn't do anything. She just turned round and made a funny noise...'

Fran was brushing past him and the rest of his words were lost on her. 'Oh God, please God, let it, let it, let it be all right.'

At first she thought the old woman was dead. Her body lay slumped to the floor like an empty suit of clothes. Then she noticed the twitching of the eyelids and kneeled to reach for the pulse. Was that Bethel's heart beating or her own? 'She's still alive, Martin. Now, please, do as I say.' As he ran for the phone she tried to arrange the twisted limbs and put a cushion to the head but there was no response.

While they waited for an ambulance Fran held the hand, flaccid now and cold. 'I need you, Bethel. I need you now.' As if in answer the face twitched again and the eyes opened a crack. 'Bethel? Bethel, I love you, Bethel!'

The old woman's breathing was audible, issuing harshly from lips that were tinged with blue.

'It's all right, mam.' Martin had got over his fright and was trying to support her. 'It's going to be OK. When they come, they'll have oxygen and all sorts of things.' And then, uncertain once more, 'Is it her heart?'

'I don't know, Martin. I think it is.'

A trickle of saliva had issued from the side of Bethel's mouth and was coursing slowly down her chin. Fran felt a momentary revulsion and then a surge of concern. She wiped it away with her hanky and patted the cold cheek. 'Here's a blanket,' Martin said, and helped her cover Bethel, tucking the coverlet tenderly around her. The next moment the ambulance men were in the room and Fran and Martin were put to one side.

'I'm coming with her,' Fran said and climbed the iron steps.

It was a stroke, a cerebral haemorrhage. As Fran heard the words she was back in that other hospital, with David lying beyond the door. '*I'm sorry*,' the doctor had said, and David had died. This time, however, there was hope.

'We won't be able to tell you anything definite tonight. Let's just keep her alive until morning ... if we can do that, she's in with a chance. Now, if you can give me some details...?'

As Fran struggled to offer up the facts of Bethel's life, she realized how little she knew of the woman who was closer to her than any other adult human being. When the doctor had gone she made a vow. '*If you let Bethel live, God, I'll make it up to you.*' But even as she bargained, she knew it was useless. It didn't work like that. If Bethel was to die she would die, and all the bribery in the world wouldn't change it. If Bethel died, she herself would be alone. She walked down the echoing hospital corridor, deserted now at seven o'clock in the evening. Without Bethel, there would be no one. Nothing.

There were decisions to make. Tomorrow she was supposed to take the Birmingham train and enter the clinic. She could still go: her presence would neither help nor hinder Bethel's recovery. Even as she acknowledged the fact, she knew that she could not leave now. And if not now, not ever. She would never be strong enough again.

As the tears started, a figure appeared at the end of the corridor. 'All right, all right, I'm here now.' Terry Malone was infinitely comforting, his arms around her like a rock. 'Your Martin came for me, he knew you'd be here on your own. Treesa's with him, and I'm with you. For as long as you want. Is she...?'

Fran was nodding and laughing, wiping eyes and nose in a

luxury of relief. 'She's alive. She's got a chance. It's a stroke ... but Bethel's strong. She is, isn't she?'

It was Terry's turn to laugh. 'By God, it'll be some stroke that carries off Sally Bethel. Some stroke! And now let's get you home.'

19

Fran sat in the church, Martin quivering with excitement beside her. Across the aisle the Malone family were together, silent and reflective except for Mike. He was wearing a grey suit, white shirt and red tie and was acutely conscious of his new elegance. From time to time he shot his cuffs and turned them left and right, just to check. In between he lifted a foot to inspect brand new lace-ups and red fluorescent socks.

The organ played quietly, and now and again a footfall could be heard on the tessellated floor. 'How much longer?' Martin whispered. Down at the front Terry stared stolidly ahead but the neck above the tight white collar was a deeper shade of pink than usual, and occasionally he tugged at the unaccustomed collar as though desperate for air.

Fran was tempted to tug at the waist of her own navy skirt. It had been difficult to get the zip up to the top and it would never have stayed there without a pin. Every time she moved, the waistband bit, reminding her of her pregnant state. Panic rose and was marshalled back into place. *Live a day at a time*,' that's what Bethel had told her years ago, after David died. '*Live a day at a time. It's as much as you can manage.*'

Now Bethel was lying in a high, white, hospital bed with a honeycomb counterpane, her lips making unintelligible sounds, only the fierce blue eyes betraying the agonized intelligence behind. At least she was still alive, that was the important thing. Sooner or later she would improve and come home, and they would all support one another. They would manage.

Mike Malone slipped from his pew and crossed the aisle. 'I can't come in your car. I have to go in the special one.'

Martin looked slightly peeved. 'We never asked you.'

Mike was not put off. Today his status was too elevated to permit of taking offence. 'Well, I'm only telling you. I'll see you at the reception.'

Fran's lips twitched. Mike's Belgate accent was overlaid with a touch of BBC received speech, as befitted the ceremony. As he returned to his seat Martin moved closer to whisper, 'He's going on as if it was his wedding.'

'Jealousy gets you nowhere,' she whispered back. Martin's eyes met hers, hostile at first and then laughter dawning in them. She reached out and patted his knees, decently covered in new, long grey trousers.

The music changed, and Terry was turning to face his bride. He looked troubled until he caught Treesa's eye, and then he smiled suddenly and was the old irrepressible Terry once more.

Treesa, on her father's arm, was dressed in a powder-blue crêpe dress, draped at the hip and broad-shouldered in true Dallas-Dynasty style. The fair hair was looped back and caught with a blue feathered band, and she carried a white missal with a single orchid attached. The outfit was formal and sophisticated, but the face above it was still the face of a child, a little chubby but serene, as though none of the trials of the last few years had occurred. Fran turned back to the altar as the bridal procession drew abreast. *Please God, let them be happy*.

Suddenly she remembered Brian's delight at the thought of his marriage to Treesa. It should have taken place in this church; instead everyone had gathered here for Brian's funeral. 'Crushed between tubs.' She closed her eyes, and then opened them to glance at Christopher, safe in Mrs Malone's arms. He would not understand as his mother made her marriage vows; for a baby, there were no complications other than hunger and wind. A twelve-year-old was different. Martin's face was rapt as he listened to the service. How was she going to explain the baby?

[146]

'*Live a day at a time.*' She reached for her hymn book and joined in, tremulous at first and then hearing her own voice gain strength at the familiar words. 'O perfect Love, all human thought transcending...'

The bridal pair disappeared to sign the register, a gaggle of family behind, and the congregation twittered. Martin was buried in the Order of Service and Fran looked around. There was something about a Catholic church, a busy feeling that she did not get from churches of other denominations. The hymn lingered on in her head: 'O perfect Love.' Love of God. God's love. Perfect as man's love never could be. Lately she had thought a lot about love, as difficult to find and hold as it was to define. She was glad when the organ pealed and the bridal procession appeared.

For the first time Fran could see Mr Malone's face. She had wondered if he would come to the wedding, until Treesa had confirmed it. 'They still don't speak, well, not what you'd call speaking, but I put my foot down. I said, "Ask him or else." Terry said, "I'll ask but that's not to say he'll come," so I said, "Leave him to me if he says no. I'll see to it."'

And see to it she had. Mr Malone was there in a dark three-piece suit, Treesa's mother on his arm in navy polka dots. They didn't speak on their way down the aisle but Mrs Carruthers' expression spoke volumes, especially when Mike, the youngest Malone, began to thread his way through the procession until he was immediately behind bride and groom. His father made an effort to grab his jacket and restrain him but in vain. Mrs Carruthers sniffed and rolled her eyes at the bride's side of the congregation to indicate that this was typical Malone behaviour and hasn't our Treesa burned her boats?

The pews began to empty and fall in behind.

The reception was held in the upper room of the Half Moon – chicken portions and salad, bread buns and bowls of beetroot, fresh cream trifles topped with hundreds and thousands in waxed paper cups, and a paper napkin by every plate emblazoned with the names of bride and groom in silver lettering.

[147]

'Very nice,' Mrs Carruthers said when it was over and she joined Fran for a chat. 'Not what I'd've wished, but our Treesa's turned very headstrong. Of course, she does what she's told now: he's got the upper hand.'

Fran glanced across to where Terry, looking distinctly hen-pecked, was obeying Treesa's instructions and cutting the cake. 'Do you think so?' she said. 'I'd've said Treesa would wear the pants. Terry'll huff and puff, but Treesa'll win in the end.'

It was too much for Treesa's mother. 'I must get round. You have to make yourself pleasant, don't you?'

Fran was relaxing into her chair when she heard Martin's whisper. 'She'll have a job!'

For anyone else she'd have told him not to be cheeky. Mrs Carruthers was different. 'You can say that again,' she said.

She had almost forgotten her own problems, but now heart-burn rose up to remind her. Soon she would have to make a plan – who to tell and how, where to go and when. She couldn't live from day to day for ever. There was a banging from the top table and she turned her head.

Terry's best man was calling for order and making the usual corny jokes. Then Terry rose to his feet. 'I would like to thank Treesa's mam and dad for giving me such a lovely lass for a bride . . .' Treesa's eyes were fixed on his face and Fran got the impression their expression was steely. Terry swallowed and looked down at the paper he held in his fist. 'And my mam and dad for everything they've done for me, bringing me up.' Fran's eyes flicked to the Malones. She was beaming above her petrol-blue crimplene; he looked ready to cry. Treesa sat back, task completed.

'Are they friends now?' Martin whispered and Fran nodded.

'They will be after this . . . or Treesa'll want to know why.' Martin's eyes met hers in perfect understanding.

At Treesa's request, Fran went to help her change. 'I've done it now,' Treesa said as Fran tugged her free of the powder-blue dress.

'You're not sorry?'

Treesa shook her head. 'No, not now. It's all right. I don't know why, but it is.'

Fran nodded. She knew the feeling.

'I used to think Terry was tough and Brian was the quiet one. You know, not pushy. And then I got to know Terry and it's all talk. He needs me more than Brian did ... Brian could always cope. Everyone liked him. Terry makes a noise but half the time he's scared.'

'You mean he's vulnerable?'

Treesa nodded. 'Yes, that's it exactly. Anyway, he's got me now. And Christopher. We'll see him all right.' She fastened the last button of her pink blouse. 'I've packed everything Christopher needs. I'm glad it's you having him. Me mam offered, but she'd only upcast it after, and Terry's mam's got her hands full. I know he'll be all right with you. I said he could stop with his gran till bedtime. Is that OK?'

Fran nodded. 'That's fine. I want to pop over to see Bethel when we leave. I won't get in as often while I have Christopher, so I'll go today.'

Treesa was stepping into the skirt of her grey going-away suit. 'How is she?'

Fran shrugged. 'Just the same. I think she knows me but I'm not sure.' To her horror her voice had an ominous break in it. She was alone and pregnant and would never look as Treesa looked now, dressing for her bridegroom to carry her away.

'I know,' Treesa said, holding out arms to embrace her. 'I know what she means to you ... but it's not hopeless. You'll see. They can do a lot now.'

Fran felt ashamed. 'I know. I'm sorry. I shouldn't do this, today of all days.'

Treesa's arms were comforting as Bethel's arms would have comforted once she got over her shock at the news. She felt the truth trembling on her lips: '*I'm pregnant Treesa. And abandoned. And bloody frightened.*' Instead she smiled and detached herself. 'I ought to be shot, behaving like this on your wedding day. I'm sure she'll pick up. Come on, let's not keep everyone waiting.'

[149]

Treesa was grinning. 'You know something, this is the first day I've known Terry that he hasn't mentioned politics!'

Fran laughed. 'Maybe he'll give it up now he's a married man.'

Treesa shook her head. 'Nee chance!'

They went off in a haze of confetti and a rattling of Ostermilk tins. 'Keep it up, Terry,' the best man roared to an accompaniment of ribald laughter.

'They're coarse, aren't they?' Mrs Carruthers said. 'And going to Scarborough. I ask you! At this time of year.'

Fran didn't reply. Her eyes were fixed on the bridal car, where Terry's hand had emerged from the side window and gripped his father's outstretched hand. The perfect ending. 'It's been a lovely wedding,' Fran said, and her tones were fervent. 'And I love Scarborough. At any time of year.'

Mrs Carruthers had missed the handshaking, and would not have perceived its significance if she had seen it, but she had a parting shot. 'I suppose it's what you're used to ... we're so used to Spain that I can't see the point of holidays at home. But if it's all you can afford ...'

There were pictures of Prince Andrew and Fergie in the shop windows as Fran drove through Sunderland. Less than a week to their wedding. There would be crowds in the streets and a world audience, but no more love than there had been today.

'I must be glad for them,' she said aloud. They would be away for three days, and when they returned she could confide in them. They would understand, but they couldn't help. No one could help. She must carry the baby alone, support it alone, care for Bethel, and make sure Martin was not the one to suffer. He had offered to come to the hospital with her today but she had persuaded him to stay with Mike. 'Well, I'm coming next time. I want to tell Bethel to get a move on and get better.'

But Bethel was deaf to exhortations, and dead almost, except for the agitated eyes. Fran sat by her bed and began to talk. 'It was a lovely wedding. You'd've liked her dress. And Terry was so

[150]

good. Like a lamb. Martin sends his love. And Walter. He's his usual self, full of beans.' In truth Walter was a shadow, seldom venturing out and devoid of his usual fire. He had been like that since Fran had broken the news, simply shaking his head and saying, 'Not Sally Bethel. Not Sally,' as though denial would alter fact.

'We all miss you, Bethel.' The hands laid on the turned-back sheet were unnaturally white and blue-veined, the nails in need of trimming. 'Oh Bethel, please get better.'

In the next bed a white-haired woman in a blue bedjacket was talking incessantly, although there was no one to hear. Across the aisle an old woman rocked back and forwards in an armchair, a doll in her arms, her skirt above her knees to reveal bare white thighs and lisle stockings held up by elastic garters.

Fran turned back to Bethel. 'I'm going to get you out of here, Bethel. Home with me ... and Martin. You'll get better there.'

A tear had formed in the corner of the old woman's eyes and Fran removed it with a fingertip. A nurse loomed up.

'All right, Sally? Not long till teatime.' She gave Fran a quick professional smile. 'Doctor's very satisfied with her. And she's a good girl, aren't you, Sally?' She twitched the pillow into place, causing Bethel's hair to straggle across the pillow. 'We'll have to get this cut, won't we, when the hairdresser comes round.'

In the other beds the women had bobbed hair, caught at the sides with clips or little girl's slides in pink and blue. Fran heard her own voice, surprisingly firm. 'I don't think she'd like her hair cut. And I'm making arrangements to have her with me, so you really don't need to bother.'

The nurse smiled again, a lighthouse grin that came and went. 'Well, we don't need to worry about it now, do we?' Another flash, and she was gone.

'I'll be back, Bethel. I'll come soon.' The face against the pillow looked smaller, somehow diminished, the eyes set further back. The lips twitched and pouted, and Fran bent closer. 'Lass ...' and then again ... 'lass'. But it had been a word. That was something.

As she left the ward she passed a side-ward, from inside which came a high-pitched voice, almost mechanical in its repetition. 'Is there anybody there? Is there anybody there?' Fran turned and looked back along the corridor but there was no sign of a nurse. 'Is there anybody there?' She put her head through the door but the figure in the bed took no notice. 'Is there anybody there?' Her eyes were fixed on the facing wall.

Fran was about to withdraw, accepting there was nothing to be done, but something in the face caught her attention. It couldn't be ... except that the chart at the end of the bed confirmed that it was. *Hilda Fenbow. Age 79.*' Miss Fenbow! Physics and Chemistry Fenbow who had terrorized Fran during her first year at Bede and then, mercifully, retired. Fran had hated and feared the woman, loathed the harsh voice and the cutting remarks that could reduce the most confident pupil to a jelly.

'*Is there anybody there?*'

Fran moved to the bedside. 'Miss Fenbow?' The eyes remained on the wall but the hands flew to Fran's arm and took possession. 'I'm here, Miss Fenbow.'

The head turned and the voice dropped to a whisper. 'Can you get my cardigan. I'm very cold. They won't get me my cardigan. The mohair one that Ivy made.'

The bobbed hair had escaped the slide and straggled the forehead. Fran stroked it back and secured it. Outside, the July sun was still high, the room like an oven. The mohair cardigan lay across the coverlet, and she picked it up and arranged it around the thin shoulders. 'I want the mohair cardigan.' She was plucking it away as she spoke.

Fran stroked her arm. 'Wear this for a moment, until I can find the mohair one. The one that Ivy made.' The hands ceased to pluck. 'I'll go and find it now.'

As she neared the door to the corridor the voice started again. 'Is there anybody there?'

20

The door was double glazed and revealed a panelled hall. 'Posh,' Fran thought and then ... 'Eve *will* be choked!'

Dennis came to greet and draw her in. 'Give us a kiss, Franny. I haven't seen you for an age.'

She wanted to put her head on his chest and give way but it wouldn't do. Instead she rearranged her shawl, knotting it at her waist. She had decided to wear it in case of prying eyes. She was thicker around the waist now and the zip of her dress proclaimed it.

'Come into the kitchen for a drink and then we'll go in. You've had a tough time lately and we want you to enjoy tonight.' He picked up a bottle. 'White?'

She nodded. 'Lovely.'

He held out the glass. 'It's not the greatest vintage, but it's wet. It's taken me years to realize what a lot of mumbo-jumbo is talked about wine. There are three categories, Fran: nice, foul, and bearable. This is bearable coming nice. I got it at cost from a guy at the market. Wheels within wheels.'

Fran sipped. 'It's gorgeous. Where's Min?'

Dennis nodded towards the door. 'In the living-room, show-ing off. She looks like the Cheshire cat, and Eve resembles Mary Queen of Scots being stoic on the block.'

Fran laughed. 'I can imagine.'

Dennis had perched on the table, one foot on a chair. 'We've been damned lucky, haven't we? I thought it was going to be all downhill. Instead, we've got this place for a year. Min's making a bob or two, keeping the wolf at the garden gate, and I'm getting a foot in on the electrical side. I still can't see us making a living from it, but it's better than nothing and you never know. We could be lucky.'

'You deserve some luck. You've both been brave.' Besides, something had to go right for someone, some time. It couldn't all be black.

'Min's been brave! I never knew she had it in her, Fran. Right from the word go. Not a word of reproach, not, "What are we going to do?" – just, "Let's get on with it."' He sipped his drink. 'It teaches you, a thing like this. What your partner's really like. Who your friends are. You'll see a few faces missing in there to-night.'

'You mean they haven't come?'

Dennis chuckled. 'I mean they weren't asked! People we've been friends with for years, off into the undergrowth at the first hint of trouble. They want back in now but I'll see them in Hell first. There was a guy we'd done business with for years. We made him, if I'm honest. Dad gave him his start, then he set up on his own. We owed him two hundred quid. Two hundred quid! He was never off the phone. "You must've known," he said, as though we'd screwed him deliberately. And Harold was very careful until he saw how things were going.' There was hurt in Dennis's voice now, and Fran couldn't think of anything to say.

'Anyway.' Dennis was standing up and holding out his arms. 'You were a brick, Franny.' He hugged her. 'You should hear Min about it. And remember, if you ever need a friend ... two friends ... you know where to come.'

As Fran followed him through to the living-room, she wondered if he knew how soon she would have to take him up on his offer. And then she was caught up in the comedy of Min seeing her day with Eve, and it was all too delicious for anything else to matter.

'I'm going to let it drop now,' Min said as they made coffee. 'I've shown her the pool, both bathrooms, the original oil in the study by the man who painted Princess Margaret, and I've pulled out every unit in here like Felicity Kendal in that advert. Now I'm going to rise above revenge, sweet as it is, and return to my usual sunny self. Bring the tray, Fran, and don't forget to tell them the

[154]

cups are Wedgwood.'

The party was deep in discussion of the royal wedding. Fergie, by common consent, had looked stunning, the bridegroom suitably reverent, and the Queen noticeably pleased. 'Relieved!' someone said. 'Fergie'll sort him out.'

Fran moved about with the tray. 'How's Martin?' someone asked, and Fran glanced at the clock. He had been alone now for two hours, without a minder for the first time in his life. '*Please mam, I'm twelve now. And there's the telephone if I need you.*' So she had given in, expecting to be worried to death. Instead she had hardly given it a thought.

'He's fine,' she said firmly, and moved on.

Eve accepted a cup of coffee and lowered her voice. 'I need this to take away the taste of that awful wine.' She sipped. 'You'd never think they hadn't a bean, would you? Entertaining! Look at Harold, his face is a study – he knows the true state of affairs. If they have any money they should be putting it aside, not splashing it on a party.'

Fran was tempted to let it go but overcame the temptation. 'I think they were right to give a party for their friends, Eve.' She put emphasis on the last word. 'And anyway, the food's homemade. Min must have baked and baked. Of course, she's got that fabulous kitchen, so I suppose it was easy. You and I have to struggle with the basics.' As she moved on she reproached herself for bitchery, but she still couldn't repress the feeling of a job well done.

'I'm going in to see your Bethel soon,' Min said as they saw Fran to her car. 'Ring me and let me know when and what ward and everything. And what she'd like taken in.'

Fran nodded. Useless to say there was nothing Bethel could appreciate. If she began on that she'd end up crying.

As she drove home she tried to think things out. It was 26 July; the baby was due in December. If she took Bethel out of hospital now, would she be able to cope later on in her pregnancy? Treesa would help, and Terry, but there were limits. And before she did anything, she must tell Martin about the baby. Before someone else did. Before, for all she knew, he noticed for himself. Then there was Walter – something would have to be done for Walter, and there was no one else but her.

The sky to the west was still tinged with pink, with clouds like mother-of-pearl. If Martin had not been alone she would have stayed in the car-park for a while, but it was time she was home. She must be careful too, showing pride that he had coped but not so much pride that it looked as though she hadn't expected him to manage on his own.

She put the car away and let herself into the yard. Light filtered through the living-room curtains, and she bit her lip. He had promised to go to bed at ten. Perhaps he had, and had simply left the light on to welcome her? There was no frenzied dog in the kitchen when she let herself in, so he was in the living-room too. She walked through the hall and pushed open the door. The television was on, but it was not Martin who rose to greet her. It was Jim. 'Hello,' he said.

She was casting around for an adequate reply when she heard Martin call from the landing. He was hanging over the banisters, bright-eyed. 'Jim's here!'

She tried to keep calm. 'Yes, I know. Now go to bed.' She waited until his bedroom door was shut before she went in to face Jim.

'I've come back, Fran.' She shook her head in puzzlement. He moved forward. 'I don't know if we can work things out. I only know I can't live without you. Not now.'

Nee-wan was looking from one to another, expecting action. 'Sit down, dog,' she said.

There was no temptation to tell him, and she mustn't let anything slip. 'I think I'd like a drink. Shall I get you one?' If he moved forward and touched her, she would tell him. She could feel it in her chest, tears that would break through as a wail if she let them come.

He turned back to his chair. 'Yes please. Whisky, if you've

[156]

got it.'

As she poured the drinks, she felt flat – that was all. Flat, uninterested, and perhaps a little angry. In fact, very angry! Walk out, walk in again: that was what men did. It was women who had to stay, tied to the fruit of a relationship as securely as branch to tree.

'I've been thinking, Fran. I could come North, if that's what you want? There are jobs up here if you look.' He was leaning forward in an effort to convince her.

'What about Desmond?' There was a taunting quality in her voice that she didn't like but couldn't help. 'He'd never let you get away from him, or be based elsewhere but London. Be realistic.'

Jim was looking hurt, and there was a devil rising up in her, a she-devil who wanted revenge for all the weeks of pain.

He had come back to her, that was what mattered. Except that it didn't matter. She was tired and she wanted him out of her house. 'We can't talk now, Jim. It's late and Martin probably has his ear to the door. There are lots of things you don't know about. Bethel's in hospital and I have to take her in here as soon as she's well enough to leave. And besides...' She would have listed other reasons, inventing them if necessary, but he had set down his glass to interrupt.

'Martin told me. How is she?' He had met Bethel several times, and concern showed in his face.

'She's had a stroke, a bad one ... but that's beside the point. What about the children? How would Kevin and Barbara survive a move up here? I won't uproot Martin, not now.'

She was building a wall, feeling safer with each added brick. Safer and more despairing with each dollop of mortar, each ring of the trowel. 'We can talk another time. If you want to.' Her tone suggested, '*If there's any point*' but she left it unsaid.

She searched his face for signs of relief. She was setting him free, making it easy, so he should be bloody grateful! Her fingers were hurting and she realized she was squeezing the stem of her glass almost to snapping point. For a moment, as she tried to relax her hands, she contemplated breaking the news. '*Oh, and by the way, I'm pregnant. Now you're sure to scuttle and run.*' Only she mustn't tell him.

'I never said it would be easy. Do you think I don't see all the problems? I don't think I've slept two consecutive hours since we split up. But if there's a will, Frances ... if we want it enough, we can find a way round everything.'

He was not going to give way. There was an air of dogged determination about him that reminded her of Martin at his most persistent. She must get him out of the house. All she wanted was to undo the zip now biting into her flesh, take off the too-tight bra, put on her towelling robe, and curl up somewhere, in the dark.

'I can't see the point, but if you've made up your mind we can meet tomorrow.'

He was getting up to go and she hadn't told him. Clever Frances. Brave Frances. Broad-shouldered Frances, who needed no help from anyone. Or any help from no one.

When she had bolted the door behind him she sat on the bottom rung of the stairs and cried until the dog brought comfort, and a reminder that Martin was probably awake upstairs and must not see her like this.

21

She had intended to miss the class reunion but now it would serve her purpose. She began to get ready at four o'clock, washing her hair and letting it dry free, until it frizzed around her face. They were all meeting in the town-centre hotel and then going on to a restaurant. 'Not that I'll eat much,' Gwen had said on the phone last week. 'I'm trying to lose a stone.'

For once Gwen's promises to diet failed to raise a smile. 'What time?' Fran had asked without interest, because there was no way she could face them, feeling as she did.

Now, though, it was different. After weeks of drifting, post-poning thought of the future let alone planning, she had a pur-pose! It had come to her in the night while she thought over Jim's insistence that they should meet.

She *would* meet him, looking her best, even blooming. And then she would leave him, as he had left her. Best of all, she would leave him to go to a party, so that he was discarded like so much used wrapping-paper. Never mind that she shrank from the pub, the happy faces of her fellow-students secure in their new jobs. It would have to be endured. She wasn't a good enough liar simply to pretend to Jim that she was going.

She felt almost excited as she put on her make-up. Lilac eye-shadow to match the cotton summer dress that floated mercifully free of her waist, pale lipstick outlined with darker pencil, two coats of mascara, and a third dip to emphasize her brows. God bless Estée Lauder, she thought as she surveyed the finished effect. She looked tarty but delectable . . . or as delectable as she was ever likely to look. Pregnancy had rounded her cheekbones and brightened eyes that glowed now with the desire for revenge. Tit for tat. Damn Jim for having reduced her to this charade.

She sat on the edge of the bath, suddenly aghast at what she was doing. It didn't make sense. But even as reason struggled to reassert itself she stood up. If she started to think, she would wind up going meekly to meet him, confessing all, and ending up in Twickenham with Desmond and Janet to oversee her rehabili-tation from the state of fallen woman. She took one last look in the mirror and went in search of her hoop earrings.

He was waiting in the foyer, rising unsmiling to greet her. 'Thanks for coming.' He followed her through to the cocktail bar, dark and cool after the sunlit streets, so that she shivered momentarily, regretting her bared arms.

They carried their drinks to an alcove, although the bar was almost empty. She felt nervous now but still determined. Driving to Sunderland she had considered his right to know about the baby, and decided her right to keep the truth to herself was greater. He didn't deserve to know – as long as she remembered that, all would be well. 'Cutting off your nose to spite your face', that's what Bethel would have said; but it had gone too far to stop now.

'You look nice.'

Here it was, the opportunity. 'Yes,' she said, 'I'm going on to a party.' She saw the shot register in a tightening of his lips, but he didn't comment.

'I suppose you think I've got a nerve,' he said at last. 'Waltzing out, waltzing back. It wasn't quite that simple.' His expression confirmed his words.

'No, Jim, I don't think it was simple for either of us. But I'm not sure there's anything we can do about it, either.'

'I love you, Fran. I knew that before, but I thought it wasn't enough to cope with all the aggro. Now I know it is.' He put his hand over hers. 'I love you a lot. And Martin. And we can make something of it, I know we can.'

If she told him now, what would his reaction be? Concern or panic? She could bear neither.

'I'll leave Desmond's business … if I'm honest, I've never been happy there … and the kids could settle up here. They're young enough to adjust.'

She was listening but somehow not comprehending. It was as though a safety mechanism had come into play, blotting out feeling. Words that would have meant so much a while ago were now just words. '*Sound and fury, signifying nothing.*' At times of stress forgotten phrases always popped up into her mind, and they were not always appropriate. He was actually speaking quietly and his words signified a great deal. The faulty reception was in her. She withdrew her hand.

'I'm not angry, Jim. I understand how you felt, I always did. But the fact remains that we each have our separate lives. I don't see how we can get over that.' She would have to listen to his arguments, keep up her own end. And then go to the Saracen, laughing, smiling … '*Yes, it's marvellous, isn't it? All of us getting schools. Good old LEA.*' She would have to watch out for Gwen,

[160]

though. Gwen was shrewd. Afterwards she could retreat, hide away in the car, and let go.

Her eyes flicked to the clock: ten past seven. Early evening, and already she was exhausted. Too exhausted to be angry, but the anger was there, whispering away. Not at Jim or the child inside her, not at men in general, or society, or any other recognizable entity. It was fate which had placed so many hurdles in her path, and left her so ill-equipped to deal with them. It was seldom others who caused your troubles, more the luck of the draw.

'I must go, Jim.' She was reaching for her bag. 'I'm meeting Gwen and the others from college in the Saracen. We're having a celebration. We've all been given teaching posts. I qualified, you know. You've never asked.'

The rebuke went home. 'I'm sorry. Congratulations. You've done well.' He pushed back his chair. 'I'll come with you. They won't mind, will they?'

She panicked. If he came with her she could never keep it up. 'Sorry, but I'm meeting someone there. Tony Lund. You remember Tony, my sociology tutor? I told you about him.' She didn't need to add, 'He was my lover'; Jim was remembering all too well. He was the only man she had ever been able to talk to properly. She had confessed her affair with Tony and he had smiled it away. Now he didn't smile.

'I'm sorry,' he said. 'I should have realized.'

He offered to walk her to the car but she left him in the foyer. 'We'll be in touch. Martin will always be pleased to hear from you.'

Relief carried her out into the summer evening and through three sets of traffic lights to the Saracen. After that she was engulfed in chat. 'I got Broad Street. What about you?' 'Pass those drinks, Steve ... don't just stand there.' 'Hi, Frances. How've you been?'

'I hoped we'd get on the same staff,' Gwen said, when the hubbub subsided. 'Still, one of us can move eventually.' She would have to tell Gwen soon, watch the plump face quiver with

[161]

concern. Or disapproval. You could never gauge reactions, not even with your friends.

'How's Bethel?' Gwen said. 'And that lad of yours? Enjoying his hols?'

Fran relaxed: Bethel and Martin were safe ground. She was about to reply when she saw Tony Lund, surrounded by female students still anxious to bask in his smile.

'I forgot to tell you lover boy was here,' Gwen said, following her eyes. 'No show without Punch, I suppose.'

Fran managed to avoid Tony. It wasn't difficult, for his eyes flicked over her as though she were a fixture. At the height of their love-making he had always used the same words – 'Oh darling, darling, Fran.' So much for passion!

She was deep in conversation with Jenny, discussing how friendly would be friendly enough with your first class, when she saw Jim come in and take a seat at the bar. At first she thought it was just a terrible coincidence, and then she remembered she had mentioned the name of the pub.

So he'd come deliberately! Emotions chased around in her head. He cared, cared enough to gate-crash. He had a cheek, barging in on her affairs! Worst of all, he would find her out in a lie: '*I'm meeting Tony. You remember Tony Lund?*' You always paid for lies. Her mother had told her that years ago and it was true.

She felt tears prick her eyes at the thought of her mother – a lifetime away, when everything had been easy, when she had played by the rules and been safe. She realized that her hand had dropped to her belly, the age-old protective gesture of the pregnant woman. She looked around, certain everyone's eyes would be on her, knowing everything. But no one was watching her except Jim, and there was no dawning knowledge in his eyes, only a steely determination. In another minute he would walk towards her and it would all be out of her hands.

She wanted to go home but if she went now Jim would follow and it would all begin again. 'Excuse me,' she said to Jenny and moved purposefully to the group around Tony.

One by one the others dropped away, some of them knowing

[162]

what had gone on before, others aware of the chemistry. 'Fran. Long time no see.' He was keeping it light but his eyes were wary.

She plunged in. 'Tony! I couldn't let you go without saying good-bye.'

His eyes were like sea-washed glass, but she fixed them with her own, batting her lashes in spite of the weary contempt on his face.

'*Please God, let it be over soon.*' When she was safe in the car she would wind up all the windows and curl up and not think. In the meantime, she must smile and flirt until the stranger sitting at the bar got the message. Impossible to believe she had shared his bed. He was a stranger now, a glowering man in a dark suit, moving his glass from hand to hand and never taking his eyes off her.

Desperation made her bold. She swayed towards Tony, putting up a hand to finger the lapel of his jacket. It was enough. It took only a moment for Jim to swing his legs from the stool and shoulder his way to the door, but it seemed much longer. She made no farewell to Tony, simply turned away. It was five minutes to eight. At eight o'clock she could go home.

She made her excuses to Gwen, pleading an upset tummy. 'I'll ring you tomorrow.' As she crossed the foyer she felt her troubles slipping away. It would be lovely to be home, to begin again. It was always all right if you could get home.

Outside, the light was going and the sky was pearly. She felt suddenly free, energetic enough to walk to Belgate if she had to ... but the car was there, waiting to be collected. She didn't need to hide in it now. She had handled things. No point in thinking how different it could have been. She had done it all for the best, that was the important thing.

She was fitting her key into the lock when he spoke from behind. 'I knew you'd have to come back to the car. I banked on him having his car with him. I'm sorry, Fran, but I only have

[163]

another day here. I can't afford to be over-scrupulous.'

He climbed into the car and sat down beside her. 'I won't keep you long, but you must hear me out. I'm sure Lover Boy will wait five minutes.'

For a few seconds she hesitated, wondering if she could maintain the charade. And then she felt herself starting to laugh, and then to cry, and only ceased to hiccup when he took her by the forearms and shook her.

'Fran? Fran, what is it? For God's sake pull yourself together . . . if he means that much I'll get out of the way.' It was too delicious an irony, that he was preparing to go when every single particle of her being was longing for him to stay.

'I don't want him,' she said calmly, as he made to get out of the car. 'I don't even like him. I did it to make you pay. It wasn't much fun for me,' she finished lamely, and saw his look of outrage give way to a twitch of the lips.

'Oh Fran,' he said at last. 'We're a pair of silly buggers, aren't we?'

22

Fran spent the next morning in a half-pleasant, half-painful daze. Thinking of her bizarre behaviour the evening before made her cringe but she could understand it. She should have realized what lay behind that irrational anger and desire to pay back Jim; she had experienced anger before, in the aftermath of David's death, a wild, unreasoning rage that was really an antidote to fear. Be mad, and you could avoid total collapse, could be fuelled by a burst of adrenalin that would carry you forward regardless. She had seen it briefly in Min after her downfall, but Min had turned it to good use and become an entrepreneur.

All the same, excuse it as she might, the thought of making up to Tony Lund and feeding that fat ego was almost unbearable.

She had hurt Jim too and risked ruining their relationship beyond repair, which had been daft.

Not quite daft enough, though, to give away her secret. She knew herself too well for that. If she had told him about the baby she would ever after believe he had stayed with her out of pity or a bad conscience. She wanted so much to believe he loved her as she loved him, madly and without reason. So she had kept quiet for the time being.

At two o'clock she roused herself. The lunch plates were still in the sink but first she must rinse her eyes, sore after a sleepless night.

She was crossing the hall when the phone rang.

'Mrs Drummond? I'm sorry to tell you Mrs Bethel is rather poorly. If you're thinking of visiting, I'd make it soon.'

Her ears were singing, the terrible Hell sounds that come with the unbearable; and then Martin was coming through the kitchen doorway and taking the phone. 'They've rung off, mam. What's wrong?'

'It's Bethel, darling. She's worse. They want me to go now.' She was trying to think, but her thoughts were woolly, running here and there like sheep, defying efforts to round them up.

'We need to tell Walter,' he said ... 'and Terry.' His mouth was trembling but his voice was firm, and she was grateful.

'Yes, that's a clever boy. Can you tell them if I go?'

He shook his head. 'I'm coming with you. We can call and tell them on the way.'

She didn't argue. He had earned his place. Instead she concentrated on her driving, changing gear scrupulously at corners and using her mirrors. It was at times like this you made mistakes.

Terry's face clouded at the news. Fran was still behind the wheel but she could see him in the doorway. 'He's going to take care of everything,' Martin said, sliding back into his seat. 'I gave him my key, and he'll see to the dog and check the plugs and everything.'

Fran felt her own lips tremble. 'Thank you. That was sens-ible.' She didn't gush. The moment your son became a man was too important for that.

She left him in the car when she went in to Walter. 'It's not good news. She's very ill. Some kind of chest infection. I think you should come, Walter.' She knew it was hopeless from the set of his body, the hands on the arms of the chair as though carved from stone.

'There's no point, lass. Besides, I'm far ower old for hospitals. Let's know how it goes.'

She wanted to comfort him, but there was absolutely nothing she could say.

'I'll go in first,' she told Martin when they reached the ward. 'And then I'll come for you.'

The sister was bustling and impersonal. 'We've moved her to a side-ward. You can stay as long as you like.' There were tiny gold stars in her ears above the uniform collar and energy seemed to surround her like an aura. 'I wouldn't bring the child in, if I were you. I'm not saying no, but I don't advise it. She's his grand-mother, is she?'

She was not expecting an answer but Fran gave one. 'Yes,' she said, 'she's his grandma.'

Bethel looked tiny against the pillow, a tiny, fretful doll of a woman who was almost a stranger. Outside the sun was shining and a painter was covering a window frame with white paint. To and fro his arm went, to and fro.

'Bethel?' She bent to the bed, hoping for an answer, but none came. She closed her eyes, trying to summon up the real Bethel. '*I went into service down London when I left school. I reckoned I might as well be paid for running after folks as do it for nothing.*' She had been the eldest of four, but three brothers had died in their youth, two in the war, one in the pit ... the same pit that had robbed her of her husband. '*I worked in one house in Chelsea ... she says, "I can't have a maid called Sally. You'll have to be Jane!" They were shouting "Jane" all round the house and I never budged. I let on I was daft and they gave in.'*

Fran realized she was smiling. If the sister looked in she would think her mad. But Bethel had been so funny. The past tense slipped from her and did not seem out of place. The figure in the bed was too still, too gentle: that had never been Bethel's way. When the strike was on she had taken on Margot, left-wing Margot of the feminist views. *'How many bellies will you fill with your token-this and token-that? You'll watch this strike drag on week after week because it suits your purpose. Get to hell out of it, before I forget I'm a lady and bash the life out of you.'* She had stood at the sink, arms akimbo, ready to take on the world.

'Oh Bethel, Bethel. I need you, Bethel.' She was crying now, wallowing in self-pity . . . and then Martin was beside her, his arms round her shoulders.

'Come on, mam. She wouldn't want you to cry.'

They sat on, watching over the figure in the bed until the restless eyelids ceased to twitch and the breathing slowed to a faint intake at intervals that drew further and further apart. 'I think you should go and find the sister now,' Fran said. 'She ought to check.'

There was one last thing to do before he came back. She took the hand from the coverlet and held it between her own. 'Thank you for everything, my darling. And thank you for saving my baby.' There was a small sigh from the bed. A faint coincidence, that was all.

'I think it's over,' Fran said when the sister came in.

'It's all right to cry,' she told Martin, when they were safe in the car. He was bearing up but now and again a gulp came and caught him unaware. She remembered that from childhood, when you had been naughty and punished and cried with remorse until you were comforted. 'Stop crying,' her mother would say, and she would try to obey but the gulp would overcome her.

She found she was taking the road to the hill – Tunstall Hill, high above Sunderland. 'My father used to bring me here,' she said when they had left the car and walked to the summit. 'We used to look out over the town and count the church spires. I think there were thirteen or fourteen ... but it might have been more.' In the distance the cranes still marked the dockside. 'He used to say this was the greatest shipbuilding town in the world.'

'And was it?' Martin asked.

Fran smiled. 'I don't know, but it was a bit of a cheat, anyway, because he never told me about the shipbuilding cities. But he made me proud of the town. I'm still proud of it.'

There was a rocky outcrop in front of them and they sat down side by side. 'More than of Belgate?' The 64,000-dollar question!

'I love them both. That's the nice thing about love – it's not something you give and have to take back to give again. The more you want to give, the more you have. It's the fastest-growing commodity in the world.' And sometimes the quickest to wither, but this was not the time to tell him that.

'How old were you when your father died?' He was trying to sound casual but she knew he was thinking of David and of Bethel.

'I was quite old, twenty-four. But it hurt a lot. And right now it's hurting that Bethel has died. But we haven't lost her. It's hard to explain, but people you love become part of you. It's as though you absorb some of them ... do you know what I mean?'

He considered for a moment. 'They teach you things, is that it? And then when you think, they're part of the thinking.'

She nodded. Bethel had taught her to stand on her own feet, to think and cope for herself ... and so much else beside.

'I expect it'll hurt for a long time,' he said and she could hear the child in the boy's voice.

'I expect it will,' she answered and stood up to go home.

Jim's car was parked outside the house, and he was sitting at the kitchen table with Terry. 'Is she gone?' Terry said and shook his head when she confirmed it. 'I can't imagine Belgate without Sally. She was a character.'

Jim was taking her coat and pouring her a cup of tea. She smiled her thanks, and knew as she did so that she was glad he was there. Martin came through the doorway, holding the evening paper. He was reading aloud. *'Belgate Colliery Reprieved. Best productivity performance in the Durham coalfield secures the future for Belgate miners.'* Terry looked unconvinced but Martin's face had brightened. 'Bethel would have been pleased about that,' he said.

23

She was ready long before time, checking and rechecking the funeral tea, laid out as Bethel would have wished it. Min stood beside her for a final inspection. 'I'm not going to say she'd be pleased with it because you know what she was like. I reckon she'd have said, "It'll do."'

It was so exactly what Bethel would have said that they both laughed. 'Cheer up, Franny,' Min said, squeezing Fran's arm. 'I know how you feel. I'm a bit choked myself, and I hardly knew her.'

'You're like her,' Fran said, suddenly seeing what she should have seen before. 'You're determined and wilful and you like to stir things up, but when you decide to stick to someone you'll do it through thick and thin. That's what she was like.'

Min looked abashed. 'I'd like to think you were right, Fran. Personally, I don't think I measure up to her bootstraps, but if it makes you happy to think so, go ahead.'

'There's something I've got to tell you, Min, but it's hush-hush for a while. I'm going to have a baby.'

Min's face was incredulous. 'Fran? I thought you *couldn't* ... is it what you want?'

Fran nodded. 'Yes. I'm not saying I'd have chosen right now, but I want it very much.'

Min was sinking into a chair. 'Dennis said there was something. I should have realized ... but I never notice anyone else, I'm so bloody taken up with me.'

Fran shook her head. 'You're too hard on yourself.'

Min was getting her wind back. 'What's going to happen? Are you...?'

Fran finished for her. 'Getting married? I think so. I haven't told Jim yet. He wants us to marry anyway, but it's complicated.'

Min's eyes had widened. 'You mean you might have it on your own?'

'If that seemed to be for the best for everyone, especially Martin. So please, Min, don't tell anyone just yet.' Min was swearing secrecy when Jim came to tell them it was time to go.

Once more she was climbing into a limousine – just as she had done three years ago, when David died. Behind her the cars lined up for Bethel's friends. She had predicted a good turn-out, but it exceeded her expectations. Martin sat beside her, with Jim and Terry on the facing seats. Last time Eve and Harold had accompanied her, but Eve was otherwise engaged today and Harold had summed it up quite succinctly: *'Don't get too upset. I know she worked for you, Fran, but you can't grieve over everyone. She'd had a good run for her money.'* Still Min and Dennis were there, in the next car, and Walter was bringing up the rear. That was all that counted.

The Salvation Army Church was small and bright, the officer respectful, and buoyed up by hope. They sang 'Fight the Good Fight' as Bethel had requested long ago, and then Martin was standing at the lectern, earnest and self-important.

Fran had found the volume of John Bunyan in Bethel's sideboard. Her husband's name was on the fly-leaf and a dedication from some long-gone Sunday School teacher. The book had opened at a marked page, and the words there came to life as Martin's young voice echoed round the hall.

'I am going to my fathers, and though with great difficulty I am

[170]

got hither, yet now I do not repent me of all the trouble I have been at to arrive where I am. My sword, I give to him that shall succeed me in my pilgrimage and my courage and skill, to him that can get it. My marks and scars I carry with me, to be a witness for me, that I have fought His battles who now will be my rewarder!

'When the day that he must go hence was come many accompanied him to the river side, into which, as he went, he said, "Death, where is thy sting?" And as he went down deeper, he said, "Grave where is thy victory?" So he passed over, and the trumpets sounded for him on the other side!'

As he sat down beside her she murmured 'Well done!' but he stared straight ahead and she saw that he was struggling not to cry. They rose to sing the final hymn and Fran closed her eyes, remembering Bethel as she had been, fur hat set firmly on iron-grey hair, determined face beneath.

'Oh Bethel, I don't think I can manage without you.' And then the voice in her head, the voice that would never leave her ... *'Let's have no more of that, miss.'* She looked down at the hymn book and blinked until the letters swam into place and she could open her mouth to sing.

There were willing hands to help with the food – Min and Dennis, Terry and Treesa, and Jim, catching her eye from time to time to reassure himself she was OK.

'Walter didn't come, then,' Terry said, when everyone had plate and cup and they could relax. Around them the elders of Belgate reminisced. One or two wiped a surreptitious tear, but for the most part they laughed, remembering their youth and their friend.

'No, he wouldn't come. I tried to persuade him. He drove away as soon as the service was over.'

Terry nodded. 'He's taking it hard, Mrs Drummond. I've known him all my life and never seen him bested, but this has got him down.'

Treesa had joined them. 'I always thought they'd get wed in the end.' She looked at Fran for confirmation. 'I know they went on at each other, but underneath it was love.' There was a tremor in her voice and Terry put his arm round her.

'Of course it was, pet. It's a pity they left it too late, that's all.'

When everyone had gone Fran went about replacing the furniture, picking damp petals from the floor, just as she had done after David's funeral. It had been a joint decision to have Bethel buried from their house. '*I know she loved her own house,*' Martin had said, deciding, '*but she loved us more.*'

So Bethel had lain in the front room amid banks of flowers, and now the carpet was imprinted by the trestles and the debris of a funeral was there to be tided away. But this time Jim was there to help her, and Martin too. Today she had noticed how thin his face had become – or perhaps it was his jaw showing through, the first angularity of youth.

When it was done, the three of them sat around the kitchen table and drank tea. Memories of Bethel, arms dusted with flour, face flushed from the oven's heat, opening her Players No 6 and offering them, crowded in, but Fran put them aside. Bethel had always had a sense·of priorities.

There was a soft plop from the hall and Martin went to collect the *Echo*. Last night he had read out the announcement: '*Bethel, Sarah Mary (née Heads) beloved wife of the late John Thomas and dearly loved friend of Frances and Martin Drummond . . .*'

Tonight he read another stark announcement, prefacing it with his own headline: 'Our coalman's gone to gaol.' Dave, the sacked miner who had brought them their coal since the strike, had been sentenced to three months for burglary of a deputy's home. The strike had been over for eighteen months but still it was claiming victims.

When Martin had finished the *Echo* he stood up. 'The dog needs taking out.' And then, fondling its head, 'Poor thing. You don't know what's going on, do you?'

As boy and dog went out, Jim smiled at her. 'He's trying hard, isn't he?'

Fran nodded. 'It seems just like yesterday he was too lazy to do anything. "Walk the dog," I'd say, and he'd say, "Wait on." And Bethel would come through from the kitchen. "Never mind 'wait on'. It's wees that dog wants, not 'wait on'."'

She was fumbling for words when the phone rang. 'Hallo, it's Barbara.' Fran was about to say, 'I'll get daddy for you' when the voice went on: 'Daddy says you're coming down soon?' and then a stern aside – 'In a minute. I said in a minute . . . get off! It's not your turn yet.'

Fran smiled. She would have liked more time to get to know Jim's children, but it would be all right. They were very normal kids.

She left him in the hall when he took over the phone, and waited in the kitchen. At last she heard the tinkle of the receiver going down and knew it had come, the moment she couldn't postpone any further, the absolute ultimate crunch.

'There's something I must tell you, Jim. I'm going to have a baby. It was my decision to keep it and I'm not asking for help, so don't feel you have to "do the decent thing". The decent thing in this situation is to be honest with each other.'

Mingled emotions were chasing across his face. 'Well,' she said at last, 'tell me how you feel?'

He grimaced. 'Absolute honesty?'

She inclined her head. 'Absolute.'

'Well then . . . I feel . . . wonderful . . . and flabbergasted . . . and bloody scared, Fran. But I expect we'll manage.' As though he had sensed his own inadequacy, he spoke again. 'I'm *glad* about it, Fran. But not because I need another child. I'm glad because it's a seal on our love, something we made together. And, oh, I do love you, Frances Drummond.'

She leaned against him, trying to quell her mounting panic. Commitment meant the prospect of pain and loss. But it meant so much more. They would be together for ever now – for as long as 'forever' was allowed to be. She closed her eyes but opened them in shock as he suddenly pulled away.

[173]

'Why didn't you tell me?' There was anger in his voice as he measured the time she had kept silent.

'I don't know. I just didn't want it to influence things. Whatever happened, I wanted it to be for the right reasons.'

He nodded. 'I know what you mean, but you were wrong. I should've known from the beginning. Anyway, I hope you're satisfied now. I didn't come back to you for any other reason than love.' He grinned and reached for her hand. 'And if I'm honest, a little bit of lust. That figured in it, too.'

His kiss had little of lust in it – it was more a search for reassurance. 'Is it what you want, Fran. That's all that matters?'

She lifted her free hand to touch his cheek. 'Of course it's what I want. Surely you realize that?'

24

Bethel's house was already taking on the odour of disuse, and everything Fran touched was chill. She decided to keep on her coat and make a start on the bureau. She had looked there after Bethel's death to see if there were instructions for the funeral, and had found the will. She and Walter were executors and could take their pick of Bethel's worldly goods. Martin got £848 in the Co-op Bank. Anything else went to the Sally Army.

Walter wanted nothing. 'I can't be bothered over what I've got already, without taking on more.' Since Bethel's death the fire had gone out of him, and with it the will to live. Apart from the day of the funeral, Fran had not seen his car on the Belgate streets and Treesa brought alarming tales of how little he was eating, which she'd culled from neighbours and the shops.

Fran smiled, thinking of Treesa. In a few years' time she would be another Bethel, strong and upright, bossing Terry, probably wearing a fur hat and a silk scarf folded inside her coat. A proper News of the World! Perhaps she would even bake

[174]

bread, although Fran doubted it. Treesa was a child of the sliced-loaf generation. Remembering Bethel's bread, Fran shivered. This kitchen used to steam gently in the glow from an abandoned fire, piled high with concessionary coal to heat the oven. There would be no more floury flat cakes, no crusty biscuit-coloured loaves to fall from their tins at the rap of an expert hand. But the memory was there, locked in her head, to be brought out reverently whenever she could bear it. Suddenly she heard Bethel's reproaching voice. *'You're sitting there as though you had corn growing!'* Obediently she lowered the lid of the bureau and settled to her task.

All she had to do was go through and remove the personal things. After that Terry had promised to see to it that everything was disposed of as the Sally Army wished. He was a good friend; so was Dennis. He and Min were to oversee the shipment of Fran's furniture to Twickenham and the subsequent sale of the house.

It had been easy for Jim and Fran to work things out once the principle of being together was agreed. She had suggested living together as an experiment and felt weak with relief when he gave a flat refusal. 'We're getting married, Fran ... and the quicker the better.' She was showing now, not to any great extent, but there was less and less point in concealment.

She had told Gwen when they met to talk about the future. 'Is it what you want?' Gwen had asked; it was the same question Min had posed, but this time Fran was more sure of the answer. 'Well, good for you,' Gwen said when Fran told her that it was.

Eve had been frosty. Her lips had mouthed uneasy platitudes but her eyes had said, *'How could you, Fran? And you a grieving widow.'* For a second Fran had contemplated explanation, but there was no way Eve would have understood the intricacies of second relationships and, anyway, Fran was not sure she cared enough about Eve to enlighten her.

Jim understood: that was the important thing. 'I understand about David because I still love Dorothy. I always will. But I love you, Fran. Not instead of or in spite of ... I just love you.' She

[175]

had shivered a little, thinking of Dorothy, for ever thirty, never growing old, or arguing, or falling from grace. She it was who would age and rage and disintegrate with time. But she had smiled and touched his cheek. Sufficient unto the day.

'It'll be a relief to have someone to look after Barbara,' he'd said. 'Kevin and I can manage, but I used to wake up in the night and think, "What do you do with a girl? How do you explain womanhood, when it comes?"'

Fran had smiled, remembering her own fears. 'I used to have nightmares about Martin and shaving. I decided when the time came I'd just go into Boots and buy him the gear and hope it had instructions. But, really, we worry for nothing. Martin is growing ... has grown up ... with very little help from me.'

It was Martin's new-found maturity that had given her the courage to face a move. That, and the fact that Bethel was no longer there to lean on. 'It makes sense for us to come south,' she said when Jim demurred. 'You've got contacts down there – you said so ... you wanted to go into marine paints? We'll talk about that in a minute. And your kids won't understand being up-rooted. Not straight away. I want to talk to Martin first, but if he agrees, we'll come to London. You never know, I might come to like it in time.'

They were lying in his hotel bed, their gentle lovemaking over. 'I'm not suddenly made of glass because I'm pregnant,' she'd told him, but he was unconvinced.

'About work,' she said. 'You said once you'd have liked to go it alone, but it was too risky. Well, I'm here now to share that risk. I'm a trained teacher, remember. I can earn a salary once the baby's here. There'll be money to come from my house and you could re-mortgage yours. We could move to Southampton if it made sense. But you must have a chance to strike out on your own!' She didn't add 'for all our sakes' but she knew he under-stood. She hoped in vain for instant agreement, but it would come with time. At least he'd agreed to consider it.

The confidence of her own thinking nowadays amazed her. Three years ago she had been a jelly, forced to recite her name and particulars to still the panic within. Now she could plot like a Machiavelli. But she still shirked telling Martin about the baby, and she would have to tell him soon. He had been a brick about leaving Belgate, and deserved better from her. She got on with clearing out Bethel's bureau.

There were the usual bills and documents. A birth certificate for Sarah Mary Heads, born to Susannah and Thomas Henry at 12 Clanny Street, Belgate, on 17 June 1917, and another for John Thomas Bethel, folded with the certificate of his death from a ruptured spleen and multiple fractures, as the result of an industrial accident, on 18 October 1949. Fran put the documents carefully aside. They were the fabric of Bethel's life and must be preserved.

The bundle of letters were yellowing and flaked at the edges and were all dated 1937; Bethel's letters written from service to the man who was to be her husband, and his letters to her. Fran read through the formal phrases, stilted at first and then warming as their acquaintance deepened. '*I felt sad, love, when I saw you off at the station and then I thought of how soon we will be together, never to be parted again, and I felt quite cheered up. I have got a poker for you, made in the pit, a stout bit of iron and our first possession.*' Fran smiled, thinking how well he had known his love and her obsession with a well-stoked fire.

Bethel's letters were full of detail about the houses she worked in and her employer's peccadilloes. '*Today we hung the winter curtains but they don't suit "madam" and will have to come down tomorrow. She says they clash with the new paper and he, poor fish, says yes dear, three bags full as usual. I'm thankful I'm marrying a man and not a soft article that isn't master in his own home.*'

She put the letters aside to be reread at leisure. She did not feel she was prying. It was as though Bethel had intended her to find them.

There was a baby's rattle in the next section, a mother-of-pearl handle topped with a silver bell, and all wrapped in tissue paper. It was not new, and had teeth-marks on the handle to prove it, so where had it come from? That too was put aside, and

[177]

she took out a blue envelope that had once held a calendar. Inside was a yellowing cutting dated 1953. At first Fran thought it was a souvenir of the coronation, but the picture of Queen Elizabeth was incomplete and when she turned it over she saw that it was an account of an accident in the pit: '*Conveyor belt tragedy at Belgate.*' A miner called Sidney Jefferson had been killed and another, Walter Raeburn, was seriously ill in Sunderland's Accident Hospital.

Fran sifted through the rest of the envelope. Christmas and birthday cards from Walter, terse messages and restrained pictures, all signed with a flourish. There was an account of his chairmanship of the local disabled drivers' club and two letters written by him to the local paper, which had been carefully clipped and preserved by Bethel.

'She did love him,' Fran thought. 'She kept every little thing connected with him. *And* she loved her husband.' So Bethel, too, had loved twice. But she had never quite had the courage to confess that second love, and now Walter was left with nothing.

'I'll get it right, Bethel. This time I'll get it right for both of us.' She put the envelope in her handbag and went on with her task, but her mind wandered. First love, second love, mother love, all fruit of the same tree, all sweet. And so different to any other emotion. She had clung to Steve, desperate for companionship, and she had lusted for Tony Lund. But she had loved David, truly loved him, and now she loved Jim. Last night she had taken his head to her breast and known, as she did so, that her love for him was strong enough to deal with whatever might come.

Martin came in, Nee-wan on the lead quivering to be free. 'I want to talk to you, darling. Yes, now. It's important.'

He settled on a chair and coaxed the dog to a sitting position. He was looking at her, waiting, but his eyes were wary. She felt the rush of love that always overcame her when she looked at her child. But children needed more than love, they needed fair play.

'Sometimes it's easy to think parents always get things right. We encourage you to think that when you're little, so that you'll feel safe. Now you're growing up, you know that I don't always

[178]

get things right.' He was smiling, trying not to look triumphant at her admission. She was seeking for words but the temptation to fob him off and delay the truth was overwhelming. She had felt like that about his father's death, knowing the secret could not be kept but hoping that if she waited it would go away.

'When people love one another they sleep together.' They were not the right words, he wouldn't understand. 'They make love . . . because they love one another.' *'Make love'*: another euphemism. She had always intended to tell him the facts of life but she had left it too late. The facts had preceded the telling.

His lips had come together now, the smile gone, and there was a flush on his upper cheeks. 'I know about sex,' he said suddenly. 'Everyone knows at school.' Of course he would know: she had known herself at twelve years old, in another and more innocent age.

It was easy to tell him, then, to discuss guilt and shame and love and the expectation of happiness. 'So I can't undo what's done, but I can try to make it better by making a happy life for all of us. If you'll help me.'

He had had enough of emotion. 'I will. Now, can I go?' He submitted to her embrace with good grace but she sensed his embarrassment and confusion. A baby like Christopher, alive and waiting to play, was one thing. A baby, mysterious within the womb, was quite another.

'I love you, Martin.'

He was frowning, uncertain of what to do next. She wanted to reach out for him but she knew it would be a mistake. Suddenly he grinned.

'It's right what Bethel used to say about you. Slop, slop, slop!'

As he quit the room she knew it was going to be all right.

When her work was done and the house left tidy for Terry and Treesa she let herself out and closed the door for the last time. The lace curtains with their bottom frills were already jaded, missing their monthly soak to bring them up white. Next week the keys would be handed in, and a new tenant would polish and dust Bethel's domain. A Belgate girl with Belgate ways; another link in the chain.

She drove to Walter's house, taking the tape recorder from the seat, the volume of Bunyan from the glove compartment, and adding the envelope of his cards and cuttings. He was sitting in front of the fire and for the first time she saw him without his tweed jacket. He was tieless, shirt neck open and cuffs flapping at the wrists. There was a stubble on his chin and a smell of urine in the air. 'He's given up,' she thought and was afraid.

'I've been to Sally's. I know you didn't want anything but there's something I think you should have. This was her *Pilgrim's Progress*: it's yours now. And these were mementoes of you she kept through the years. She loved you Walter: for all the sparring and the ding-dong battles, you were the apple of her eye. And I don't know what she'd make of you today.'

She had hoped for some retaliation, a burst of anger as the barb went home, but there was nothing. He fingered the book and the envelope for a moment and then laid them on the side table.

'You're off tomorrow, then?'

She nodded. 'Yes, Martin and I are driving down together. We'll sort things out there, and our furniture will follow later. Some friends of mine are seeing to it for me ... and Terry's going to see to Bethel's house.'

'That young communist.' Once the words would have been flung like a lance, now they were simply a comment. Fran decided to ignore them.

'I'll be coming back often, Walter. Martin has friends here and so do I. So we won't lose touch. In the meantime, I want you to have this.' She held out the tape recorder. 'There's a tape in it, I made it last night. It just says a few things I want you to know. When you've heard it, you can record a message and send it back to me. It's better than letters.'

The massive head rolled slowly from side to side as if in amazement at her foolishness. 'I'm far ower old for that sort of thing. Tapes, buttons ... why not get a space machine and I'll fly down?' She remembered Bethel's injunction: *'Don't give way to him. He likes everyone to dance to his tune.'*

'Well, it's there, Walter. Whether or not you use it's up to you. I'd like to keep in touch and so would Martin, but we can't make you.'

As she drove away she wondered if he was right: perhaps an old dog couldn't learn new tricks, not even push-button ones. She drove into her back street and got out to open the garage door. From a house further up a figure emerged, wheeling a bicycle. It was Fenwick, the miner whose pigeons had been slaughtered to punish him for his opposition to the strike. There was a basket on the back of his bicycle, and as he drew level she saw activity behind the wickerwork. 'New birds?' she said. For a year or more he had walked the streets of Belgate like a zombie, an outcast with no purpose in life other than work and sleep. Today he looked more relaxed. 'Aye, Mrs Drummond. I don't know if they're any good. We'll have to wait and see.'

As she let herself into the house she felt comforted. Fenwick was flying pigeons again. Birds to soar and circle, symbols of hope. And then again the memory of Bethel, floured arms akimbo, bringing her back to earth. *'Pigeons is nothing but shit-machines, miss. And don't you forget it.'*

25

They gathered for the last time in the kitchen: Dennis and Min, Mike Malone, Terry and Treesa, Christopher on unsteady legs, and Frances Mary in her carrycot. Fran had held them both in her arms from birth. Soon she would have two more children to care for and a baby of her own. After all the years of hoping, a child had crept up on her unawares and her son had grown to be a comfort. He was grinning at her now. 'Cheer up, mam. Everything's under control.'

Mike Malone was fidgeting and Martin heaved a sigh. 'Come on then, Mick. Let's get loaded.' Mike flew to the stairs and Terry tut-tutted.

'He's a right little vulture, that one. I don't know where he gets it. As soon as your Martin said there was some gear he could have, he was like a cat on hot bricks.'

Treesa smiled indulgently. 'He's only a bairn.' She turned to Fran. 'What time will you get to London?'

'About seven o'clock. I want to miss the rush-hour traffic. It should be over by then.'

Dennis's mouth had opened. 'Six hours to get to London! I thought you were going by car!'

Min gave him a playful rap. 'All right, Stirling Moss. Some of us quite like living. We're not all speed merchants.' Last night she had confided her chief ambition to Fran. *I mean to get him some decent wheels again, Fran. It'll take a long time but I'll do it.*

'There now.' Treesa put the tray on the table and began to pour. 'You can't beat a good cup of tea. And don't you worry about Walter, Fran. Me and Terry'll see to him.'

Terry grinned. 'I'll snap him out of it. A few digs about Scargill, that'll get his dander up.' It was true. Perhaps a good argument was what Walter needed.

'Arthur's a red rag to more than one around here,' Treesa said. 'I was talking to Ella Bishop's man the other day. You know the wife with the gold earrings, the one that was big in the strike? When the support group closed down she joined the Party. At it day and night, keen as mustard. I was saying to her man she'd gone very political, and he shakes his head and says, "I'll never forgive Scargill. He's ruined our lass."'

There was general laughter, and then Min returned to the subject. 'Terry's right, Fran. You're not to worry about a thing. He'll sort out Walter, and Dennis and I will see to things here. And then we'll all come down for the wedding, no matter where we get the cash. I'm planning a really snazzy outfit.' She thought for a moment. 'Of course, I won't go too far, I'll dress down. It's your day, after all.' She said it in generous tones and looked puzzled as Fran and Dennis burst into laughter.

'What about Eve and Harold?' Dennis said when the mirth had subsided.

'They won't be able to get away,' Fran said. 'Well, they have got a lot on. Isn't it a shame!' This time everyone laughed.

The next moment the door from the hall rocked back on its hinges and a flushed Mike Malone came through almost concealed behind a pile of books, comics, boxed games and half-completed models. He gave not a glance to the group around the table merely steered for the back door. 'I'll come straight back for the rest,' he called as he exited.

'See what I mean?' Terry said. 'Mention something for nothing to that one and his motor starts.' Fran smiled, remembering Mike years ago, describing his grandmother's funeral. '*We had meat ... not just gravy ... git lumps of meat. And cream cakes. You could eat as much as you liked and the priest gave us all 10p. I've still got one nana left.*'

The next moment he crashed back into the kitchen and through it without pause. 'He's a man in a hurry,' Dennis said. 'They're the ones who make the world go round.'

When Mike had tottered out under the second and final load, Martin said, 'I'm going to say tarra to Walter. I won't be long.'

Fran had made her own good-byes to Walter earlier, once more exhorting him to keep in touch and receiving little response. 'We have to leave at one o'clock,' she said. 'Don't hold me up.'

Min and Treesa were clearing the fridge of perishable food and washing the teacups while the men amused the children, so Fran mounted the stairs for a final check. She was sure to have forgotten something.

She had meant to check wardrobes and drawers, but she found herself drawn to the window. Three years ago she had looked out on the snow-covered garden and made her decision to stay. Now she was leaving but Belgate always would be her 'land of lost content'.

[183]

'We'll come back often, won't we?' Martin had asked last night and she had promised that they would.

Down below in the kitchen she could hear laughter, and her eyes filled with tears. Her friends! She had thought of them the night before as she walked on the beach with Martin and the dog. In the distance the sea-coalers toiled on the moonlit tideline. Beside her, Martin had walked, hands in pockets in case she was mushy enough to reach for one. Nee-wan, amazed at this night-time ramble, had run back and forth like a dog possessed.

'Do you know what I'm thinking about?' he said suddenly.

She shook her head. 'I don't know, darling. Is it about London? We'll be all right there, you know.'

He bent for a stone and sent it skimming across the surface of the sea. 'No, it's OK about London. Mike says he'll come down on the coach once we're settled in and you said we'll come back. And Jim's OK.' There was a chuckle. 'He's the best boyfriend you've had. Since dad.'

She felt her cheeks flush. 'I haven't had that many ... you make me sound like Henry the Eighth.' If she wasn't careful he would start listing them! 'What *are* you thinking about?' she said hastily.

'I was thinking about the pit. Being here, under the sea. Men we know working down there with the North Sea above them. Mike's going to be a miner if he can get an apprenticeship, and he says he can. He says his dad and Terry can fix anything at the pit. Anyway, I was thinking I might be a mining engineer. Or an architect. Except that I'd quite like to work the market like Aunty Min.'

She was tempted to ask if he fancied brain surgery or fire-fighting but decided against it. At least he was thinking about the future.

'It's hard to believe the strike's been over for a year and a half,' she said. 'Except that it still rumbles on.' Yesterday she had seen '*UDM is sods*' on a wall, fresh painted. And another slogan blaming the NUM for all the miners' troubles, as though to answer the first.

[184]

'They'll get over it eventually,' Martin said easily and bent for another stone.

Fran was still remembering that moonlit walk on the beach when Min tapped on the bedroom door. 'Fran?' She pushed the door to behind her and stood, arms at sides. 'Fran, there's no easy way to ask this but someone has to. You're not marrying Jim because it's the respectable thing to do, are you? Because if you are, you mustn't! Dennis and I are behind you every inch of the way, and you know you could cope. Don't say it's cheek to ask, because I'm not a bit ashamed. What's the good of having a brass neck if you don't stick it out occasionally?'

Fran went to Min, arms outstretched and they clung. 'Thanks for saying that, Min. You sounded just like Dad. He offered me a final get out before we left for church, and when I said I was sure I wanted to marry David he said, "Thank God. Your mother would've killed me if you'd called it off."'

'It's a lifetime ago, isn't it?' Min said, suddenly awestruck.

'Ten lifetimes,' Fran said, 'but I'm sure this is right, Min. Very sure. I love Jim.'

Min smiled. 'We've grown up, kid, you and I. A bit late, but we've done it all the same.'

They went out to the cars at one o'clock. 'I told Martin we were leaving at one,' Fran said, beginning to fret.

Fenwick was coming towards them, for once without his bike. 'You're off, then.'

Fran held out her hand. 'Good-bye, Mr Fenwick. But we'll see you again before long.'

He nodded and released her hand. 'Good-bye, Mrs Drummond. Watch out for that lad of yours.'

His eyes flicked to Terry – militant Terry, who had been known to spit at the sight of scabs. Fran held her breath until Terry inclined his head.

'Aye, aye, Tom lad.'

Fenwick merely bobbed his head in return, but Fran could see

[185]

he was pleased.

'Oh Terry Malone, you're a jewel,' she said when Fenwick was out of earshot.

'By,' Treesa said, putting her hand through the crook of her husband's arm, 'you're in my good books now, and no mistake.'

Terry was embarrassed and had to make a joke of it. 'Listen that,' he said to Dennis. 'The way they're going on you'd think I was a right sod usually ... excuse the language.'

Martin came running up, panting. 'I'm not late, am I?' Neewan was shooed into the back seat. The babies were held up to be kissed, and Martin was hugged in turn. 'I'll see you, Mick,' he yelled – and they were away.

'Don't cry, mam,' he said as she tried, through her tears, to negotiate the corner. 'They're still your friends. Besides, wait till you hear about Walter! He was trying to use the recorder and the air was blue. You know what he's like when he gets stuck. So I showed him, and he says he might send a tape. Which means he will, only he can never just say so.'

They were leaving Belgate behind and the rounded tops of the Cleveland Hills appeared in the distance. Once beyond the hills the north-east would be lost to view. 'It's a long way, isn't it?' Martin said suddenly, echoing her thoughts.

The comic he had begun to read was lying on his knee, and for the first time since London had been talked about he looked a little woebegone.

'Two hundred and sixty-five miles,' she said, sticking to facts. 'But it's only three hours by train.' He was silent. 'You'll like London ... lots to see, heaps of history.' Perhaps they would learn to love the South in time, both of them.

They were approaching the junction with the A1. Soon she must turn west and then south. Instead she turned east and began to climb into the hills. The blue, remembered hills of Housman's poem. 'Why are you going to the Cleves?' Martin asked but she didn't reply.

She drove to Look Out Point, where they had picnicked so often with David, where she had driven in anguish after his death. 'Is this a kind of good-bye to Dad?' Martin said.

'No. We'll never say good-bye to Dad or Bethel. Or anyone we love. There's no need.'

Martin was grinning now. 'Dad fried sausages up here once, didn't he? And he set the pan on fire and said, "Hell's bloody teeth," and you said, "Shush, David, Martin's listening."'

Fran shook her head. 'You always have had *big* ears.'

She turned back to look out on a grey landscape, touched here and there with colour as the leaves turned with autumn and the fields, raped of their crops, blackened at the approach of winter. Ancient Northumbria, a kingdom by the sea.

She could not see the towns and cities or the mighty rivers of the North, but if she closed her eyes she could summon them to view. The grey, luminous mouth of the Tees, the yellow cranes of the Wear, the bustle of the Tyne, the grey towers of Durham, the green parks of Sunderland, and Cleveland waiting to stir its great limbs at the promise of work.

Most of all, Belgate and its people. Not better or more friendly than southerners, but special because they were her people. Inside her pocket her fingers closed around the piece of sea-coal she had carried up from the beach the night before. Solid and tangible, a talisman to take her safely along the sliding stream.

'It's time to go, mam,' Martin said. 'Jim'll be waiting.' She turned away obediently. No need to stay and no need to look back. The kingdom of the north was in her heart and she would take it with her wherever she might go.

H